WINTER'S
JUSTICE

Talon Winter Legal Thriller #4

STEPHEN PENNER

ISBN: 978-0-578-81138-3

Winter's Justice

Joy Lorton, Editor.
Cover design by Nathan Wampler Book Covers.

WINTER'S
JUSTICE

Arguments to a jury to "declare the truth" or to return a "just verdict" misstate the law and are improper.

State of Washington v. Anderson, Washington Court of Appeals
153 Wash.App. 417 (2009)

CHAPTER 1

"Private prison! Hell no! Shut it down and let them go!"

Talon Winter, full-time criminal defense attorney and part-time criminal justice reform advocate, frowned at the chant being led by the young, purple-haired woman at the front gate of Tacoma's brand new private jail, the Pierce Regional Institute for Correctional Endeavors, a.k.a. 'P.R.I.C.E.'

"Catchy," Talon allowed. "But you'd get more support if you changed 'let them go' to 'transfer them to a publicly owned and operated detention facility that is more directly responsible to the voters'."

Shayla Jackson, full-time public defender at the Pierce County Department of Assigned Counsel and the new friend who had dragged Talon to the protest, matched Talon's frown, and added a raised eyebrow and a fist on her hip.

"I know, I know," Talon raised her own hands defensively. "It doesn't rhyme."

The new private jail was the result of a battle between the county and its public jail on the one hand and on the other hand, a group of cities who wanted to arrest every vagrant and ne'er-do-well on their streets but didn't want to pay the county jail's daily rate for housing and feeding said vagrants and ne'er-do-wells. It was expensive to run a fully staffed jail that provided not only three hots and a cot, but also full medical care and adequate mental health facilities for the myriad afflictions prevalent in a population that consistently ran afoul of society's rules. P.R.I.C.E. offered the bed and meals, but little else, and so they could offer those basic services for considerably less. The cities could still book the diabetics and schizophrenics into the county jail, which was obligated to accept them because of their status as a public jail, but everyone else was headed to P.R.I.C.E. It was a win-win. The cities paid less, and American Corrections Enterprises, Inc., the nation's third largest private prison corporation and owner/operator of P.R.I.C.E., could enrich their stockholders on the backs of the aforementioned vagrants and ne'er-do-wells.

But that really wouldn't rhyme.

"Private prison! Hell no! Shut it down and let them go!"

"Remind me why we're here again?" Talon asked Shayla. "I think we can do more good just doing our jobs and keeping people out of jail in the first place."

"It's not either/or, Talon," Shayla scolded.

Shayla wiped some sweat from her forehead with the back of her hand. It was an especially hot day, which made standing out in the sun even more irritating to Talon. Shayla's brown skin glistened in the sun and her long black braids were tied back behind her neck. Talon wished she'd brought a hair tie for her own long black hair; instead, she scooped it to one side and twisted it into a loose ponytail over one shoulder, her lighter skin also uncomfortably hot in the midday sun.

"Besides, it's easier for you," Shayla continued. "You're a private attorney. Your clients have money. Mine are all indigent, by definition. Yours can post bail, but mine are part of the seventy-five percent of the jail population who are supposedly presumed innocent but wait for their trials behind bars because they're poor."

Talon shrugged and glanced around the protest. "Not all of mine can post bail. Depends what they did, and how high the bail gets set."

There were maybe three dozen people at the protest. That was actually a good turnout for something as esoteric as opposition to private prisons. Mr. and Mrs. Middle America wanted prisons and jails, and they really didn't care how they were funded. If anything, they probably preferred private prisons, if it meant lower taxes. That left the diehard social justice warriors to come out on a blazing hot afternoon to chant quixotically in front of the latest franchise of America's industrial prison complex.

In fact, even Shayla probably wouldn't have been there if it hadn't been for one other protester in the crowd: Karim Jackson, her little brother—or rather, her younger brother. He was anything but little. He towered several inches over the rest of the crowd, and despite his relative youth, his hairline was already receding. He tried to make up for it with an eager, but struggling beard, but that just left a manly face framed in an oval of boyish fuzz. He was still in college, almost done with a double major in philosophy and criminal justice, and he intended to follow in his sister's footsteps as a lawyer. So, even though he couldn't help people professionally quite yet, he and his classmates could organize a noisy protest against an injustice about to open up in their own backyard.

"Full of sound and fury," Talon quoted the Bard under her breath, "signifying nothing."

"What's that?" Shayla asked.

"Oh, nothing." Talon shook her head. She wiped some sweat off the back of her neck. "Can we get going soon? How long is this supposed to last? You promised me iced lattes after this. There will still be iced lattes, right?"

Shayla sighed. "Yes. Sure. Of course. I think we're almost done anyway. Everyone is hot and tired. No one's even responding to the chant anymore."

Sure enough, the young woman who had been leading the chant was lowering her megaphone as the crowd's energy started to ebb away with the heat rising from the pavement.

Thank God, Talon thought.

But not everyone was done protesting injustice in the hot sun. Karim himself jumped up on the overturned plastic milk crate and took the megaphone from his weary compatriot.

"Fuck court! Fuck bail! Fuck the cops and fuck this jail!"

Edgy, but effective. The crowd seemed to regain some of its energy from the very rawness of a profanity laden chant.

Talon nodded approvingly. "Now, that's to the point," she laughed.

Shayla was less enthused. She covered her face with her hand. "That's embarrassing. He can do better than cussing."

"I don't know. It looks like it finally got someone's attention." Talon looked past Karim, through the gates, at the approaching uniformed, and armed, jail guards. "For better or worse."

They weren't just uniformed and armed, they were also escorting a not uniformed, not armed, but very angry looking man in a shirt and tie. He was a bit on the short side, a bit on the heavy side, a bit on the bald side, and a bit on the old side, with sweat stains under his arms and a scowl under his mustache. His pink skin seemed to be sunburning before their very eyes.

The guards pulled open the gate with a loud clatter and short, heavy, bald, old, sweaty, angry mustache man marched right up to the gathered protesters.

"I am James Dank, Director of the Pierce Regional Institute for Correctional Enterprises!" he shouted. "You are on private property. I am ordering you to leave at once, under threat of arrest."

There was a pause as the crowd hesitated, unsure how to respond. Then Karim turned the bullhorn directly at Dank. "Fuck court! Fuck bail! Fuck *you* and fuck this jail!"

Talon winced. Bullhorns were loud, really loud. That was the entire point. Having someone point one right at your face and shout would be not just irritating, but painful. Dank jerked away and covered his ears. When he turned back, that pink in his face had turned to a fiery red.

"Give me that bullhorn!" Dank screamed. He closed the distance between them and grabbed at the bullhorn, but Karim turned away and blocked Dank with his body. Dank scrambled after it, reaching around Karim's body, half bearhugging him and half pushing him forward with the weight of his body. Karim pulled the bullhorn against his chest, shouting at Dank to let him go. Dank refused and wrapped his arms fully around Karim, screaming for the bullhorn and shaking Karim side to side.

But Karim was bigger than Dank. Karim was younger than Dank. And Karim was stronger than Dank. So, when Karim exploded his arms outward, breaking Dank's grip and pushing the Director of the Pierce Regional Institute for Correctional Enterprises away, Dank had no chance of holding on. To the contrary, he went flying backward, off balance and out of control. His butt hit the ground first, followed almost immediately by the base of his skull. The sound was a combination of a home run off a wooden baseball bat and a watermelon hitting the pavement from thirty stories up.

Everything went silent. Dank was motionless. Blood started pooling under his head. Karim stared at him, bullhorn barely held by a limp hand. Nothing moved for several seconds. Then all hell broke loose.

The guards jumped on Karim. Five at least, maybe more. It was hard to tell because several of the protesters jumped onto the guards. The result was a pile of people with Karim at the bottom, pressed against the pavement, face driven into the cement. As the rest of the guards wrestled Karim's arms behind his back, one of them stood up and unholstered his handgun, leveling it at the crowd surrounding them.

"Get back!" he screamed. "Everyone get back!"

It took a moment, but the protesters started to comply. They raised their hands and took a few cautious steps back from the weapon. Two more guards drew their own guns and pointed them at the crowd as well. The resultant space allowed the remaining guards to yank Karim to his feet, hands cuffed behind his back, blood running from his nose and lip.

"This man is under arrest!" the first guard shouted. "Everyone else, back the fuck up! This is a fucking crime scene. You are ordered to disperse. Everyone leave, right fucking now!"

Stunned, but outgunned, the protestors slowly turned to leave. But not Talon.

She stepped forward and extended a business card to the officer bellowing orders.

He looked at the card but didn't take it. "Who the fuck are you?"

Talon waited a beat, then dropped the card at his feet and pointed to Karim. "I'm Talon fucking Winter. And I'm this man's lawyer."

CHAPTER 2

Somewhat ironically, Karim was booked into the public county jail after his arrest. P.R.I.C.E. wasn't quite open yet; it was the impending opening they were protesting. It took Talon a while to confirm where Karim had been taken, and even longer before Karim had completed booking and been assigned to a cell. By then, it was well after visiting hours, even for attorneys. That meant Talon and Shayla had to wait until the next morning before they could finally see him.

"Do you think he knows how much trouble he's in?" Shayla asked as they waited for the door to the visitor area to be buzzed open.

Talon frowned. "*We* don't even know how much trouble he's in. It depends on what the prosecutor decides to charge him with. Some level of assault, probably, but we won't know for certain until court at one o'clock."

Shayla looked around the jail lobby. "Well, he knows he's in some sort of trouble. That's why he's here."

Talon nodded. "That's why we're all here."

A loud buzz and an even louder clank filled the lobby and Talon reached forward to pull open the heavy metal door between them and Karim. There were also two remotely controlled, barred gates between them and Karim. They had to wait behind each until an unseen guard in a video control room waited for the one behind them to close before opening the next. But eventually, they were past all of the checks and into the holding area for 3-West, the west wing of the third floor, where Karim was housed. There was one last door, the door into the 3-West living quarters, but they weren't going through that one. Karim would be coming out of it, to meet them in one of the private attorney-client meeting rooms just outside the door. Talon pressed the large red button imbedded in the metal speaker and waited.

After a moment, a deep, electronically scratchy voice boomed, "You here for Inmate Jackson?"

"Correct," Talon answered into the grating. "Attorney visit."

"Step away from the door," was the reply.

Talon and Shayla did as instructed and a moment later, the door unlocked with another, albeit quieter, buzz and clank. A guard pushed open the door and held it ajar as Karim walked through with a second guard behind him. Karim was handcuffed again, but in the front and to belly chains. The blood on his face was gone, but the swelling on his nose and the cut on his lip served as a reminder of the last time they'd seen him.

"Which one of you is the lawyer?" the guard behind Karim demanded.

"We're both lawyers," Shayla responded before Talon could say anything.

"Same firm?" the guard asked.

Shayla hesitated.

"No," Talon admitted. "I'm the main lawyer. She's, uh…"

"She's my sister," Karim informed the guard.

"Nope." The guard shook his head. "Family visiting hours

are afternoons from three to five. Otherwise, it's attorneys only."

"I am an attorney," Shayla repeated.

"You're not his attorney." The guard pointed at Karim. Then turned to ask him, "Right? She's your sister, not your lawyer? The other one's your lawyer, right?"

Karim nodded. He gestured at Shayla. "She's my sister." Then at Talon. "And she's my lawyer. I guess."

"I'm his lawyer," Talon confirmed. "No guesses."

It was pretty obvious, to Talon anyway, that Karim wanted to be able to talk to her, without his big sister present. That was probably the right call. And easier for Talon as well.

She turned to Shayla. "Why don't you wait out here?" Talon suggested. "This won't take too long. I just need to explain where things stand. We'll know a lot more this afternoon."

Shayla hesitated, a worried frown unfurling across her lips.

"She's right, sis," Karim agreed. "Stay out here. Let me talk to Talon alone."

Talon nodded. "We don't need any arguments that the conversation isn't confidential because you aren't really his lawyer. I need Karim to be able to speak freely."

Shayla's frown deepened, but after a moment she rolled her eyes and sighed. "Fine. But I can stay right outside the meeting room, right?" she asked the guard. "I don't have to go all the way back through the hallway of a thousand gates? In case they need me after all or something."

The guard who'd been doing the talking looked back to the other guard for guidance. That guard shrugged, then nodded. "Sure. Just don't cause any trouble."

Shayla's eyebrows shot up. "Because I'm Black?"

The guard frowned. "No. Because you're a lawyer."

Talon smiled at that and put a hand on Shayla's shoulder.

"We'll be quick. See if you can find anything out online. Maybe they've already filed the charging documents."

That was unlikely, but it gave Shayla something to do while Talon and Karim, still cuffed to his belly chains, entered the attorney-client meeting room. The guard closed the door behind them and waited outside with Shayla.

Karim and Talon each took a seat in one of the two lightweight plastic chairs that were in the room. There was also a lightweight plastic table. Basically, nothing that could be used as a weapon. Once seated, Karim started the conversation.

"Why the hell am I in here? That dude attacked me. I was just defending myself. It's not my fault he tripped. It was an accident."

Talon nodded. "Yes. All of those things. But also, angry young Black man knocks old white prison warden unconscious."

"I wasn't angry! He was the one who was angry. He was the one who laid hands on me."

"Right," Talon agreed. "But you asked why you're in here, and that's why you're in here. You knocked out a prison warden— well, 'private jail director'—and you did it in front of like six or seven of his guards. There was no way you were walking out of there yesterday."

"Is there any way I'm walking out of here today?" Karim asked, shrugging his shoulders at his surroundings.

"Maybe," Talon gave the ultimate lawyer answer. "It depends on what they charge you with."

"Charge me?" Karim shook his head hard. "That dude attacked me."

Talon leaned back a little in her chair, as much as the weak frame would allow. "Well, there's a chance they don't file charges," she allowed. "Or maybe not right away anyway. Depends on how the victim is doing."

"Victim?" Karim laughed. "I'm the victim. Did you see what those cops did to me?" He gestured up toward his face, as well as he could in the cuffs.

"I know, I know," Talon agreed. "But look, I'm not your therapist. I'm your lawyer. I'm here to tell you how much trouble you're in and to figure out how to get you out of it."

Karim shook his head again and sighed heavily. "Okay. So, how much trouble am I in?"

"That depends," Talon repeated. "If they charge you with assault in the second degree, not that much trouble. It's a felony, but it's only three to nine months for a first offense."

"Three to nine months?!" Karim exclaimed. "I can't be in jail for three to nine months. I've got school. I've got a job. I didn't do anything!"

"Right," Talon acknowledged before moving on. "The real danger is if they charge you with assault in the first degree. The high end of the sentencing range for that is a hundred twenty-three months. That's ten years."

"Ten years?!" Karim gasped. "Oh, hell no."

"Well, assault one is a lot harder to prove," Talon went on. "With assault two, they only have to prove you intended to assault him and he suffered substantial bodily injury. Losing consciousness is always substantial bodily injury, by the way; there's case law on that. But for assault one, they'd have to prove you not only intended to assault him, but that it was your specific intent to inflict gross bodily harm. That's a stretch, even in the strongest cases. So, I think assault two is a lot more likely."

"Assault two," Karim repeated. "So, three to nine months in here?"

"Probably less," Talon answered. "If they charge you with

assault two, they'll probably offer to knock it down to assault three or even assault four. Assault four is a misdemeanor. You'd get credit for time served. And if they only charge assault two, I can probably get you released on your own recognizance this afternoon. Or at least a low bail that Shayla can post. If all goes well, you won't do more than the one night in jail you just finished."

Karim looked down and shook his head. "That's crazy."

Talon couldn't disagree. "Yes. But it could be worse."

The door to the meeting room opened then and Shayla stepped inside, holding her phone up.

"Did they file the charges already?" Talon asked, a bit surprised.

Shayla shook her head. "No. I mean, I don't know. I didn't even look for that. No, I have a friend who works at Tacoma General. I asked her to find out how that warden guy was doing."

"How's he doing?" Talon asked.

"He's dead, Talon."

Talon took a moment to process that information, then turned back to her client. "It's worse. They're gonna charge you with murder."

CHAPTER 3

All new arrests had to be brought before a judge within 24 hours for a determination of what the lawyers called 'probable cause'—basically, was there at least some evidence the defendant had committed a crime? If so, the prosecutor could file charges. If not, the defendant was released. In Pierce County, Washington, those hearings were heard in the Criminal Presiding courtroom every day at 1:00 p.m.

Which meant Talon arrived at that courtroom at 12:50.

Any earlier, she would have been wasting her time. Any later, and she might not have the time she needed to confirm Karim was indeed on the docket, find out who the prosecutor was going to be, determine what charges were being filed, and make any necessary adjustments to her already mostly prepared argument for a release on personal recognizance.

Although that dead victim wrinkle made a full P.R. release less likely. Still, she might manage a bail low enough Karim's family could post it. Better yet, there was still a chance the State might not file charges. It was an accident after all. If so, Karim's name wouldn't even be on the docket, and they would be processing him out of the jail even as she was preparing to ask for the same result from the judge.

The bailiff was already in the courtroom. Apparently, he didn't care about wasting his own time. That meant the docket was complete, printed out, and resting on the bar for all to see. All who were ten minutes early anyway.

Talon knew there was only the smallest chance Karim wasn't on the docket. She also knew, she wasn't that lucky. She slid the calendar over and flipped to page four. Sure enough, right there between Ms. Johnson and Mr. Kemp, was 'JACKSON, KARIM.' That meant the State wasn't letting him go. That meant Karim was back in one of the holding cells behind the courtroom. And that meant the prosecutor assigned to the case would be showing up any minute.

There were a couple dozen prosecutors in their office who handled homicides, some better than others, like in any vocation. Talon had wondered who would get assigned to Karim's case. It wasn't a particularly complex case. The facts were undisputed, and there were literally dozens of witnesses. It wouldn't take much talent to elicit the testimony establishing what happened. Even the worst homicide prosecutor could do that. The challenge would be in convincing the jury why the undisputed facts added up to a crime. Not every unnatural death was a crime—automobile accidents came immediately to mind. In this case, there was also the whole self-defense angle. It would take some skill to convince a jury, beyond a reasonable doubt, that what happened out there that day was murder. On top of that, the victim was one of theirs, a prison warden—on the same team, so to speak. All of that meant the prosecutor's office might assign one of their top homicide people to the case. And if that happened, if someone smart and experienced handled the case, then Talon could possibly appeal to their logic and empathy to convince them to drop the charges.

But again, Talon wasn't that lucky.

The door from the gallery opened and in walked Jonathan Cobb, veteran prosecutor. Homicide prosecutor. Karim's prosecutor. Talon knew it, and her heart sank a little. Cobb was very tall; he was very mediocre; and he was very unjustly confident. Getting him to see reason was going to be like convincing a brick wall to fly up into the sky. He would never agree with her. Not because he was right, but because he always thought he was, no matter what anyone else told him.

Half of the murder cases that the State Supreme Court had overturned for prosecutorial misconduct had been his cases. His misconduct. Usually for egregiously unfair and prejudicial statements made in closing argument, but also a handful for withholding evidence and even a couple for racially inappropriate questioning of prospective jurors. The kind of stuff you do when you don't think the rules really apply to you, or you're too privileged to bother knowing the rules. He should have been disbarred years ago, or at least fired, but he was in and of The System. And part of the system was not changing the system.

"Talon, right?" Cobb offered her a squint and finger gun point. "We've met, I think. You here on the Jackson case?"

Talon resisted the urge to offer an exaggerated and mocking squint/point back at him. "Yeah, I know you. And yes, I represent Mr. Jackson. You're the prosecutor on his case?"

"Guilty as charged," Cobb guffawed. "See what I did there? A little prosecutor humor to lighten the mood."

"Letting my client go would lighten my mood," Talon suggested. "Please tell me you're not filing charges."

"Oh, wow. I wish I could tell you that," Cobb replied. He set his file on the counsel table reserved for the prosecutors, then looked up and grinned at her. "Oh, wait. No, I don't. We are definitely filing charges against Mr. Jackson. But..." he pulled a document out of his file and handed it to Talon, "not today."

Talon looked at the paper. "Motion for Seventy-Two Hour Hold," she read aloud. "You want the judge to find probable cause, then set it over for two days? Why? Nothing's going to change in two days."

Cobb shrugged and maintained his grin, cheery but hard at the edges. "We just want to make sure we have all the information we need before we make a final charging decision."

Talon scoffed. "You read the police reports. It was an accident. The most you have is manslaughter in the second degree."

Cobb returned the scoff. "I can tell you one thing, Talon. It's not going to be Manslaughter Two. You kill the director of a jail, you're getting charged with murder."

"Even if it was an accident?" Talon challenged.

"Even if it was an accident," Cobb admitted, "which, by the way, it wasn't. It was homicide. We just haven't decided which level of homicide yet."

"You know it's not really a jail, right?" Talon continued. "It's a private entity, profiting off the misery of others."

Cobb laughed. "So are you and I."

At that point, the ten minutes were up and the judge entered the courtroom, to a call from the bailiff of, "All rise! The Pierce County Superior Court is now in session, the Honorable Robert Harvey presiding."

Talon frowned. She'd seen Harvey's name at the top of the docket but had held out some small hope he might be out sick and they would get a *pro tem* judge. Again, not that lucky. Harvey wasn't the worst judge on the bench, but he wasn't the best either. He was just a sixty-year-old white guy who went to a fancy law school back east, but thought he was progressive because he'd moved to the Left Coast to practice. He wasn't, but he thought he was, which was the worst possible combination.

"Are there any matters ready?" he asked after taking his seat above the rest of the people in the courtroom.

Cobb stepped forward. Of course. The prosecutors usually ran the calendar. Harvey's question was directed to Cobb even if he didn't use anyone's name. Talon stepped over to the defense spot at the bar and waited for the announcement from Cobb: "The Jackson matter is ready, Your Honor."

"Very good," Harvey replied. "Bring in the defendant."

There was a single guard by the secure side door that led to the holding cells, and Talon knew there were a half dozen more guards inside. The courtroom guard opened the door and bellowed inside for "Jackson!" A few moments later, Karim walked into the courtroom. He was wearing the exact same jail garb Talon had seen him in that morning, right down to the belly chain and handcuffs. The guard directed him to a spot next to Talon.

"Any good news?" Karim asked in a whisper.

Talon shook her head. "No news at all. Yet."

"What does that mean?" Karim asked, but Talon didn't get a chance to respond.

"Are we proceeding with the arraignment?" the judge asked Cobb.

"No, Your Honor," Cobb answered. He handed his motion to the bailiff who in turn handed it up to the judge. "Pursuant to Criminal Rule 3.2.1, the State is asking for an additional forty-eight hours to review the evidence and make a charging decision."

Judge Harvey nodded approvingly. It was pursuant to a rule. It had to be okay. He turned his head toward Talon but didn't quite raise his eyes to look at her because he was already signing Cobb's order. "Any objection, counsel?"

'Would it matter?' Talon wanted to ask, but she knew better. It would not matter, in fact, so there was no point in objecting. "No, Your Honor. But I would like to be heard on conditions of release."

Harvey nodded as he finished signing the order setting the arraignment over two days and handed it down to his bailiff. "Of course. I'll hear first from the State."

Of course, Talon repeated in her mind.

"Thank you, Your Honor," Cobb began, He really was very tall. At least 6'6". But rather than his height making him imposing, it made him awkward. Talon thought it was probably from the way he carried himself. Rather than standing up straight, Cobb always had a slight hunch, like he was trying not to be quite so much taller than everyone else. Or maybe it was just the natural posture for villains and other creatures of the night. "The State has every intention of filing homicide charges in this matter, however the autopsy had not been completed as of noon today. The State, of course, wants to be thoughtful and deliberate in pursuing justice in this matter, and the court rules, promulgated by our State Supreme Court, allow for exactly this sort of scenario by providing for additional time to make a just and true charging decision. Accordingly, we are asking the Court to maintain the status quo, to include the pretrial detention of the defendant, by setting bail at the sum of one million dollars. We, of course, reserve the right to ask for an increase in the bail at the arraignment should the facts and circumstances warrant it, which I suspect they will. Thank you, Your Honor."

"Thank *you*, Mr. Cobb," Judge Harvey gushed. Then he finally looked at Talon for the first time. "Ms. Winter?"

"Thank you, Your Honor," she began. "I'd like to start by thanking the State for wanting to be thoughtful and deliberate, and for wanting to make—how did Mr. Cobb phrase it?—a 'just and true charging decision'. We applaud that. We encourage that. Indeed, we believe the more thoughtful and more deliberate the State is, the more likely they will come to the conclusion that the just and true charging decision in this case is to not file charges at all."

She turned to Cobb and opened her arms encouragingly. "So, by all means, take all the time you need. But in the meantime, Your Honor," Talon turned back to look up at the judge, "let my client go. He shouldn't have to sit in a jail cell while the prosecutor's office tries to figure out the right thing to do here. If they haven't figured it out yet, I'm not sure what else they will need, except maybe a backbone. This was an accident. A terrible, tragic, fatal accident. But it was still an accident. The facts are hardly in dispute. There were multiple witnesses. The autopsy report is unlikely to show anything not already readily understandable from the eyewitness accounts. The decedent wrapped his arms around my client, my client broke free, and the decedent fell backwards, striking his head on the pavement, which ultimately led to his death. Tragic, but not criminal. The State could have forty-eight more hours, forty-eight more days, even forty-eight more months, and nothing will change the basic facts in this case. But Mr. Jackson should not be deprived of his liberty while the State tries to figure out what is 'just and true' here."

Talon paused and put a hand on her client's shoulder. "As the Court is well aware, the factors to consider when setting bail are whether the defendant poses a danger to the community and whether he is a risk to flee the jurisdiction. In addition, he is not a flight risk. In fact, he is enrolled in college right here in town, and his sister is even a lawyer with the county's Department of Assigned Counsel. He will be looked after and available if the State ever decides to file charges against him.

"In addition, Your Honor, Mr. Jackson poses no threat to the community. To the contrary, he is a benefit to his community. He was attacked while protesting against the blight of yet another private prison in our community. There are significant First Amendment issues in this case, Your Honor. This was an isolated incident set off, not by Mr. Jackson's actions, but by a physical attack of a privatized agent of the state attempting to violate Mr. Jackson's constitutional rights to free speech, peaceably assemble, and petition that government for redress of grievances, even when that government has outsourced its governance to a corporation feeding off the misery of its citizens."

Talon was pleased. She would have to remember some of that argument for the jury, if the case got that far. It was time to wrap up.

"In summary then, Your Honor, the court rules mandate a release in this case. Mr. Jackson is not a flight risk, and he is not a risk to the community. Just the opposite, in fact. The State may want more time to figure out how to charge him with a crime he didn't commit, but he should not, he need not, he *must* not be deprived of his liberty while that decision is made. Thank you."

Judge Harvey nodded approvingly at Talon's argument. "Thank you for your advocacy and your eloquence, counsel," he said. "Bail will be set at one million dollars as requested. Next case."

Karim grabbed at Talon's coat with cuffed hands. "That's not fair!" he gasped.

Talon sighed. "You're right. It's not. Get used to it."

CHAPTER 4

Not being lucky was, in its own way, lucky. Lucky people got lazy. They invented sayings to justify stumbling into successes, like: 'Luck is the residue of planning.' Unlucky people had to work for things, and work hard.

Talon Winter knew hard work.

The hard work on Karim's case was going to be decoupling Karim's actions from the law and the facts. The law that said you can't kill people, and the fact was that James Dank would still be alive if Karim hadn't pushed him away. It wasn't exactly the stereotype of a lawyer arguing black is white and white is black, but it wasn't that far off either. It was the source material for that caricature.

She knew she had a lot of legal research ahead of her on the different forms of legal causation, but when the autopsy report appeared in her email in-box, she also knew the law would take a back seat to the facts. It usually did, in the end. She just needed to be able to study the medical examiner's findings without interruption and—

"Hey, Talon! Whatcha doing?"

Curt Fairchild. Her on-again, off-again investigator. More on than off it seemed lately. He was sweet on her—an open, and unspoken, secret between them—so he charged her less than he should. She supposed she probably shouldn't take advantage of that. But she did anyway. Especially on murder cases that needed a lot of hard work.

"Heyyy, Curt," she looked up from the autopsy report she hadn't even started reading yet. "How are you this fine morning?"

Curt smiled, but nervously. Like a mouse realizing it was cornered by the cat. "I'm okay. I guess. I was going to ask you that, but you seem... happy?"

"Is that surprising?" Talon knew the answer, but cats liked to play with their mice.

"Um, well," Curt stammered. He hadn't stepped all the way into her office yet. He ran a nervous hand back through the black hair falling over his eyes, offering a nice view of his bicep. Talon wasn't interested in a relationship with Curt, but that didn't mean she couldn't appreciate some of his more pleasant qualities. "It's just, well, you're usually serious, even when you're happy. Like how a really intense athlete looks angry after scoring, shouting and punching the sky, even though they're happy inside. You're like that. Angry happy, not smiling happy."

Talon's tactical smile became a little more genuine. It was nice to be known.

"Sit down, Curt," she said. "Let me run a case by you. I may need some help on this one."

Sometimes that cornered mouse is relieved to be played with. It meant he was still alive. Maybe they could even team up against the dog, à la Tom and Jerry.

"Sure, Talon," Curt agreed. He took a seat opposite her and she could tell he was trying not to stare at her. It was nice to be seen too. "What kind of case is it?"

Talon grinned. "Well, that's the million-dollar question, actually. Somebody's dead, but the State hasn't filed charges yet. It could be anything from a tragic accident all the way up to murder."

Curt thought for a moment. "So, it's probably manslaughter."

"Maybe," Talon allowed with a slight cock of her head. "I hope that's what the State settles on too. I can push manslaughter down to an accident. It's a lot harder to push murder all the way to an acquittal. It's not like my guy has an alibi. He definitely did it. Well, he did something."

"What did he do?" Curt asked.

So Talon told him. She had the advantage of having been there, rather than just recounting facts from a report narrative written by a cop with an agenda to convict her client. She did her best to be objective and neutral when breaking down the details of how Dank ended up on the concrete, bleeding out of his head.

When she finished, Curt nodded. "That does sound like an accident."

"I know, right?" Talon agreed. She turned to her computer and clicked on the report attached to the email from the medical examiner's office. "But let's see what the autopsy report says."

She scrolled down quickly, past the initial observations and descriptions of the body. "There are four manners of death," she explained as she skimmed the document. "Natural causes, accident, suicide, and homicide. If the medical examiner ruled it an accident, I don't see how the State can file charges."

"That would be nice," Curt commented. "Over before we even start. We could go grab coffee at that new place around the corner. I hear it's really—"

"Shit!" Talon cut off Curt's attempt to bootstrap a date. "Homicide. The medical examiner ruled it a homicide. Damn it."

"How do they make that determination?" Curt wondered.

"That's just it," Talon answered without looking away from her monitor. She was scrolling back up to read the description of the injuries after all. "They pretend it's all objective, based on just the forensic examination, but there's no way to determine if this kind of case was a homicide or accident based solely on that. If he'd fallen off a forklift or something and suffered the exact same injuries, it would definitely be classified as an accident. It's only a homicide because the cops said someone pushed him."

Curt shifted in his seat. "Well, there's some logic to that, right? I mean, the victim wouldn't have died but for your client pushing him away."

Talon finally pulled her eyes away from the computer screen, but only to shoot daggers at her investigator. "That's called 'but for' cause, Curt, and it's not enough. The defendant's actions have to be a 'proximate' cause of the death."

"Proximate cause," Curt repeated.

"Yeah." Talon looked back at the autopsy report.

"What does that mean?"

Talon considered for a moment, then laughed sardonically. "No one really knows."

CHAPTER 5

Although the most celebrated part of a criminal case was the trial, there were a series of preliminary hearings before the lawyers would stand up before the jury to deliver their opening statements. The first of these hearings was the arraignment. The filing of the criminal complaint initiated the criminal case and once that was accomplished, the defendant would be arraigned. It was at the arraignment, a formal hearing designed to give the accused full and fair notice of the accusations against him, that the defendant would be given a copy of the criminal complaint and informed, on the public record, what he was being charged with.

"Murder in the first degree?!" Talon yanked the proffered copy of the complaint out of Cobb's hand. "Are you fucking kidding me?"

They were back in the Criminal Presiding courtroom two days after the previous hearing. The judge hadn't taken the bench yet, although he'd be doing so at any moment.

"Murder in the first degree is intentional *and* premeditated," Talon shook the papers at the prosecutor. "This was neither. It was an accident."

"Well, Murder One doesn't have to be premeditated," Cobb

defended. "It can also be a death caused during the commission of a serious felony."

"Yeah, robbery, rape, burglary, arson, or kidnapping." Talon knew the statute. "None of which apply here. Or are you really that stupid?"

Cobb forced a smile. "Those are two of the three ways to commit Murder One," he growled through clenched teeth. "The third is extreme indifference."

"Extreme indifference?" Talon repeated. "Are you fucking kidding me?"

Cobb looked down at his own copy of the complaint and read the statutory language reproduced there. "Under circumstances manifesting an extreme indifference to human life, he or she engages in conduct which creates a grave risk of death to any person, and thereby causes the death of a person. So, no, not kidding."

"That means firing a gun into a crowd," Talon protested. "Not this."

Cobb pretended to examine the criminal complaint, even turning it over and looking on the blank backside. "Nope, it doesn't actually say that. Extreme indifference, risk of death, cause a death. Murder One. Don't confuse the classic example with the actual elements."

Talon shook her head. "I can't believe you're doing this."

"Now, as to that felony murder you alluded to," Cobb continued. "Death during the commission of a felony?"

"Robbery, rape, burglary, arson, or kidnapping." Talon reminded him.

"Yes, right. Those are the predicate crimes that make it Murder One," Cobb agreed. "But if it's any other felony, then it's murder in the second degree. If you'll turn to count two of the complaint." He pointed at the paperwork in Talon's hand.

She took a moment, her own angry eyes locked with Cobb's, then turned the page and discovered that Cobb had also charged Karim with murder in the second degree.

"You're charging him in the alternative?" Talon was incredulous. "Murder One based on extreme indifference, and Murder Two based on death during the commission of—what?" She read the charging language. "Assault in the third degree? You're bootstrapping Murder Two from assault three? That's like the lowest felony there is."

"And yet, still a felony," Cobb preened, "and therefore Murder Two. But keep going. There's more."

Talon scowled as she turned to Count III. "Manslaughter in the first degree. Being aware of a substantial risk of death and disregarding that risk. That's still not what happened here. Is this just in case the jury doesn't buy your ridiculous arguments for Murder One and Murder Two?"

"It's to give the jury an option to hold your client responsible for the death of James Dank," Cobb responded. "Which, by the way, he is."

Talon checked to see if there was a Count IV, but the documents ended with Manslaughter One. "What, no Manslaughter Two? Criminal negligence plus death. That's the only type of homicide he might actually have committed."

"It's also the only type of homicide where you can get less than two years in prison," Cobb explained. "You don't kill the warden of a prison and get less than two years."

"Regional director for a private jail," Talon corrected.

"To-may-to, to-mah-to," Cobb rejoined. "It won't matter. I fully intend to obtain a conviction on Murder One. The lesser charges will just merge into that one."

"Unbe-fucking-lievable," Talon huffed, spinning away from Cobb for a moment, only to turn back, arms wide. "It was an accident. They should just sue my guy."

"Your guy doesn't have any money," Cobb replied. "Or else he would have posted that bail by now."

"So, you're going to do the family's dirty work for them?" Talon complained. "You don't represent them. You know that, right? You're supposed to seek justice, not vengeance."

Cobb unfurled a cold grin. "As I said: to-may-to, to-mah-to."

"You're the fucking worst, Cobb," Talon blurted out.

But Cobbs' smile remained. "You ain't seen nothing yet, Winter."

Judge Harvey took the bench at that moment, punctual as ever as the clock struck one. The bailiff announced his entry into the courtroom, everyone stood, the judge sat, and everyone else sat down too. Except the two lawyers ready to step up to the bar.

"The parties are ready on the matter of the State of Washington versus Karim Jackson," Cobb announced, almost cheerily.

Talon declined to say anything. She took the same spot at the same bar in front of the same judge and waited for the same guards to bring out her same client. She was ready.

Judge Harvey accepted the originals of the charging documents from Cobb via the bailiff and looked down at Talon and Karim. "Has the defense received copies of the criminal complaints from the State?"

"Yes, Your Honor," Talon answered, "We acknowledge receipt, waive a formal reading, and enter pleas of not guilty to all charges."

Harvey nodded approvingly. "Excellent. Pleas of not guilty will be entered and the matter set for a pretrial conference. Next case?"

"Next case?" Talon questioned. "May I be heard regarding bail first, Your Honor?"

Harvey's eyebrows knitted together. "We addressed bail two days ago, Ms. Winter. Has anything changed since then?"

"My client has now been formally charged, Your Honor," Talon reminded the judge.

"That would seem to cut against him," Judge Harvey suggested.

But Talon shook her head. "No, Your Honor, it doesn't. He is now formally presumed innocent. And we now know the State's case has no clothes. These are the emperor's new charges. Take a look at the exact language the State is relying on to charge Mr. Jackson. If you just read the boldfaced crime names, it sounds bad. Terrible, in fact. Murder in the first degree, murder in the second degree, manslaughter in the first degree. But it's not intentional and premeditated murder in the first degree; it's extreme indifference murder. It's not intentional murder in the second degree; it's felony murder. And manslaughter in the first degree, which, by definition, is unintentional. Accident, accident, and accident again. This may be tragic, but it's not criminal."

"Plenty of accidents are criminal," Judge Harvey replied. "Vehicular homicide for example."

"Perhaps," Talon allowed, "but that sort of case usually involves drugs or alcohol, and it's reasonable to conclude the defendant may pose some risk to the community from reoffending. But that's not the case here. This was a very particular set of facts that led to a very particular outcome. Mr. Jackson poses no danger to the community, and he's not a flight risk either."

"You argued all this two days ago, counsel," Harvey sighed.

"Two days ago, Mr. Cobb made it seem like my client had

intentionally murdered someone," Talon answered. "Now we know the most they are accusing him of is being reckless. That's not a basis to hold someone, Your Honor."

The judge just frowned at her. So, she pressed on.

"Your Honor, the court rules presume a personal recognizance release," Talon continued, "unless there is a specific danger to the community, or the defendant is a flight risk."

"I know the court rules, counsel," Judge Harvey warned her. "And you better not be about to repeat your argument that it's okay to attack the director of a private prison if you disagree with the privatization of corrections facilities."

Talon frowned. "That's not what I said."

"It's what I heard," the judge replied.

"Me too," Cobb put in eagerly.

"I don't want to hear it again," Harvey repeated.

"Fine," Talon replied. "I will stick to the court rule that Your Honor knows so well. Flight risk and danger to the community. Neither of these things exist here and so the only proper bail decision is to P.R. my client."

"I am not going to P.R. a murderer," Judge Harvey scoffed.

Talon took a beat to make sure she'd heard what she thought she'd heard. "Did you really just say that, Your Honor? Did you really just call my client a murderer? You've already made up your mind based on charging documents you barely skimmed before asking for our plea?"

"*Accused* murderer," Harvey corrected himself, albeit with a poorly concealed eye roll. "Bail will remain at one million dollars. And I would advise you to tone down your advocacy, Ms. Winter, lest you find yourself in a cell next to him for contempt of court."

"Reduce my advocacy?" Talon was stunned.

"I didn't say 'reduce'," the judge responded. "I said tone it down. Watch your tone. No one likes to be talked to in that tone."

"By a woman, you mean?" Talon challenged. "You're tone-policing me?"

"I did not say that." Harvey sat up and set his jaw. He lifted his gavel and hovered it menacingly over its strike plate. "But one more suggestion like that, and I will hold you in contempt. Is that perfectly understood?"

Talon understood all too well. But she also understood that it wouldn't do any good for Karim to have his lawyer in jail with him. At least that's what she tried to tell herself as she left the courtroom after swallowing her words—and her pride.

CHAPTER 6

Swallowing your pride was bad enough in the moment, but the aftertaste was even worse.

"I can't believe I chickened out like that." Talon shook her head, eyes cast downward. Her view was her own legs, along with those of her desk and office chair.

"Don't beat yourself up," Shayla consoled her from across the desk. "You were right. It might have felt good to say something back, but it wouldn't have done Karim any good. In fact, it could have created a conflict and gotten you kicked off the case. You did the right thing."

Talon looked up again. She wasn't convinced. Or rather, even if she was, it didn't make her feel any better. "Whatever," she gruffed. "Let's get to work. You're not here to make me feel better. You're here for a strategy session."

"So, let's strategize." Shayla smacked the top of the table. "What's our strongest line of attack?"

Talon considered for a moment, then answered, "Proximate cause," even as Shayla answered her own question, "Self-defense!"

"Self-defense?' Talon questioned.

"Proximate cause?" Shayla spluttered.

"No way," they said in unison.

Talon leaned back and laughed. "We're off to a great start."

"Should we try to convince each other?" Shayla suggested.

"No, that would never work," Talon answered. "We're lawyers. No one can change our minds. I have a better idea."

She picked up her phone and a few minutes later, in walked their jury, in the form of Curt Fairchild.

"What did you want to see me about?" Curt asked as he entered Talon's office. Then, noticing Shayla, he introduced himself. "Oh, hi. I'm Curt. I'm Talon's investigator. Well, sometimes."

"This time," Talon confirmed. "This is Shayla Jackson, Karim's sister."

Shayla stood up and shook Curt's hand.

"Karim's sister?" Curt said. "Oh, wow. I'm really sorry. That sucks."

Shayla nodded even as she grimaced a little. "Yeah, it does. Can you help us?"

"Of course," Curt answered. "Talon already brought me onto the case. Right, Talon? I'm on this case, right?"

"Yes, Curt, you're on the case," Talon assured him. "But that's not what we mean. We need your help right now."

Curt looked around. "Okay. Sure. Of course. What do you need me to do?"

"Sit down," Shayla said.

"Shut up," Talon added.

"And listen," Shayla concluded.

"When we're done," Talon explained, "you tell us which one of us is right."

Curt sat down, as instructed, in the other guest chair. Talon swung it out to the side of her desk, exactly halfway between her and Shayla. "I'm probably going to say Talon is right," he admitted.

Shayla raised an eyebrow. "Do I sense some partiality from our juror?" She threw a sideways smirk at Talon. "Is there something going on here you want to tell me about, Ms. Winter?"

"There is nothing going on, Ms. Jackson," Talon replied. "He's just afraid I won't hire him anymore if he pisses me off."

Talon turned to Curt. "You help me the most by being honest. Got it?"

Curt thought for a moment. "Got it."

"Good," Talon said. "I'll go first."

She stood up, tipped her head to one side to crack her neck, then began.

"The key to this case is causation, and specifically proximate cause. Or rather, the lack thereof. It's undisputed that the victim died from injuries sustained when the back of his head struck the pavement. The impact fractured the plate under his brain, causing a brain bleed and swelling which ultimately led to his death. However, there is insufficient causation between Mr. Jackson's actions and Mr. Dank's death. While there is 'but for' causation, there is not proximate cause. The victim would not have died 'but for' Mr. Jackson pushing him away, but that act alone is not a sufficient contributor to the ultimate result. The courts have struggled to define exactly what 'proximate cause' really means, but they have been clear that it is more than 'but for' causation. Proximate cause is also a higher standard in criminal cases than in civil actions. Not only does there need to be sufficient connection between the defendant's actions and the criminal result, but there must also be no sufficiently intervening causes and the result must be a foreseeable consequence of—"

"Can I hear from her now?" Curt interrupted, raising his hand and pointing to Shayla.

"Wha? Um..." Talon was taken aback. There was a lot left to

explain. But she acquiesced. "Okay. Yeah, sure." She sat down and gestured for Shayla to take the floor.

Shayla stood up. She nodded to herself and cleared her throat. Then she began. "He was defending himself." And then she sat down again.

"That's it?" Talon barked.

But Curt pointed at Shayla. "She wins. Shayla wins." Then, remembering himself a bit, he added, "Sorry, Talon."

"She can't win with that," Talon complained. "That was like three words."

"Four," Shalya corrected. She double checked on her fingers. "Yeah, four words."

"Sometimes four words are better than more words," Curt rhymed. "I understood her, Talon. I didn't understand you. If the courts don't know how to define 'proximate cause', how are you going to? And if you can't define it, how can you convince the jury it doesn't exist?"

Shayla nodded at Curt. "He's right, Talon. It needs to be simple."

"It needs to be accurate," Talon returned. "Simple is good. I get that. But sometimes it's not enough."

"So, do both," Curt suggested. "Self-defense and proximate cause."

"It's never a good idea to argue alternative defenses," Talon cautioned. "But maybe that could work here. He didn't proximately cause the victim's death, but if he did, it was self-defense."

Curt grimaced a bit. "Something like that."

Talon ran her hands through her hair, but started nodding. "Okay, okay. This could work. But self-defense is always tricky. It's going to come down to exactly what happened. Exactly what the threat was to Karim. Exactly what his response was. He can defend himself, but it has to be no more force than necessary."

"That's okay," Shayla said. "There were dozens of witnesses."

"No." Talon shook her head. "There were dozens of people there, but no one knew what was about to happen. A few of them may have been paying attention, but most of them were probably looking for the exits because it was starting to get out of control."

"I was paying attention," Shayla offered.

"You're his sister," Talon frowned. "You will have zero credibility. Their side is going to take the stand and say Karim's response was excessive and unprovoked, and they're going to be wearing badges."

"You mean," Shayla frowned as well, "they're going to lie, and the jury is going to believe them."

"That's exactly what I mean," Talon confirmed. "We need more."

"What?" Curt asked.

"We need something that prevents them from lying," Talon knew. "Or better yet, something that proves that what they already wrote in their reports is a lie. We need cell phone video."

Shayla nodded. "I bet we can find that. Somebody must have been filming."

"We need to tell our story," Talon explained. "Not fight against theirs."

"That makes sense," Curt agreed.

"Of course, it does." Talon grinned. "I said it."

She turned to Shayla. "We're going to need a use of force expert, those cell phone videos, and one more thing."

"What?" Shayla asked.

"Their medical examiner classified the manner of death as homicide," Talon explained. "As long as that's left unchallenged, the best we can do is manslaughter. We need it to be classified as accident. We need another autopsy."

"Gross," Curt commented.

"Yeah." Talon laughed, if a bit coldly. "Now, come on. We have a funeral to stop."

CHAPTER 7

Talon waited in the lobby of the courthouse the next morning, sitting in a chair against a far wall, but still with a view of the elevators. Cobb's day was supposed to start at 8:30, but it was almost 9:00 before he sauntered through security with a latte in his hand.

Just as well. It gave Talon time to file the paperwork with the court clerk before beginning her surveillance. Surveillance/ambush.

"Jonathan!" Talon called out from her seat across the lobby. She waved her papers in the air. "Oh, Jonathan Cobb! Over here, Jonny!"

Cobb's head swiveled around trying to locate who was calling his name. After a moment he caught sight of the motion in the corner, and the person attached to the motion.

"Talon," he sneered.

Talon stood up and crossed the cavernous lobby, decorated in faux marble in a jarring combination of orange and gray. "Mr. Cobb," she extended the papers she had waved at him, "I believe these are yours."

Cobb took them with his coffee-free hand and frowned at

them. "What are these?"

"Emergency motion for temporary restraining order," Talon explained. "Motion to shorten time on hearing for temporary restraining order. Proposed order to shorten time on hearing for temporary restraining order. Notice of hearing on motion to shorten time on hearing for temporary restraining order. Proposed temporary restraining order. And," she reached into her jacket and extracted one more piece of paper to hand to him, "proof of service of the aforementioned motions, orders, and notices."

Cobb chewed his cheek for a moment, but he couldn't look through the documents with a coffee in his other hand. "Restraining order for what?"

"For the funeral," Talon answered. "James Dank's funeral. We need to stop that. Temporarily, of course."

"Why would you want to stop a murder victim's funeral?" Cobb questioned through an increasingly tightening jaw.

"I don't," Talon answered. "I want to stop James Dank's funeral. Or rather, his burial. I don't really give two fucks about his funeral. But I want to stop the disposal of his body. And specifically because he is not, in fact, a murder victim."

Cobb rolled his eyes and sighed through his nose, long and loudly. "You want to inspect his body? That's morbid. You got the autopsy report. You got the autopsy photos. You don't get to look at the body too. You can't cross-examine a dead body, counselor."

"Not cross-examine," Talon replied. "Re-examine. Your medical examiner's conclusion that it was homicide is bogus. I want a second opinion."

"You want to carve his body up a second time?"

"Not me," Talon said. "I want someone else to carve it up a second time. I can't do that if it's buried in the ground, or worse, burned to ashes. Hence," and she tapped the papers in Cobb's hands.

"What if it's already too late?" Cobb suggested.

"I bet it's not," Talon said. "But that's why I set the hearing for this morning at eleven. It was the soonest I could get it in front of a judge."

"Two hours' notice?" Cobb scoffed. "The court rules say I get five days."

"Five days and that body will be in an urn," Talon knew. "That's why I also filed the motion to shorten time for the hearing. And it would have been two and a half hours if you'd shown up to work on time. Must be nice to have a cushy government job where you can walk in late, commit reversible misconduct, and not get fired."

"Must be nice keeping murderers out of prison," Cobb fired back.

But Talon just smiled. "It has its moments. See you at eleven. Don't be late."

CHAPTER 8

Talon had a couple of hours to kill, but no brain for anything legal. That part of her mind was waiting patiently for 11:00, sharpening its sword and quivering its arrows. Court was the fun stuff. Law and arguments and especially winning. But there was more to being a lawyer than just smiting foes and taking names. There was also paying the rent. Literally. And renewing the lease so she could pay that rent, plus a probable 5-10% increase, for the next twelve months.

Technically, she was subletting, sharing space with several other attorneys, chipping in for communal amenities like the copier and the receptionist. She didn't deal directly with the building owner; she dealt with one of her fellow office-share attorneys, Greg Olsen. He was a civil practitioner and, Talon felt after all their time together, a friend.

She was wrong.

Olsen's office was right off the main lobby. Talon's was at the end of the hall leading to the break room. When she got back from court, she greeted the receptionist, Hannah—who replied with a grunt and a finger in the air until she finished whatever task she was in the middle of when Talon walked in. "One sec. There. And send." She dropped the finger and raised her eyes. "Hey, Talon."

Hannah was the bright face the attorneys had jointly hired to greet potential new clients and anyone else who might wander into their shared office space. It turned out the attorneys themselves were included in those 'anyone elses' and Hannah always had a bright face for them too.

"Is Greg in?" Talon asked, with a glance down the hall toward his office.

Hannah's bright face seemed to dim a bit. She checked her computer screen. "Looks like he's on the phone."

"Oh." Talon frowned. She could wait. She just didn't want to.

"So, how are you doing?" Hannah asked, her voice chipper again. "Any cool new cases?"

"Yeah, actually." Talon nodded. "A new murder case. Total bullshit charge, but the judge is almost as dumb as the prosecutor, so I've got my work cut out for me."

"You always have the best cases," Hannah enthused. "And the best stories. Not like those civil guys. Boring."

"Oh my God, right?" Talon laughed. She put a wrist to her forehead, mocking her colleagues on the civil side of the bar. "Oh, no, I have a deposition tomorrow. Oh, look at these interrogatories I drafted. Oh, oh, I gave opposing counsel all of my exhibits in advance, and they're automatically admissible at trial because if he objects and they're admitted anyway, the judge will impose costs against him, so no one ever objects which is good because I don't know the evidence rules and I have no idea how to try an actual case, oh, oh, oh!"

Hannah laughed. Her smile warmed and filled her eyes. "Yes, that. You're the best." Then the smile drained from those eyes as she glanced again at her screen and said, "He's off the phone now."

"Cool," Talon answered, and she stepped down the hallway to Olsen's office.

"Hey, Greg," she rapped on his doorframe. "I need to renew my lease. Is now a good time to get the paperwork from you?"

Olsen did look up from whatever he was working on. He grimaced slightly, then leaned back in his chair and ran a hand over his head. "Uh, yeah... About that."

Talon cocked her head. "What?"

"Um, so, funny thing..." Olsen started.

Talon doubted it.

"It turns out," Olsen went on, "the company that owns this building is owned by another company that's part of a conglomerate or something that's associated somehow with A.C.E."

"Ace?" Talon repeated. "What's 'Ace'?"

"American Correctional Enterprises," Olsen answered. "The company that built that new jail outside of town."

Talon crossed her arms. "You mean the for-profit human cages?"

"Uh, sure," Olsen responded. "I guess. I don't know. I don't do criminal work. You know that. All I know is they own this building, and they own that jail, and so..."

Talon raised an eyebrow. "So?"

Olsen shrugged. "So, you know."

"Yeah, I do," Talon agreed, "but I'm going to make you say it out loud."

Olsen sighed, then leaned forward and rested his elbows on his desk. "They won't renew your lease. Your sublease, technically. They won't let me renew your sublease."

Talon nodded. "Uh huh. And what did they say when you told them they should? You know, when you stood up for me, went to bat for me, took a stand for me?"

Olsen sighed again. "Talon…"

"Yeah, that's what I thought." She couldn't believe it. And yet a part of her could. She hated it when that part was right.

"Talon, try to understand," Olsen entreated. "I don't have any control. We have a great lease here. You know that."

"I do know that," Talon confirmed. "That's why I wanted to renew. But never mind. Somehow, it's lost its luster. But you go ahead and enjoy it, knowing what you're giving up to keep it."

"Come on, Talon." Olsen threw his hands open. "It's just business."

"Funny," Talon said, "I thought we were in the business of justice."

She turned to leave, then looked back one last time at her former officemate. "Oh, and fuck you."

CHAPTER 9

Talon didn't have time to be angry. Or rather, her schedule required her to channel her 9:30 anger at Olsen into her 11:00 argument against Cobb. Maybe not a bad thing, actually. Passion was good, and what was more passionate than anger?

"Talon," Cobb greeted her as she walked into the presiding courtroom again.

"Fuck you," she shot back without bothering to look at him. She dropped her file on the counsel table reserved for the defense attorneys who rotated in and out during the day.

"Wow," Cobb half laughed. "Is that any way to greet a colleague? Just because we're on opposite sides doesn't mean—"

"Just because we're on opposite sides," Talon interrupted, "doesn't mean I'm going to give you a pass for charging a man with murder for defending himself against some jackass who couldn't keep his balance. You're only doing it because he was part of your team, your system. A system that harvests young men for pain and profit. But you know what?"

Cobb didn't get the chance to try to guess what.

"I'm glad you charged him," Talon answered her own question immediately. "I'm glad the dirtiest prosecutor in this county is going to help me bring all of this out in the open. Let's daylight this fucking travesty of a criminal justice system, where corporate interests run the show and pay pieces of shit like you to keep everything pacified so they can buy their hundred-foot yachts and California beach homes. Enjoy that pension, Cobb, because I am definitely going to enjoy making you crawl through broken glass to earn every penny of it."

"Wow," Cobb repeated. "Who pissed you off?"

"Who didn't?" Talon growled. Then she regretted giving Cobb even that vague bit of information. "Never mind, Cobb. Just get ready to argue. I sure as hell am."

That was a good thing, because the clock struck 11:00 and out came Judge Harvey once again. Not only were all the arraignments in front of whichever judge had rotated into the criminal presiding for their six-month stint, but all preliminary motions on criminal cases were also scheduled there. The good news was, at least Harvey was familiar with the facts of the case. The bad news was, Talon was one snide remark away from being held in contempt. Harvey wasn't one to forget a slight. Then again, neither was Talon.

Normally, the defendant was present for all hearings on his case, but there hadn't been time to arrange for transport from the jail. It was okay, though, because the criminal court rules allowed a defense attorney to waive their client's presence for any hearing that wasn't a 'critical stage' in the case. What exactly was a 'critical stage' in a criminal case? No one was quite sure, but you know it when you see it. Like obscenity. Or proximate cause.

"Good morning, counsel," Judge Harvey began amicably enough. Maybe he had forgotten his threats to Talon. "I understand we're here for some sort of emergency motion, is that right?"

"Something like that, Your Honor," Talon confirmed. "I'm

sure you recall the case of the State versus Karim Jackson. I have filed a motion for a temporary restraining order to prevent disposal of the victim's body until after it can be examined by an independent defense expert."

Judge Harvey grinned slightly. "Which is it, counsel? An independent expert or a defense expert?"

Ha fucking ha, Talon resisted the urge to say. Instead, she answered, "Both, Your Honor. And thank you for clarifying the point that no expert is truly independent. The medical examiner who conducted the autopsy in this case works for the same county and is paid out of the same budget as Mr. Cobb here."

"And myself," Judge Harvey pointed out.

Talon took a hard pass on that softball. "The medical examiner here concluded the death was a homicide," she continued. "That could only have happened if someone, likely the police or the prosecutor's office, maybe both, advised him that the decedent was pushed. There is nothing inherent in the injuries suffered which could lead to that conclusion in the absence of such subjective information being provided by agents of the State."

"How do you know that?" the judge challenged. "You're not a doctor." He hesitated. "Are you?"

"No, Your Honor," Talon sighed. "But that's exactly the point. I'm not a doctor, Mr. Cobb isn't a doctor, and Your Honor isn't a doctor. The only doctor involved to date is the State's doctor, and that's simply not fair to the defendant. We shouldn't have to just accept the opinion of the State's doctor."

Judge Harvey pursed his lips in thought for a few seconds, then turned to Cobb. "Are you objecting to this, Mr. Cobb?"

"Am I objecting to a murder victim being carved up a second time by some hired gun defense expert?" Cobb asked rhetorically. "Am I objecting to the murder victim's remains being kept in the county morgue rather than being released to his family? Am I objecting, Your Honor, to the family being prevented from laying the murder victim to rest at the time and in the manner they wish? Am I objecting to the murder victim and his family being re-victimized all over again by ridiculous defense attorney games, designed not to seek truth or justice, but only to harass, embarrass, and delay? Yes, Your Honor. Yes, I am objecting. I am proudly objecting, to all of that."

"Did you want to say, 'murder victim' one more time?" Talon whispered at Cobb out of the corner of her mouth. He ignored her. Judge Harvey didn't seem to have heard it.

Instead, the judge seemed surprisingly interested in doing the right thing. Or maybe he was just turned off by Cobb's hyperbole, which was something at least.

"There's no jury here to impress, Mr. Cobb," he chastened. "In fact, there's no defendant here either, which I find a little troubling. Even more troubling is the fact that there are no doctors here. We have three lawyers arguing over what a doctor might say about a forensic examination of a murder victim."

Talon raised a finger to object, but Harvey cut her off. "Alleged murder victim," he corrected.

"In any event," the judge continued, "I don't think the three of us are the best people to be discussing the necessity of the defense request. I know I don't want to make a decision based on the paid arguments of two lawyers, whether paid privately or out of the county budget. I'd rather make that decision on the paid arguments of two doctors, again paid privately and out of the county budget."

He nodded to himself, then motioned to his bailiff to hand him the papers Talon had filed that morning.

"I am going to set this hearing over two days," Judge

Harvey announced, signing Talon's temporary restraining order.

"Your Honor, I object," Cobb interjected.

"Yes, I was here when you did that," Harvey responded without looking up. "I gave you forty-eight hours to review information and prepare to file charges. It seems only fair that I give the defense that much time to prepare to change my mind."

He looked down at Talon. "And that was not a slip of the tongue, Ms. Winter. I am dubious about setting a precedent that the family of every alleged murder victim must endure the indignity of a second forensic examination of their loved one's remains. That being said, I will order the medical examiner's office to hold onto the body and not release it for final disposal until such time as we have had our hearing and you have or have not changed my mind regarding the necessity of such an extreme request."

There was a lot in the judge's statement that Talon wanted to take issue with, but she knew when to accept 'Yes' as an answer.

"Thank you, Your Honor," she said.

"Forty-eight hours," Judge Harvey repeated. "You better have a doctor here, and he or she better be ready to explain to me why any of this is absolutely necessary."

"Understood, Your Honor," Talon nodded, then she quickly stepped away from the bar before he could change his mind.

She'd won the first hearing. Now all she needed was to find an independent medical examiner in only two days' time to help her win the next one.

CHAPTER 10

"A private medical examiner?" Curt questioned. "Like a coroner for hire?"

"A coroner is different from a medical examiner," Talon replied. "Anybody can be a coroner. A medical examiner has to have a medical degree."

Curt cocked his head. "Is that true?"

Talon rolled her eyes. "Yes. But I don't have time to cite the statutes for you. I just need to know if you know anyone who might know someone who would know such a person."

Curt thought for a moment. "I don't know."

"Ugh!" Talon threw her head back. She was about to call him useless, but she caught herself. It wasn't his fault he was useless on that particular occasion. She didn't know any private body carvers either.

"Maybe one of the hospitals?" Curt suggested. "Don't they do autopsies there sometimes? Maybe Harborview has someone."

Harborview Medical Center was the regional trauma hospital about thirty miles north in Seattle. It served as the Tier One trauma center for four states, including Alaska. It was exactly wrong. But Curt's idea was right.

"No, not Harborview," Talon replied. "Everyone who dies there dies from some sort of major trauma. Exactly the sort of thing that would lead the county medical examiner to doing the autopsy. No, we need a small, private hospital. The kind where rich people go to die. The kind where the hospital does a quick, minimally invasive forensic exam on site, just to confirm Grandpa Moneybags died of a stroke and not something a greedy nephew slipped into his drink."

"That's pretty dark," Curt remarked.

"Yeah, well, life's dark, Curt," Talon grumbled. "I hate to be the one to break it to you."

But Curt just grinned. They both knew she kind of liked being the one to break it to him.

"Which reminds me," Talon continued, "I don't know if you've heard anything from Greg yet, but—"

"Not from Greg," Curt interrupted. "From Hannah. She knows everything. She told me they aren't renewing your lease."

"Yeah, so, I guess that means—"

"I'm going to need a new office too," Curt stepped on her words. "I gave them my thirty-day notice. I'm not staying here if you can't."

"You don't even rent space with us," Talon questioned. "You're down the hall."

Curt shrugged. "Same building. Same owner. Same landlord. I just don't have to deal with a coward like Greg."

Talon frowned. "I'm not sure I'd call him a coward," she tried.

"What would you call him?" Curt asked her. "Whatever it is, it's not a friend."

Talon had to nod at that. "But you're a friend?"

Curt cocked his head at Talon. "You have to ask that?"

She smiled. "No," she admitted. "But sometimes it's fun anyway."

Curt didn't pick up that thread of the conversation. Instead, he suggested, "So, why don't we look for new office space together? Maybe something with a view of the water?"

"Or closer to the courthouse," Talon suggested.

"Yeah, or that," Curt conceded. "Maybe even this afternoon, if you're not—"

Talon's phone rang just then. She held up a finger to Curt. "Hold that thought."

"Talon Winter, attorney at law," she answered the phone. "Oh. It's you, Cobb." She made no attempt to hide her derision. Then Curt got to listen to one half of the ensuing conversation.

"Oh, now you want to talk?

"Today?

"Ha, I doubt it.

"No, no, I'll make the time.

"Better be worth it.

"Fine. See you then."

She hung up without the formality of a 'Goodbye' then looked across her desk to Curt.

"Sorry, friend," she said. "Office hunting will have to wait. I've got a rattled prosecutor and a chance to get a good deal for my client. Need to strike while the iron's hot."

CHAPTER 11

Cobb had a much nicer office than he deserved. All of the prosecutors did. Their offices were on the top floors of the 11-story County-City Building, which sat near the top of a large hill overlooking Commencement Bay. Cobb's office had a peekaboo view of the water and a sweeping one of Mount Rainier, the 17th tallest mountain in the United States and an inactive volcano that took up about a quarter of Pierce County's land area. On a clear day, every purple and white detail was visible for a hundred miles. Talon grunted at it as Cobb welcomed her into his office and commented, "Nice view, huh?"

"I didn't come here to discuss your view," Talon grumbled. "I came here because you said you had an offer for my client."

"What? We can't be civil, too?' Cobb protested.

Talon sat down and set her mouth into a thin line. "Fine. Nice view," she allowed. "Now, what's your offer? It better be credit for time served."

Cobb sat down, too, laughing. "Oh, no. It's not going to be credit for time served. Not unless we push the plea out until you and I are both retired."

"How old do you think I am?" Talon asked instinctively,

then thought better of it. "Never mind. What's the offer?"

Cobb nodded. "Okay, fine. Straight to business. I like that. So, first order of business: you drop your motion for a second autopsy and let the family bury the victim."

"Alleged victim," Talon corrected. "You're as bad as Harvey."

"I'm allowed to say 'victim'," Cobb countered. "I'm the prosecutor. I wouldn't be prosecuting this unless he was a victim. I don't care what the judge says, although he isn't wrong."

"Agree to disagree," Talon crossed her arms. "And no way. I'm not dropping my motion."

"Well, that's just it," Cobb went on. "The only reason I'm even making this offer is because the family is freaking out that they can't give Mr. Dank a proper funeral. Plus, they really don't like the idea of some defense doctor carving up their loved one. They find it disrespectful."

"I have no sympathy for them," Talon answered. "You're holding an innocent man in jail. That's worse than a doctor performing a forensic examination on a body that's already dead."

"Agree to disagree," Cobb parroted with a grin. "But you have to agree to releasing the body. That's non-negotiable."

"I can give you a hard maybe on that," Talon answered. "It really depends on what the offer is. If it's good, I can live with that—although I will need iron clad assurances you don't back out of the deal because, to be perfectly honest, I don't trust you. Like, at all. I do not trust you in any way, shape, or form. In fact, I would probably want the offer in writing, signed by your boss and maybe a priest or two, before I'd be willing to let go of that body. Especially now that I know it's a negotiating chip."

"You're using a dead man as a negotiating chip?" Cobb sneered.

"I am, now that you told me I can," Talon answered. "Now, hurry up and tell me the offer already. I'm starting to think it can't be that good if you're taking this long to spit it out."

"Fine, fine." Cobb threw his hands up. "Murder Two."

"Murder Two," Talon repeated. "That's your amazing offer?"

"Yes, but," Cobb raised a cautionary finger, "he has to agree to exceptional sentence upward to twenty years, the minimum for Murder One."

Talon nodded. "So, plead guilty to murder in the second degree, but agree to be sentenced as if he were convicted of murder in the first degree. Do I have that right?"

"And release the body for burial," Cobb reminded her with a jab of his finger. "That's key."

"That's ridiculous," Talon shot back. "That's what that is. Absolutely ridiculous."

"It saves him ten years in prison," Cobb defended.

"Ten years off your absolute best-case scenario," Talon countered. "If you get a conviction for Murder One, which you won't, and if you convince the judge to give the maximum sentence, which you won't."

She stood up. "I'm actually surprised at what a complete waste of my time this has been. I shouldn't be, but I am. I let myself believe you had actually come to your senses."

"So give me a counteroffer," Cobb said, also standing up. "The family is pissed. They want to bury him, but they don't want his murderer to walk away with nothing."

"He's not a fucking murderer!" Talon shouted. "It was an accident! How many more times do I have to say that?"

Cobb crossed his arms. "Well, at least one more. To the jury when this thing goes to trial. If you're not going to take my offer."

Talon shook her head. "I'm not going to take your offer. I'm not going to make you a counteroffer, because the only counteroffer I would make is a misdemeanor with credit for time served, and even that I would advise my client to reject. This entire prosecution has been a travesty, and I for one will see to it that justice prevails."

Cobb chuckled and started to reply, but Talon cut him off. Don't laugh at Talon Winter.

"And you know what else I'm going to see to?"

Cobb took a moment, then went ahead and asked, "What?"

"I'm going to see to it," Talon growled, "that James Dank's body gets carved into so many pieces they won't need to cremate him to fit him into an urn."

CHAPTER 12

Big words required big actions to back them up. Or, for lawyers, even more big words from a person with a big resume. And, as it turned out, a big name. Giannina Evangelopoulos.

"It's Greek," she explained as she invited Talon to sit in her office on the first floor of the Greater Puget Sound Tahoma Medical Center, a private hospital in Steilacoom, Washington, a waterfront resort and retirement town just south of Tacoma. She had a view of an interior courtyard that was mostly empty except for one nurse pushing a patient in a wheelchair, and two other nurses taking an ironic smoking break, while likely complaining about the other nurse, or the patient, or both. Or doctors like Giannina Evangelopoulos. "Don't ask me to spell it," she joked. "We don't have time for that."

"No worries," Talon responded. "I'll make sure I can pronounce it correctly in time for our hearing."

"Right." Dr. Evangelopoulos pointed steepled fingers at Talon. "And when is that hearing again? This week?"

"Tomorrow," Talon admitted. "Which is technically this week."

"Tomorrow," Dr. Evangelopoulos repeated. "That seems

like kind of short notice. What is it you want me to say again?"

Talon took a moment. This was always a tricky response. She didn't want to be accused of coaching the witness about what to say on the stand. On the other hand, Dr. Evangelopoulos was a professional and an expert. She was unlikely to agree to say anything that wasn't true. Not that Talon would ever ask her to do that, but her question suggested at least that possibility as an answer.

"The truth, of course," Talon was sure to start with. She always answered that type of question with that preamble, followed by the inevitable, "But... I'm hoping the truth lines up with what I'm arguing."

"And what are you arguing, Ms. Winter?" the doctor asked with a grin. She was about the same age as Talon with similarly long black hair, although hers was curly and pulled back into a loose ponytail.

"I'm arguing that I need more information so I can argue other things," Talon answered.

Dr. Evangelopoulos laughed. "You sound like a lawyer."

"I guess that's a good thing," Talon supposed. "To be more specific, I'm arguing that I need a second autopsy to be able to challenge the findings of the first autopsy."

"What if I agree with the first autopsy?" Dr. Evangelopoulos asked. "Do you still want me to tell the truth?"

"Of course," Talon was quick to answer. "But just to me. That's not the kind of thing I need a jury to hear. You tell me that, then I thank you and send you on your way. No need to testify at all."

"That doesn't seem completely forthright," Dr. Evangelopoulos observed.

"Like you said, I'm a lawyer," Talon answered. "I have a job to do and that job is to protect my client. If you can help me with that, then I will use you for that purpose. If not, then I will thank you and release you from any further obligation. It's not dishonest; it's just not candid."

Dr. Evangelopoulos laughed slightly and shook her head. "I can't imagine having a career where the distinction between honesty and candor is significant. I wouldn't omit a relevant fact just because it might hurt my patient's feelings."

"You might omit it," Talon suggested, "if it was the difference between your client spending thirty years in jail or not. Especially when he's innocent."

Dr. Evangelopoulos leaned forward. "Is he innocent, Ms. Winter?"

"Does that matter?" Talon deflected.

"It may not to you," the doctor said, "but I think it does to me."

Talon nodded. "That's fine. Because he is definitely innocent, and he definitely needs your help."

It was a good mic-drop line, but they weren't done talking yet. Talon knew she had the good doctor on board. But she still needed to explain what the hearing was about and why she was so important.

"So, how does this work?" Dr. Evangelopoulos asked. "Do you have the reports for me to review or what?"

Talon nodded and pulled out a copy of the autopsy report from her briefcase. "Yes. Here you go. The prosecutor is going to argue that you can be just as effective by simply reading their medical examiner's report and pointing out areas where you might disagree with his methods or conclusions. My argument is that would be far less persuasive than you performing an independent examination and testifying as to your own findings and conclusions."

"Well, obviously, it would be preferable to conduct my own examination," Dr Evangelopoulos said.

"Obviously," Talon agreed.

"But that doesn't mean it's necessary," the doctor continued. "I would assume the medical examiner did a thorough job, and his conclusions were made in good faith based on the available information."

"Hold that thought," Talon suggested. She pointed at the report. "Read that first. But I'm not sure how you can tell if it's accurate without looking at the body yourself. Otherwise, you're just kind of taking his word for it."

Dr. Evangelopoulos considered for a moment, then shrugged. "I suppose so. But I think deferring to him may well be justified, Ms. Winter. I've certainly conducted forensic examinations here at the hospital, but I've conducted very few full autopsies, and never where murder was suspected."

Talon raised a cautionary finger. "Let's leave the m-word out of it, shall we, doctor? Murder is a legal concept. It places criminal responsibility and hinges on several other legal concepts like self-defense and proximate cause. Let's have you stick to the h-word. Homicide. I just need you to look at the body and tell me whether, looking only at the body, you can really say whether it was a homicide."

Dr. Evangelopoulos put a hand to her chin. "I would want to know more information than just what trauma I find on the body. I don't know how anybody could decide whether a death was homicide without some outside information about the circumstances surrounding the death."

Talon smiled and pointed at the doctor. "That. Say that. I mean, read the report, examine the body, write your own. Do all that. But then turn to the jury and say exactly that."

"Jury?" Dr. Evangelopoulos's eyes widened. "I thought this was just in front of a judge."

"Oh, it is," Talon assured. "But that's just the opening act. Juries are the main event, and you're going to be the star of the show."

Dr. Evangelopoulos chuckled nervously. "I am?"

"Actually, no," Talon admitted with a grin. "You're a very important supporting actor. But the star? That's me."

CHAPTER 13

The biggest stars made those around them shine too. That was true in any sort of competitive or performative endeavor, whether sports or theater. Or lawyering. Talon was definitely the star of the show, but in the early scenes, she could afford to direct the spotlight onto a bit player. Indeed, it was a sign of her stardom that she could dictate where the spotlight fell. And that next afternoon, it fell on Dr. Giannina Evangelopoulos.

And also Michael Smith, assistant medical examiner for the Pierce County Medical Examiner's Office. Cobb got to call witnesses too.

What Talon hadn't expected was the surprise guest star at the end of the show.

But first, the show had to start, and all courtroom scenes always started with the judge taking the bench.

"All rise! The Pierce County Superior Court is now in session, the Honorable Robert Harvey presiding!"

Harvey took the bench over a busy courtroom. They had scheduled Talon's motion onto the afternoon criminal motions calendar, which was supposed to start at 2:30, right after the day's arraignments were over. But often as not, they started late because the 1:00 arraignment calendar always had too many arraignments and/or too many long-winded lawyers to complete everything in 90 minutes. That meant Talon and Cobb sat in the back of the attorney area at the front of the courtroom, and Drs. Evangelopoulos and Smith sat at the front of the public area in the back of the courtroom, surrounded by other lawyers and litigants waiting their turn to sway the judge to whatever their request of the day was.

It was also stuffy in the windowless courtroom and that time of day when everyone was tired from too much lunch or, as often as not, not having had time to eat lunch. Talon fought off her own sluggishness as Harvey finished the last two arraignments, informing both the prosecutor and the public defender to be as concise as possible, if not more so. Thirteen minutes later, the arraignments were finished, and Harvey was ready for Talon and Cobb. Talon took a moment to scan the courtroom. There were still a lot of attorneys in the gallery. Some of them she knew, a few of them she didn't. It seemed that most of the attorneys who had come for the 1:00 calendar might have been sticking around to watch the main event on the 2:30 card.

"Are the parties ready on the matter of the State of Washington versus Karim Jackson?" Judge Harvey asked formally. He could be pretty sure of the answer—they would have already rescheduled it with the bailiff if they weren't ready—but it was a nice way to get everyone on the same page.

"Yes, Your Honor," Talon answered first, as she stood up. It was her motion after all.

"The State is ready, Your Honor," Cobb added as he, too, stood and stepped forward to sit at the tables in the front of the courtroom. It was going to take a lot longer than an arraignment; no one wanted to stand at the bar right below the bench the entire time.

Talon gave a nod to the guard by the side door, and a few

moments later, Karim was escorted in to sit next to her for the arguments. She'd told him what he needed to know: it was a motion for a second autopsy; she would be doing all the talking; he didn't need to listen, but he absolutely couldn't speak.

"This is your motion, Ms. Winter," Judge Harvey began, "So I'll hear first from you and your witness."

Talon's witness was, of course, Dr. Evangelopoulos, but she didn't like the dynamic of Smith being able to testify second and rebut whatever Evangelopoulos said. Fortunately, like the judge said, it was her motion. She could call any witnesses she wanted.

"The defense's first witness," she stood up and announced, with a look over her shoulder at the assistant medical examiner in the front row of the gallery, "is Dr. Michael Smith."

Cobb sprang to his feet. "I object, Your Honor," he wailed. "Dr. Smith is the State's witness."

"As you said, Your Honor," Talon responded, "this is my motion. I can call any witnesses I want, in whatever order I want. Dr. Smith is present in the gallery. He doesn't belong to the State, Your Honor. He is *a* witness, not *their* witness, and I am calling him to the stand."

Judge Harvey allowed a faint smile. He could appreciate the advocacy. And she wasn't wrong. "Call your witness, Ms. Winter."

"The defense calls Dr. Michael Smith," Talon repeated, even as Cobb flopped into his chair, again with a pouty huff.

Smith stood up tentatively, offering a sheepish glance at Cobb. If he was asking for guidance, he got none. Cobb was still pouting, his head down, staring hard at the table in front of him. Smith nodded to himself, then stepped forward to be sworn in by the judge.

There were several advantages to Talon in calling Smith herself. In addition to allowing Evangelopoulos to contradict him rather than vice versa, she could also limit his questioning to only the bare bones. Just enough to help her make her point, without all of the extra dog and pony show about how experienced and expert he was like Cobb undoubtedly would. Then Talon could do the extended version with Dr. Evangelopoulos, ensuring her star got more screen time than the State's star.

"Please state your name for the record," Talon began after Smith was seated in the witness box to the side of Judge Harvey.

"Um, Michael Smith," he responded. He was clearly uncomfortable. He didn't know Talon from Eve, but he knew she was the enemy, and he was obviously concerned with being seen consorting with said enemy. Medical degree aside, he was just another middle-aged bureaucrat, pulling in an adequate salary and the promise of a pension in exchange for the security of a government job. Talon guessed his age at about 45, with receding brown hair that needed a trim, and a neglected, puffy body hiding under his brown blazer.

"How are you employed, sir?" Talon continued. She knew the answer, but part of being a lawyer was asking stupid questions so the answers would be in the record.

"I, I'm an assistant medical examiner," Smith answered, "with the Pierce County Medical Examiner's Office."

"Do your job duties include performing autopsies?" Talon continued. She decided to completely skip the part about Smith's medical degree and years of experience.

Smith nodded. "Yes."

Short response. *Good*, Talon smiled to herself. "Did you conduct the autopsy in this case?"

Smith nodded again and placed a hand on the case file folder he'd brought to the stand with him. "Yes, ma'am."

"Please tell the Court what you determined the cause of

death to be," Talon instructed.

Smith hesitated, glanced at Cobb who still had his head down, then looked up at Judge Harvey to answer. "The cause of death was blunt force trauma to the posterior skull, resulting in a fracture to the occipital bone, cranial hemorrhage, and swelling of the brain."

"Okay," Talon said. "And did you also determine a manner of death?"

Smith turned himself to face forward in the witness stand again. "Yes, ma'am."

"And what did you, Assistant Medical Examiner at the Pierce County Medical Examiner's Office, determine was the manner of death?"

"The manner of death was homicide," Smith answered. He seemed relieved to be able to say something that helped the prosecution.

"Was it?" Talon immediately challenged. "My question was, 'What did *you* determine was the manner of death?' Could you please answer that question, doctor?"

Smith took a moment, his expression confused. "You want me to add 'I determined' to the beginning of my answer?"

"That's exactly what I want you to do," Talon confirmed.

"Okay," Smith replied slowly. "I determined the manner of death was homicide."

"How did you determine that, doctor?" Talon shot back immediately. Then, before he could try to answer that question, she interposed another. "Were you present when the decedent suffered his injuries?"

"Um, no," Smith admitted. "No, I was not."

"Was there a note taped to the back of his head that said, 'someone killed me'?" Talon demanded.

"Obviously not." Smith sat up a bit in his chair.

Talon noted that Cobb had finally looked up from the table, but he hadn't objected yet. Not that she would have minded. She'd know she was getting to him.

"So then, how did you decide it was homicide?" Talon repeated her question.

"Someone pushed him," Dr. Smith answered.

"And that makes it homicide?" Talon asked. "It's that simple?"

"Well, nothing is ever simple—" Smith started, but Talon cut him off.

"Well, that's one thing we can agree on," she said. "Who told you he had been pushed?"

"I'm sorry?" Smith cocked his head at the question.

"You said he was pushed," Talon reminded him. "Who told you that?"

"Um, I'm not sure," Smith admitted. "Probably the detective."

"The detective," Talon repeated. "Do you remember the name of this detective? Was it someone you know?"

"Um, yes," Smith answered. "It was Detective Louise Crenshaw."

"Detective Louise Crenshaw told you the decedent had been pushed, and that's how he suffered the injury to the back of his head, is that right?"

Smith nodded. "Yes, that's correct."

"And you used that information to determine that the manner of death was homicide?"

"It was one piece of information I considered," Smith acknowledged, but qualified, "among others."

"Like the actual injury itself?" Talon knew. "Did you also

consider that?"

"Yes, of course," Smith agreed.

"So, tell me, doctor," Talon leaned in toward the witness, "could a person suffer that sort of injury falling off a back porch onto a cement patio?"

Smith thought for a moment. "Yes." He knew which side he was on, but he wasn't going to lie.

"Could a person suffer that sort of injury," Talon continued, "by being struck in the back of the head by, say, a loose beam at a construction site?"

Smith took a moment to answer, tilting his head slightly as he considered the hypothetical. Finally, he nodded. "Yes, this sort of injury could also be caused by an object striking the back of the head, as opposed to the person falling and striking their head on the ground, if that's what you're asking."

Talon nodded back. "That's what I'm asking," she confirmed. "The injury you observed on the back of Mr. Dank's head, that was caused by the collision of his head and a very hard, unyielding object, regardless of which hit which, correct?"

Smith thought again before answering. "Correct."

"So, why homicide?" Talon pressed. "Is it just because some cop told you he was pushed?"

Smith set his jaw a bit. "A detective," he clarified, "informed me that he was pushed down by another human being. Thus, it wasn't an accident. He didn't fall off his porch. He wasn't hit in the head at a construction site. He didn't push himself to the ground. Someone else pushed him. That's homicide."

Talon rubbed her chin and let out a long sigh. "What exactly did the detective say happened?"

Cobb finally intervened. "Objection, Your Honor," he called out. "Calls for hearsay."

Talon scowled at him. "Hearsay? Are you kidding me?" Then she remembered to address the judge. "It's not hearsay, Your Honor," she defended. "I don't care if it's true. I just care what she said and how it impacted this witness's conclusions. If anything, I think it's not true. Therefore, I'm not offering it for the truth of the matter asserted, so by definition, it's not hearsay." She thought for a moment, then added, "Also the evidence rules don't apply at preliminary hearings like this, so Mr. Cobb's objection is doubly stupid."

Judge Harvey frowned at Talon. "That sort of language is inappropriate, Ms. Winter. I won't have you calling opposing counsel stupid. As to the applicability of the evidence rules or the existence of non-hearsay uses for the expected testimony, I will avoid making those rulings and sustain Mr. Cobb's on other grounds. Namely, you have made your point. I don't need to hear the exact wording the detective used when describing the incident to this witness, even assuming he could remember that after this amount of time. Move on."

"Fine," Talon replied. "I will move on. I'll move on to Dr. Evangelopoulos. No further questions for this witness."

She spun on her heel and returned to her seat next to Karim. He tried to ask her a question, but she waved him off, placing a finger to her lips and pointing at Cobb making his way to the front of the courtroom, gesturing generally that she needed to pay attention to the prosecutor's cross-examination of his own witness. Karim seemed to understand and returned his attention to the proceedings.

Cobb stepped up to the witness box, came to a complete stop, then just stood there for several seconds. He waited two seconds too long, ensuring everyone was uncomfortable, before finally asking his one and only question. "So, there's nothing from the injuries themselves that would allow you *or any other doctor* to differentiate between homicide and accident, is that right?"

"That's right," Smith agreed.

Cobb nodded, almost to himself, then turned back toward his own counsel table. "No further questions," he announced without looking at the judge.

Talon frowned. It was the best question Cobb could have asked for that particular hearing. Anything more would have been superfluous.

"Any redirect exam," Judge Harvey asked her, "based on that, um, one question?"

"No, Your Honor," Talon answered. "I'm done with Dr. Smith." But she wasn't done with the hearing. "The defense calls Dr. Giannina Evangelopoulos to the stand."

Dr. Evangelopoulos rose from her seat in the gallery and walked toward the witness stand, exchanging nods with her colleague, Dr. Smith, as they passed each other. Judge Harvey swore her in, and she took a seat on the witness stand as Talon stood up to begin her direct examination.

"Could you please state your name and occupation," Talon prompted.

"Giannina Evangelopoulos," she answered. "I am a staff physician at Greater Puget Sound Tahoma Medical Center in Steilacoom, Washington."

"So, you're a medical doctor?" Talon followed up. Again, a silly question, but the witness has to say it or the lawyer can't argue it.

Evangelopoulos knew it was silly and grinned a bit as she answered. "Yes, I have an M.D."

"Great," Talon responded. "Let's take a moment then, and have you please advise the Court of your education and experience as it pertains to forensic pathology."

There was a reason Talon didn't ask Smith to detail his experience; it would have dwarfed Evangelopoulos's. His entire job was doing autopsies, all day every day. He'd likely done thousands of them. Dr. Evangelopoulos, on the other hand, was more of a generalist. So, after she listed her undergraduate and medical degrees, and her residency—not in forensic pathology—she explained that she had been at Greater Puget Sound Tahoma Medical Center for just over four years and in that time had conducted, "Perhaps a dozen autopsies or partial autopsies."

A lot less than Smith had done, but a dozen more than Talon or Cobb. Most importantly, it was twelve more than Judge Harvey had done, so Talon could only hope the judge would at least defer to her experience, even if he wasn't overwhelmed by it.

But rather than try to gauge the judge's reaction with a quick glance up at the bench, Talon kept her attention focused on the witness before her and soldiered ahead.

"Are you familiar with the four manners of death?" she asked. "And if so, could you please list them for the record?"

"Yes, of course." Dr. Evangelopoulos nodded. "While there can be any number of causes of death—from heart attack to gunshot wounds to drowning—all of those causes fit into one of four broad categories we call the manners of death. Those four categories are natural causes, accident, suicide, and homicide."

"Who makes the determination of what the manner of death is?" Talon asked.

"Typically, the pathologist who conducts the autopsy makes that determination," Evangelopoulos answered.

"And what information should a pathologist consider when making that determination?"

"Well, ideally," Evangelopoulos glanced up to deliver her

answer directly to the judge, "that determination should be made using just the information from the forensic examination."

"No outside information?" Talon followed up.

"I would say no," Evangelopoulos confirmed. "Again, that's the best practice."

"Why is that the best practice?" Talon asked, as if she didn't know the answer she had specifically retained Dr. Evangelopoulos to give.

"Pathology is a science," Evangelopoulos explained. "It should be objective. Outside information, especially outside information from someone untrained in forensic pathology, will be subjective. Therefore, you would be introducing subjective information into what is supposed to be an objective determination. It risks undermining the conclusion. It's also unnecessary."

Talon was a little surprised by that last bit. But she liked it. So she followed up. "Unnecessary? Why?"

"Earlier I said there are four manners of death," Evangelopoulos replied, "but there is actually a fifth: undetermined. The objective pathologist will describe the injuries and explain the cause of death from those alone. In this case, blunt force trauma to the back of the head. If the manner of death cannot be determined from those same injuries alone, then the pathologist can and, in my opinion, should leave the manner of death as undetermined."

Talon nodded as she allowed the answer to settle in on those assembled in the courtroom, most importantly Judge Harvey. It was an important point, one that might impact the jury come trial, but it wasn't enough for the current battle. Or rather, it wasn't exactly the point of the current battle.

"Have you had a chance to review the autopsy report prepared by Dr. Smith in this case?" Talon asked.

Dr. Evangelopoulos nodded. "Yes."

"Now, he went ahead and made a determination that the death in this case was homicide, is that correct?"

"He indicated his opinion that the manner of death was homicide," Evangelopoulos restated the question a bit more precisely. "Yes."

"And that was based at least in part," Talon followed up, "on subjective information from a police detective, is that correct?"

Evangelopoulos nodded. "Yes, that appears to be the case."

And finally, the point: "Are you able to determine, from Dr. Smith's report alone, what the manner of death would be if one were to ignore the subjective information from the police officer?"

"From the autopsy report alone?" Evangelopoulos emphasized. "No."

"Why not?"

Dr. Evangelopoulos took a moment to collect her thoughts, like a teacher trying to explain a math problem to a particularly dense group of students—probably not a far cry from how most doctors viewed most lawyers. "This report documents those observations which Dr. Smith felt were relevant to support his conclusions as to cause and manner of death. The report does not necessarily include any observations which might not support those conclusions. It's impossible to tell from the document itself because, by definition, it doesn't contain the information it didn't include." She cocked her head at Talon. "Does that make sense?"

It made sense to Talon, but it didn't need to make sense to her. She looked up at Judge Harvey, who probably shouldn't have, but provided Talon the slightest nod to signal that he, too, understood the witness's assertion.

"Yes, doctor," Talon returned her gaze to her subject. "That makes sense." Everything was teed up for her final question: "Is there any way you could effectively assess and, if need be, challenge the findings of Dr. Smith's conclusions as to cause and, especially, manner of death in this case? And if so, how?"

"Yes." Again, Dr. Evangelopoulos looked up at the judge. "I need to examine the body myself."

And that was the whole point. "No further questions," Talon confirmed and turned back to her counsel table.

"Any cross-examination?" Judge Harvey invited.

The prosecutor stood up. "Of course, Your Honor. Thank you."

Cobb approached Dr. Evangelopoulos and came to a stop just a little too close to her.

"Do you agree with Dr. Smith's statement that no doctor, not even you, could tell the difference between homicide and accident solely from the injuries in this case?"

Dr. Evangelopoulos thought for a moment, then gave a very lawyerly answer. "It depends."

"On what?" Cobb demanded. "How would a second autopsy reveal anything related to how the blunt force trauma was inflicted on Mr. Dank's skull?"

"It probably wouldn't," Evangelopoulos conceded, "but there may be secondary injuries. Things like scrapes to the hands or elbows. Anything that might indicate efforts to break his fall and how he ended up striking his head."

"But can't that sort of information be gleaned from the report?" Cobb pressed ahead.

"Possibly," Evangelopoulos allowed, "but only if it was included in the report in the first place."

"Of course it was included in the report," Cobb defended.

Evangelopoulos took a moment, then asked, "Is that a question?"

Talon smiled. She loved a witness she didn't have to defend

with objections.

Cobb exhaled loudly through his nose. "Fine. Why would it not be included in the report?"

"I don't know why information wasn't included," Evangelopoulos answered. She looked up at the judge again. "I don't even know whether there's any information that wasn't included. That's why I need to see the body myself."

Cobb ran a hand over his head, then squeezed his arms tightly across his chest. "Doctor," he growled. "I'd like you to assume for a moment, just one moment, that your colleague over there, Dr. Smith—who, by the way, has far more experience and expertise in this area than you have—actually did his job properly, upheld his oath solemnly, and executed his duty with the professionalism and honor attendant to his position. Assume all that, for just one moment. Can you do that, doctor?"

Evangelopoulos suppressed a bemused smile. "Sure," she said after a moment. "I can do that."

"Okay, good," Cobb huffed. "So, assume he included everything in his report. Assume he did a thorough job and didn't miss anything. Assume he wasn't some second-rate quack from a local nursing home. Are you telling me you can't just look at his report and criticize it to the jury in whatever manner you've been paid to do? Do you really need to dig up the body and defile it further? Is that really what you're saying, doctor?"

Talon would have objected to the *ad hominem* attacks against both her and the doctor, but she had a feeling Dr. E was going to do just fine on her own.

"What I'm saying, sir," Evangelopoulos added the honorific to show she didn't mean it, "is that I cannot assume any of that. I do not know whether Dr. Smith did a thorough job. But I do know I am not a second-rate quack. I do know Greater Puget Sound Tahoma

Medical Center is not just a nursing home. I do know I have not been paid to say anything but the truth. And I do know that your grasp of the case generally, and today's hearing specifically must be sorely lacking, if you think the remains need to be dug up, since everyone else in this courtroom knows they are still at the county morgue. What I'm saying is, your question is unprofessional and uninformed, bordering on nonsensical, but I hope you are able to understand my answer. If not, perhaps Ms. Winter can try to explain it to you again,"

Cobb's face reddened. Harvey saw what was coming and cut it off.

"I think that answer was sufficient, doctor," the judge advised. Then, to Cobb, "And your question was enough too, counselor. Again, I think you've made your point. I suggest you sit down, and we excuse this witness." The judge looked to Talon. "I assume you have no redirect exam, Ms. Winter?"

Talon knew to give the judge the answer he wanted. She was ready for argument anyway. "Correct, Your Honor. I have no further questions for this witness."

But before Judge Harvey could formally excuse Dr. Evangelopoulos from the witness stand, a woman in the front row of the gallery stood up and called out, "I have questions for this witness, Your Honor!"

She was tall, even more so in three-inch heels. She was older, with thin pale skin under expert makeup and gray hair sweeping back in a smooth bob. She was affluent, with plenty of gold jewelry flashing on her ears, neck, and wrists. And she was prepared for court, dressed in a dark suit and holding up a set of pleadings she clearly intended to file with the clerk.

The judge didn't recognize her immediately. Talon did.

"Who are you?" Judge Harvey demanded, obviously

perturbed at the audacity of the interruption.

"I am Helen Hampton Montclair, Your Honor, of the law firm Gardelli, High & Steinmetz." Talon's old firm, when she still did civil litigation, what seemed like a lifetime ago. "I represent the estate of the murder victim, Mr. James Dank."

Talon looked up at the judge. "*Alleged* murder victim," she reminded him. "Also, I object. Obviously."

"I don't know, Your Honor," Cobb put in, his previous anger replaced with barely concealed glee. "This could be fun."

Helen Hampton Montclair stepped forward, but stopped just short of the counsel tables Talon and Cobb occupied. "May I be heard, Your Honor?"

Judge Harvey pulled a hand down his face. "Sure," he sighed after a moment. "Why not?"

Talon knew Helen Hampton Montclair, or rather she knew of her. Part of climbing the corporate ladder was knowing when not to make eye contact with the ones at the top who would push the ladder off the parapet. Talon was a young up-and-comer, trying to make partner at Gardelli, High & Steinmetz; Hampton Montclair was one of the senior partners who would have decided her fate, if Talon hadn't left of her own accord. Well, mostly of her own accord, choosing ethics over advancement, and money. A lot of money. More than she sued for when she left. But that was another story.

The important thing was, right then, Hampton Montclair was one of the city's top civil litigation attorneys and a senior partner at one of the city's most expensive civil litigation firms. She was used to being respected, feared even. And catered to. Harvey probably knew her, and probably knew all that too.

"Thank you, Your Honor." Hampton Montclair strode forward purposefully, between the counsel tables, and stopped just short of the lower bar. Rather than hand her pleadings to the bailiff, whose hands were extended in anticipation of the documents, Hampton Montclair raised them again for all the world, or at least all the courtroom, to see. "If Your Honor grants the defendant's motion, I will immediately file a motion to intervene, a motion to quash the order, a direct appeal to Division Two of the Court of Appeals, and a writ of mandamus against Your Honor with the State Supreme Court."

"Jeez, Helen, are you gonna shoot his dog, too?" Talon whispered to her old boss.

Hampton Montclair ignored the jab from her former subordinate. She either didn't remember Talon or didn't want Talon to know that she did. "This entire proceeding is outrageous, Your Honor. It's bad enough that Mr. Dank was murdered by this," she gestured toward Karim, "this person."

"Oh wow, I wonder what you were really going to say," Talon commented, no longer in a whisper. "Never mind. We all know."

"But to subject his family," Hampton Montclair continued, "to this invasion, this intrusion, this *indignity* is nothing less than unconscionable."

"Indignity," Talon laughed. "Indignity? That's the big one? Have you seen what Mr. Jackson has had to endure? He is literally in chains."

"That's enough, Ms. Winter," Judge Harvey admonished.

"Is it, Your Honor?" Talon spun to face the judge. "Is it really? Let's remember why we're all here, shall we? We're all here because the State wants to put my client in prison for the rest of his life, or damn close to it."

"We're here because your client murdered someone," Cobb contradicted.

"So says you," Talon shot back at him. "But the law and the

jury will say otherwise." She looked up at Harvey again. *"If* you allow us to present the vigorous defense he's entitled to, Your Honor. We're talking about taking a man's life away. Another young Black man thrown away. Why? For the dignity of a dead white man?" A quick glare at Hampton Montclair, then back again to the judge. "Really? I don't know what's worse. Denying my motion to preserve the theoretical dignity of a dead man over my client's right to a fair trial, or denying it in order to prevent Mr. Jackson from presenting the strongest defense possible. Either way, it stinks. And Ms. Hampton Montclair should sit down, wait for you to make your ruling, then do whatever she's been hired to do, without inflicting on me and my client the actual indignity of interrupting and hijacking our duly noted and well-founded motion."

Hampton Montclair huffed audibly. "May I be heard, Your Honor?"

"No," Harvey barked. "It's my turn to talk."

Talon was fine with that. She'd said her piece anyway.

"Ms. Hampton Montclair," Harvey began, "I don't like being threatened. Ms. Winter, I don't like being disrespected. And Mr. Cobb, as ever, I appreciate it when you don't say much. I understand that you all have jobs to do. I respect that. Believe it or not, I actually appreciate the passion you've brought to your advocacy. But I have a job to do, too. My job is to protect this man's rights while allowing the State to seek to hold him responsible for his," a nod to Talon, *"alleged* crime. The way I do that is by ensuring he has a fair trial. The fairest trial possible. I won't bore you with the theoretical underpinnings of the jury system or quotes about cross-examination being the greatest invention ever devised for discovering the truth. What I will say is this: the fairest trial is the trial with the most information. The best decisions are made with the best information. And in any criminal trial, but especially a murder trial, we want the best possible decision."

Talon was liking where the judge was heading.

"But," the judge raised a pointed finger, "there are other considerations. Dignity for the alleged victim is not to be dismissed out of hand. If this crime was, in fact, committed, it would be adding insult to injury to defile the body."

Or maybe not, Talon thought. She wasn't that lucky, she recalled.

"As I said, each of you has a job to do," Harvey continued, "and it is the judge's job to seek justice and find compromise. Accordingly, this is my ruling."

Talon steeled herself for the disappointment inherent in being a criminal defense attorney.

"And if any of you interrupt me," Judge Harvey warned, "you will be held in contempt. Ms. Winter knows I'm serious."

She did.

"Dr. Evangelopoulos," Judge Harvey announced, "will be allowed to examine the body, but only externally. She will not be allowed to cut or do anything else invasive. Her examination will be limited to whatever she is able to observe without the use of a scalpel or other similar tool."

Talon looked to Evangelopoulos. The doctor nodded back, communicating, *Yes, that's good enough.*

"Further," Harvey continued, "the examination will take place today. As in *now.* Go directly from here to the medical examiner's office. I want nothing to delay the final rest of Mr. Dank. The family has waited long enough."

A bone to Hampton Montclair, but also a shot across her bow. "So, Ms. Hampton Montclair, you can appeal me if you want, but that will freeze everything in place until the appellate courts have time to hear your plea. That is what will delay the funeral, not a brief external examination conducted this very afternoon. You and your clients have a decision to make."

Hampton Montclair didn't respond, but she did react: a twisted frown and a glance back at the gallery where Dank's family was presumably hidden among the rest of the gathered crowd.

Harvey scanned the attorneys before him. "I would ask if there are any questions," he said, "but I won't, because I won't answer them anyway. My ruling is clear, and this hearing is over."

He banged his gavel and stood up to take his leave.

Karim turned to Talon. "Did we win? It sounds like maybe we won."

"We won a little." Talon nodded. "And for our side, that's big."

CHAPTER 14

The Pierce County Medical Examiner's Office was located just east of downtown, out on Pacific Avenue, past the ships on Thea Foss Waterway and the city's iconic Tacoma Dome stadium, up a large hill and next to a condominium high-rise whose builders either didn't know they were building next to the morgue, or figured their prospective buyers wouldn't think to ask while admiring the views. The M.E. building itself was unassuming enough, with a brick façade, a small parking lot off to one side, and a line of thin deciduous trees in front of the structure obscuring the name on the building, another reason local residents might not know who their neighbor was. It was a single story, above ground anyway. The real work happened in the lower levels.

Talon rarely got the opportunity to attend autopsies. It was the same with crime scene investigations or suspect interrogations—those all occurred before charges were filed and the defense attorney finally got onto the case. In truth, there wasn't a particularly strong need for Talon to observe Dr. Evangelopoulos conduct her examination of Dank's body, but there was no way she was going to miss it.

Cobb apparently didn't share Talon's enthusiasm. He opted

out of observing Dr. E's examination. Talon wasn't surprised. Some early advice she'd gotten when transitioning to criminal defense was to always visit the scene of the crime because the prosecutors never did. They were used to having the cops do all the work for them, content to experience the case through paper and photographs. Skipping Dr. Evangelopoulos's re-examination was in the same vein, especially if you realized the body was its own type of a crime scene.

The other good news about Cobb not attending was that Talon wouldn't have to share the observation room with him. It would have been brutal to try to make small talk with him, and they could only argue about the case for so long. Luckily, instead of an hour of hiding her contempt for a pompous ass—or letting it shine through, more likely—she got an hour by herself, her eyes tasked with watching Dr. Evangelopoulos through the window to the examination room, but her mind free to float along the expanses of the case. And everything else.

Evangelopoulos and Smith entered the examination room at the same time, along with a technician rolling a gurney with a sheet over what was very obviously a dead body. The technician locked the gurney into place at one of the examination stations, then she and Smith stood off to one side, but still in the room. Evangelopoulos wasn't going to be allowed to examine a body in a murder case all alone. It was evidence, after all.

Evangelopoulos pulled back the sheet, exposing the bone white corpse underneath. Whatever blood had been in the body had drained to the bottom, leaving the top almost transparent. Evangelopoulos carefully slid a gloved finger under the neck and began her examination. Talon didn't know exactly what the doctor was doing but she trusted her, and that allowed those thoughts she was alone with to bubble to the surface.

Helen Hampton Montclair. Did that self-important witch really not recognize Talon? They'd worked at the same law firm for nearly seven years. They might not have been friends, they might barely have spoken, but they knew each other. At least, Talon certainly knew Hampton Montclair. Was she pretending not to know Talon just to try to keep that power dynamic? Maybe she just didn't want to give Talon the satisfaction of acknowledging her. Talon hadn't left the firm on good terms. In fact, she'd sued them for constructive wrongful discharge. Maybe acting as if Talon was beneath her was Hampton Montclair's petty revenge for daring to stand up to her and her firm. Talon didn't know, but she expected that she might get to find out. She had a feeling she hadn't seen the last of Helen Hampton Montclair and outrageous demands from the Dank family. Talon wondered whether Judge Harvey would be as adept at dealing with whatever bullshit motion Hampton Montclair brought next.

Judge Harvey. Talon had to admit, Judge Harvey came up with a pretty impressive solution to the puzzle Hampton Montclair had launched into his lap. Maybe he was coming around to treating the defense fairly. Probably not, Talon suspected. He was still an old white guy with power in a system that punishes other people for not being old white guys. Talon might be sipping coffee at the Medical Examiner's Office; Dr. Evangelopoulos might be in the examining room doing the inspection Talon had demanded; but Karim was still sitting in the county jail in lieu of a million dollars bail. Talon wondered whether she should maybe ask for a reduction in bail, especially if Evangelopoulos found something that cast doubt on Karim's guilt. If Judge Harvey lowered the bail and let Karim out, that would be a huge red flag to Cobb about the strength of his case.

Cobb. What a jackass. He possessed the usual traits of a

prosecutor: self-righteous, self-important, self-serving. The expected result when you give power over the fringes of society to people affluent enough to go to college and law school and privileged enough never to get arrested for the drugs they did at those same colleges and law schools. Talon really disliked him. Sometimes, she wanted to win the case just to best him. Well, that, and also to save Karim from life in prison.

Karim Jackson. The client. The one who almost gets forgotten in all of it. Remaining silent can mean remaining forgotten, or at least overlooked. But really, everything was all about him now. All about Karim's life and what would become of it. Murder or accident, Dank was gone. What was done was done. One view through the observation room window confirmed that. But unlike the blanched remains of James Dank, Karim Jackson had his whole life ahead of him. Maybe. If Talon could win. *No pressure.*

Shayla Jackson. Karim wasn't the only one counting on Talon. Shayla was too. Everyone who loved Karim was. They had put their trust in Talon. A lot of people were starting to do that. Talon wasn't sure if she liked it. Trust could lead to dependence, and dependence could lead to burden. She didn't want a bunch of puppy dogs following her around.

Curt Fairchild. He was definitely turning into a puppy dog that wanted to follow her around. Actually, he wanted to do more than that to her. But Talon wasn't letting that happen again. Still, he trusted her enough to do whatever she asked, which was helpful in an investigator. And he was going to follow her to her new office, wherever that ended up being. It definitely felt burden-y. Still, she appreciated the loyalty. It was a lot better than disloyalty.

Greg Olsen. It turned out he was also a jackass. But worse than Cobb, in a way. Cobb was paid to be a jackass. His jackassery was part of the system. It came from a place of privilege and overconfidence, or overcompensation. But at least he didn't shrink from a fight. Olsen's jackassery was spawned from fear, from weakness. That was definitely worse. Maybe the worst. Was that a harsh assessment of a lawyer who was just trying to hang on to his choice office space? Maybe, but Talon didn't hold anyone to standards she wouldn't hold herself to.

Herself. Well, no reason to dwell on herself. She chuckled, almost nervously, and took another sip from her rapidly cooling coffee. She had stuff to do. All the time. Clients to defend, offices to find, autopsies to observe—or external forensic examinations, anyway. And by the look of it through the observation window, that examination was just about done. Whew.

Dr. Evangelopoulos was pulling off her gloves and the technician was pulling the sheet up over the corpse's face again. Evangelopoulos nodded toward the observation room to signal she was indeed finished, then turned back to offer a 'thank you' to Smith. She walked toward the observation room and dropped her used gloves in the trash outside before opening the door and joining Talon inside. A faint smell of death followed her into the observation room. Talon reflexively stuck her nose into her coffee cup for another swig to mask the odor.

"Well?" Talon asked after a hasty drink.

"Well," Evangelopoulos parroted, "I examined everything. Head, neck, shoulders, back, hands, arms, legs, everything. I was looking for anything to suggest exactly how the fall happened."

"Right." Talon knew that. "And?'

Evangelopoulos shrugged. "It's hard to say."

Talon's shoulders dropped. "Great."

"Well, there's more," Evangelopoulos continued. "Maybe more important too, if I understood our hearing before."

Those shoulders rose again. "More important than how it

happened?"

"Maybe," Evangelopoulos answered. "It goes to how the autopsy happened. Smith missed something."

"He did?" Talon allowed herself to get a little excited. "What?"

"Does it matter?" Evangelopoulos asked.

Talon considered for a moment. "Maybe not. Missing anything dents his credibility. But missing something big is even better. What did he miss?"

"Bruising," Evangelopoulos answered. "On his knuckles. It's faint, but it's there."

"His right hand?" Talon hoped.

"Yes," Evangelopoulos confirmed. "So, you might want to confirm he's right-handed. But if he is, it could be evidence he threw a punch."

"And Smith missed it," Talon grinned. "Or intentionally left it out."

"Even better," Evangelopoulos said. "Right?"

"Right." Talon nodded to herself as she allowed the potential of the discovery to unfold in her mind. She grabbed the doctor by the shoulders. "This is perfect. I could kiss you."

"Maybe later," Evangelopoulos smiled coyly. "Right now it would be a conflict of interest."

CHAPTER 15

Being a solo lawyer meant also being a business owner. Being bad at either one meant doom. Talon had a case to win, but she also had a new office to find. One she could reasonably afford, but one she also didn't mind coming to every day. Cheap was easy to find. Luxurious was too. The hard find was the bargain. The Goldilocks office, but on a holiday weekend sale.

Even though Curt had expressed his horny puppy dog desire to move his office with her, Talon had embarked on her office hunt alone. She didn't need his input, largely because she didn't really value it. He wasn't a lawyer. His clients were lawyers. Talon's clients were people accused of crimes and their families, facing serious charges and lengthy prison sentences. They needed to be immediately impressed at her apparent success, lest they conclude she wouldn't be successful on their case too. Curt just needed four walls and an internet connection.

After checking out yet another promising, but ultimately disappointing, office prospect, Talon returned to her soon-to-be ex-office to consider next steps, either on the office search or the Jackson case. She wasn't sure which. She'd decide when she sat down.

Unless Curt interrupted her at that exact moment, which he did.

"Hey!" He rapped on her doorframe even as he slid into her office uninvited. "I saw you get off the elevator."

Talon squinted at him. "You can't see the elevators from your office."

Curt grinned. "I may have been waiting for you."

"Creepy," Talon observed. "Please don't do that. Although kudos to you for me not seeing you."

"Hey, it's what I do for a living," Curt responded. He sat down across her desk from her. "Speaking of which, I did a little digging."

Looked like her decision was being made for her. The office could wait. "Karim's case? Did you finally find some cell phone videos?"

"What? Oh, no," Curt admitted. "No videos yet. But no, I was talking about our new office. I got a lead on something that hasn't hit the market yet."

Ok, twist, Talon thought. *Office, not Karim.*

"You got a lead?" Talon went ahead and asked. "On an office? How did you do that? Spying on a landlord getting off the elevator?"

Curt laughed. "No. Of course not. I mean, I would do that, but I don't think that would really be very helpful. No, I put the word out with some of my contacts."

Talon narrowed her eyes again at Curt. It surprised her somehow that he had contacts. She hired him mostly out of convenience, and price, and because he was always pushing himself on her. But she supposed he must have other clients. Maybe he was better at his job than she expected. "Cool," she approved. "So, what's the lead?"

She still didn't expect much. Curt thinking something was good wasn't the same as Talon thinking something was good. It needed to meet her needs first.

"It's a little far from the courthouse," Curt admitted.

Talon nodded. Here we go.

"But it's got a great view of the water."

Talon raised an interested eyebrow. "Go on."

"It's right out on Schuster Parkway, just before Point Defiance," Curt said. "They're building a new complex, mixed retail and condos, right on the water."

Talon's eyebrow dropped. "I've seen that already. It's not finished yet, and the prices they're advertising are way too high. Plus, I don't want to be smashed in between an organic pet food store and an upscale cupcake shop."

"No, no. Not there." Curt shook his head. "Across the street. When the developers bought the plot for the upscale retail on the water, they also bought a smaller plot across the street to park all the construction equipment and materials. Once they didn't need it for that anymore, they built a little three-story office building. But it's on the wrong side of Schuster, jammed between the road and the train tracks, so they sold it to some guy and now he needs tenants."

Talon put a hand to her chin. "And you know this guy? The one who bought the building?"

Curt shrugged. "I know someone who knows him. Well, someone who knows someone who knows him."

Talon rolled her eyes slightly. Still, it sounded not terrible.

"I guess it's a quick drive up Schuster to the courthouse," she considered.

"Right," Curt agreed. "You can also cut up past Wright Park and come in the back way by the jail."

Talon looked at her empty desk, her not-turned-on-yet computer, and the clock on the wall indicating the day had just begun. She was right: her decision had been made for her. She stood up. "You're driving."

Curt stood up too. "Sounds good. I already got you a coffee. It's in the passenger seat cupholder."

Talon's eyebrows knitted together. "Again, creepy."

Curt smiled. "Thanks. I'm better than you think I am."

CHAPTER 16

The office building wasn't much to look at it. Tucked between the three-lane Schuster Parkway to the east, and train tracks atop a steep hill to the west, there were no other buildings on that side of the road. Just a three-story box, painted an inoffensive taupe, and a smallish guest parking lot, although it seemed large enough to handle any client meetings, Talon was sure to note as Curt pulled in and parked in a strangely random spot in the middle of the lot.

"Why here?" Talon gestured toward the empty spots closer to the door. There were no other cars in the lot.

"Why not?" Curt responded. "It's a nice day for a short walk."

Talon supposed that was true. She stepped out into the sun, unfiltered as there were no trees on that side of the road either. The calls of seagulls floated over from Commencement Bay, visible past the grassy park across the street. She also noted it would be a short walk to the inevitable coffee shop at the upscale retail complex next door to the park. Although there was no crosswalk, so she'd have to dodge traffic a bit to secure her morning latte.

She frowned down at the cup in her hand. It still bothered

her that Curt knew not only her coffee preference, but her schedule sufficiently to time his ambush so the coffee would still be hot when they went down to his car, not to mention his presumption that she would agree to his suggestion in the first place. She felt known. She didn't like it.

She put the coffee back in the car and closed the door. "Come on. Let's go find the guy you don't actually know."

Curt locked the car with his key fob and hurried after Talon, barely catching the front door as it closed behind her. For a moment, Talon felt bad for not holding it open for him. She didn't like feeling that way either.

"The lobby is nice," she offered, without looking at him. "Maybe this will work out."

"Sure, it will," Curt replied happily. "Or it won't. Either way, it will be the right decision."

"How are you like this?" Talon grimaced at him. "So positive?"

Curt shrugged. "Why not be positive? None of this matters anyway. We're all just going to die eventually, and the world will go on without us. We might as well be nice to each other and enjoy what we can."

He stepped over to the reception desk, even as Talon tried to process his 'none of this matters' comment. Unexpectedly dark. That she liked.

"Hi," Curt greeted the woman seated at the receptionist desk. She was young, pale, and skinny, with a green tank top that showed off her tattoos and her dull brown hair twisted into an off centered knot on the back of her head. "Is Mr. Delgado in? We wanted to talk to him about renting some office space. Tony Jacoby sent us."

"Tony Jacoby?" Talon whispered. "Seriously? Is that his real name?"

Curt thought for a moment. "Well, I mean, I think it's Anthony."

Talon rolled her eyes again and turned away, as her nascent respect for Curt drained away again.

"I know he's here." The receptionist reached for her computer mouse. "I'll message him and see if he's available."

As they waited, Talon inspected the furnishings, with an eye toward what impression it would leave on a potential client. Overall, she approved. It was fairly neutral, with vases of dried reeds and abstract watercolors on the wall. The main color was beige. It wasn't flashy, but it was new and wouldn't leave clients with the idea that she was struggling, short on both cash and victories.

"Paul will be right out," the receptionist informed them. She pointed to a minifridge in the corner. "You can grab a water or something, if you want."

Talon didn't want, so instead she took a seat on the beige leather couch against the far wall. She continued her appraisal of the lobby, now seated where a prospective client would be while the receptionist messaged her to come to the lobby. Curt took a can of Diet Coke from the fridge.

He opened it, loudly, as he plopped down next to her. "Nice place," he observed. "I could get used to walking in here every day."

Talon agreed, but didn't feel like sharing the sentiment. Thankfully, Paul Delgado walked into the lobby to spare her from more small talk with Curt.

He was a big person. Not extremely tall, although not short, but very stocky, with broad shoulders and a barrel torso. He had short black hair and a goatee, and was wearing a button-up shirt in a sort of teal shade, with black pants and shoes. Rolled up sleeves revealed thick forearms and a very expensive looking gold watch.

"Hello, I'm Paul Delgado." He extended a hand to his guests. "Riley said you're interested in office space? We haven't actually started advertising for that yet, but since you're here..."

"Tony Jacoby sent us," Curt put in as he shook Paul's hand.

Paul took a beat. "I don't know who that is."

"Me neither." Talon stood up and shook Paul's hand. "Talon Winter. I'm an attorney. This is Curt Fairchild. He's an investigator. He used his amazing skills to find this place before anyone else did. We'd love it if you could show us what's available."

Paul smiled and opened an arm toward the hallway he'd emerged from. "Right this way, then. I bet we have what you're looking for." Then, after they started walking down the indicated hallway, he asked, "What are you looking for?"

Talon answered for both of them. "I'm a criminal defense attorney. I spend a lot of time in court, but when I'm not there, I'm here meeting clients. I need a receptionist who knows how to deal with people from diverse backgrounds. I need a lobby that impresses people. I need a conference room for interviews and depositions. I need a printer, a copier, a fax—yes, the court still uses faxes—and a coffee maker, although I could probably get my own of some of those. And I need an office large enough to hold a potential client and their family, furnished in a way that lets them have enough confidence in me to put their loved one's fate in my hands." She jabbed a thumb at Curt. "He needs four walls."

"And internet access," Curt added.

Paul nodded. "I think we can manage all of that. Riley is super cool and can get along with anybody unless they piss her off and then she can deal with anybody. You'll like her. We have a shared printer/copier/fax machine on each floor. And this," he gestured to the glass doors at the end of the hallway, "is our shared conference room. You just have to book your time with Riley."

Talon liked what she saw. It wasn't ultramodern with all steel and glass or anything, but the furniture was classic and clean. The windows faced the road, but that meant there was a view of the water too. She could see hosting meetings there. "Nice," was all she said. "Do any of the offices have a water view too?"

Paul smiled at her. "There is one. On the top floor. Would you like to see it?"

"Obviously," Talon answered. She walked over and punched the elevator button. "Is it a corner office too?"

"Sorry." Paul shook his head. "I have the corner office on three. But it's pretty nice just the same."

Curt was lingering in the conference room but hurried over when the elevator doors dinged open. It was one of those elevators in small, short buildings. Perfectly adequate, but somehow still rickety-feeling. That would be a negative as Talon took clients up to her office. But it was a short ride. The doors dinged open again and they stepped out on the third floor.

The hallway was decorated similarly to the lobby, with a matching vase of dried whatever on a stand directly in front of them as they stepped off. It was a nice touch that brought the feel of the lobby up to the offices. Talon wondered if Riley had done the decorating. Or maybe Paul. He dressed better than Riley after all.

"Right this way." Paul directed them to the left. "I think you'll like it. You said you want your clients to leave impressed. This office should help with that."

He wasn't wrong. Talon stepped into an office at least twice as large as her current one, with picture windows offering an obstructed view of that park across the street and the steel blue waters of Commencement Bay beyond. The office furniture matched that of the conference room. Nothing amazing, but nice and new—which meant it would be a while before it wasn't nice anymore. There was just a desk and two chairs, but there was definitely enough room to add a small table and chairs for her own mini-conference room. A great place to get someone to sign a fee agreement.

"Okay, what are the terms?" She was ready to move forward. Possibly.

"One-year lease, then month-to-month," Paul answered. "Sign the lease now, and we can knock ten percent off the rent."

"Sounds like a bargain." Talon looked around the office again then narrowed her eyes at Paul. "What's the catch?"

Paul chuckled and spread his arms wide. "You have to deal with me."

Talon took a moment to appraise the man before her. She could imagine dealing with him and not hating it.

"You're not a lawyer, are you?" she questioned. "I'm getting tired of dealing with lawyers."

Paul laughed again. "No, I'm definitely not a lawyer."

When he didn't offer more, Talon followed up. She did that for a living. "What do you do?"

He hesitated. "Well, I'm a sort of data analyst, let's say." Another chuckle, but more forced. "I could tell you more, but I'd have to kill you."

Talon frowned. "That joke isn't as funny as it used to be."

"Yeah, you're right," Paul admitted. "So, what do you think? Are you interested?"

Talon glanced around the office again. "You said this is the only one on the third floor with a view," she recalled. "Where would Curt's office be?"

"I'm afraid this is the last available office on the third floor,"

Paul admitted. "Curt's office would be on the first floor."

Talon stuck her hand out. "You've got yourself a deal."

CHAPTER 17

Out with the old, in with the new. That was how things were supposed to go. But in Talon's experience, The Old usually didn't leave without a fight. The Old tended to hang on far longer than it was wanted, or worse: it figured out a way to circle back around and pop up in your face again.

Helen Hampton Montclair was waiting in the lobby of Talon's soon-to-be old office when Talon returned from securing her soon-to-be new office. Talon made no effort to hide her disgust.

"Ugh. You?" she grunted. "What do you want?"

Hampton Montclair stood up from her seat at the far end of the lobby, a saccharine smile pasted on her face. "Oh, come now, Talon. Is that any way to greet a former colleague?"

"First of all," Talon pointed a finger at her, "if we're going to use names, it's Ms. Winter to you. Second of all, we're not former colleagues. We're still colleagues. We're former co-workers, although I don't recall ever actually working with you directly. I do remember suing you, though."

That saccharine smile curdled. "Yes, well, Ms. Winter, regardless of the circumstances under which you departed, I would think you would show more respect for your former firm. We are the largest civil litigation firm in the city. That's nothing to sneeze at."

Talon thought for a moment, then faked a sneeze very much at Helen Hampton Montclair and her law firm.

"Delightful," Hampton Montclair sneered. "Do you have any idea how much money flows through our firm every month?"

"No," Talon answered. "How much?"

Hampton Montclair was a bit taken aback. "Well, I'm not exactly certain of the precise number, but I'm sure it's thousands. Tens of thousands even."

"Wow, not impressive." Talon shook her head. "Not impressive at all. Don't ask a question like that if you don't have the answer ready. Here, let me show you. Do you know how little I care about you and your fucking money? Go ahead, ask me."

Hampton Montclair stood up straighter. "I'm not going to ask you that," she sniffed.

"Not at all," Talon answered anyway. "Not one fucking bit. Now, why are you here? I already defiled your client's body. Do you want a blow by blow of the atrocity? I think we have pictures."

Hampton Montclair narrowed her eyes at Talon. "I am here, Ms. Winter," she growled, "to ensure that you never do anything like that ever again. Here. Consider yourself served."

She pushed a letter-sized envelope toward Talon. Talon took a beat, then shrugged and snatched it out of her hand.

"What's this?" Talon asked, even as she pulled the single folded sheet out of the envelope.

"It's a cease and desist letter," Hampton Montclair declared. "You are hereby directed to cease and desist any further defamation of James Dank, his businesses, or his family."

Talon actually burst out laughing. "Are you fucking kidding me? First of all, you can't direct me to do anything. This is a letter from a lawyer, not an order from a judge. It doesn't mean shit. Second, if you think I'm going to do anything other than my absolute most and best for my client, as mandated by the Fifth and Sixth Amendments and Article One, Section Twenty-Two of the Washington Constitution, which, I can assure you, will involve defaming the fuck out of James Dank and his private jail, then not only do you not know shit about how criminal law works, you don't know shit about me."

Hampton Montclair didn't say anything for a moment. She set her jaw and raised a disapproving eyebrow. "I'm not certain all of that profanity was really necessary."

"Did you understand me?" Talon asked. "Then it was necessary. Or at least, it was fun, anyway."

"Yes, well," Hampton Montclair sniffed. She gestured to the letter still in Talon's hand. "You've been warned, Ms. Winter."

Talon looked down at the letter as well. Then she tossed it carelessly onto the lobby's coffee table and turned her back on her former boss. "Yeah, whatever," she said as she turned toward her office. "You. Door. Ass. Out."

Talon could hear Hampton Montclair huff again—a well-practiced sound, Talon could tell—and then turn to leave. Hampton Montclair did, in fact, not let the door hit her ass on the way out. Talon stopped and waited a moment, then turned back to fetch the cease and desist letter off the coffee table after all. She wasn't about to abide by it, but she wanted to keep it for her records. Something told her it could maybe even help Karim somehow, although she knew she'd have to wait for that possibility to reveal itself.

CHAPTER 18

Talon had fastened the cease and desist letter into the very back of her case file, behind the charging documents and scheduling orders. She only let it take up space in the back of her mind, so it seemed fitting that it only take up space in the back of her file. The file she brought with her to the courthouse for the pretrial conference listed on the most recent of those scheduling orders.

The pretrial conference was a mandatory hearing between the arraignment and the trial. Most criminal cases settled short of trial—well over ninety percent, in fact. Part of that was plea bargains for all of the lower level crimes, like car theft and drug possession, to clear the way for the more serious cases. Like murder.

Not that Karim's case should have been a murder charge. It was manslaughter at worst, self-defense at best. Not a crime at all. But she didn't get to make that decision. The prosecutor and the jury got the first and last say on that. She was just piloting the boat of Justice on the river rapids of The System.

Or something like that, she thought, as she arrived at the conference room filled with prosecutors and defense attorneys, all gathered for the hundred or so cases set for pretrial that morning. It wasn't so much a court hearing as a non-court hearing. If all went well, they could just fill out a form in the conference room and wouldn't have to appear in front of the judge. But things probably wouldn't go well. After all, Cobb was the prosecutor. And Talon was the defense attorney. And she wasn't that lucky.

Talon strolled into the crowded, frenetic room. It was about the size of a full courtroom, but instead of a bench and witness stand, there were a series of conference tables, pushed together into different sizes and shapes, with doors at either end to enter the actual courtrooms if a judge actually needed to resolve some dispute that (1) the attorneys couldn't work out, and (2) couldn't wait for a properly noted motion hearing. The length of one entire wall was a row of closet-sized attorney-client meeting rooms for the defendants who were being held in custody pending trial. Defendants like Karim. Talon was there to talk with Cobb, but she was damn sure going to talk with Karim first.

"Jackson, Karim," she barked into the communication box next to the last room on the left. That was the procedure. No face-to-face interaction with the guards watching the defendants. Press the button on the squawk box, state the defendant's name only—no small talk—and then wait for the faceless voice on the other end to announce which room they would put the client in.

"Seven," a guard's voice scratched after a few moments.

Talon made her way down the row to the closet door with a plastic numeral '7' stuck on its frosted glass. It was barely wide enough for the chair she sat down in on her side of the glass partition. After a few seconds, a guard opened the door on the other side of the room and Karim walked in. He didn't look good. Talon wasn't surprised, but it was still disheartening. It always was.

Incarceration was punishment. Apart from the death penalty, it was the ultimate and really only punishment meted out for crimes. It was the worst society could do to you in response for the worst you could do to it. And yet incarceration wasn't reserved for the guilty. It was routinely imposed, by way of pretrial detention, on those who were supposed to be presumed innocent. If it was punishment for the duly convicted, why wouldn't it also be punishing to the presumed innocent? It was. Maybe more so. County jails, with their crowded conditions and lack of windows, were notoriously less pleasant than state prisons, with their yards and educational programs. Karim had been suddenly arrested and shoved into a cage. He hadn't seen the sun in weeks, and whatever reserve allows humans to brace for enduring extended hardships was starting to run out. At first, he had been righteously angry at his predicament and eager to fight against it. But when he shuffled into the conference room to meet with Talon, she could see the fire in his eyes had gone out. He was tired, undernourished, and while perhaps not quite yet broken, he was bending.

He needed a shave, his hair was matted, and he avoided eye contact with Talon. But he did manage a weak greeting. "Hey."

"Hey," Talon replied. "How are you holding up?"

Karim shrugged. "Fine."

"No. Seriously." Talon tapped on the glass to make sure she actually had his attention. "I'm not being polite. I need to know how you're doing. You're in the worst place we have for people. You shouldn't be doing fine. But I need to know how not fine you are because I still need you to pay attention and fight. I need you to help me, even through glass."

Karim finally raised his gaze and stared at her with dark-rimmed eyes. "How am I doing? Seriously?" he questioned. "That's what you want to know? Fine. The honest answer is, I don't know. I don't know how I'm doing. I don't know what to think about all of this. I know I got arrested for something I didn't do. I know I'm in jail for something I didn't get convicted of. And I know there's a very good chance I'm never getting out again. Tell me I'm wrong."

"You're wrong," Talon said. "It's not a very good chance. But it's definitely a chance. You're not wrong about that."

Karim chuckled and shook his head. "Oh, okay. Only a normal chance I'm going to spend most of my life in here for something I didn't do. Only a normal chance I'm another casualty of a fucked up criminal justice system. Only a chance I won't finish college, find a job, get married, have kids, have grandkids. Only a chance my entire life will be erased because I dared to push back when some old guy grabbed me. Only a chance. Fucking great. Yeah, that's how I'm doing. I'm fucking great. How are you, Talon?"

"Better now," Talon answered. "I need you angry again. They're going to try to break you in here. It's what they do. It's not even personal. They don't give enough of a shit about you to want to break you personally. They just set up a system and a place that breaks people all by itself. The longer you're in there, the harder it is not to break."

"So, get me the fuck out of here!" Karim slammed his fist down onto the narrow counter under the glass partition.

Talon took a moment. After that moment, she started nodding. After another moment, she stood up. "Okay."

She pointed behind him. "Go back to the holding cells. If things go right, I'll see you in the courtroom in five minutes."

"What if things go wrong?" Karim asked.

"That's the thing, Karim." Talon grinned. "They can't really get any worse."

Talon exited the consultation room and scanned the conference room for Cobb. She found him in a back corner, leaning his chair onto its back legs, and yukking it up with some other socially stunted prosecutors. She strode directly over to him, keeping her eyes fixed on her prey.

"Hey! Cobb!" She smacked his shoulder with the back of her hand. "Get up. Judge Harvey wants to see us on the Jackson case."

Cobb dropped the chair back onto the floor. "He does? Why?"

"I'll explain when we get in there," Talon answered without answering. Then she marched toward the courtroom, knowing Cobb was watching her, trying to sort out all the different feelings he was having being bossed around by a better woman than he'd ever be while looking at her ass. He was definitely looking at her ass.

It was easy enough to lie to Cobb. He was a jerk. She would explain it off as a poor choice of verb tense. 'I meant the judge will want to see us—after I tell him why he should.' But she couldn't pull that on the actual judge. She knew Cobb would take a minute to gather his thoughts and those feelings, make some crass joke with his buddies, then trudge his way, unsettled, into the courtroom. That gave Talon a minute, maybe two, to convince the bailiff to greenlight Karim's case being put on the record for something.

It had to be something the attorneys couldn't resolve. That part was true. But it also had to be something that couldn't wait the five days normally required to give the other side notice of the motion. That was debatable. But debatable gave her just enough of an opening.

"Hey there, Sherry." Talon leaned onto the lower bench next to the bailiff, Sherry Norton. She had been a bailiff longer than Talon had been an attorney. She'd seen it all, and somehow was still pleasant to everyone who bothered her like Talon was doing just then. "Is there room on the docket to squeeze in a quick hearing on the Karim Jackson case?"

Sherry raised a penciled eyebrow behind her pearl-framed

glasses. "Quick?"

"Super quick." Talon nodded.

"Super quick?" Sherry questioned.

"Ultra quick," Talon assured her. "Don't blink or you'll miss it quick. Really."

"Really?" Sherry allowed a slight grin in the corner of her mouth.

Talon returned the smile. "Well, maybe not that quick. But pretty quick. It's just a follow-up on that motion from the other day."

"The one that took forever and had extra attorneys popping up out of the gallery?" Sherry remembered.

"Yes. Yes, that's the one," Talon admitted. "But no extra attorneys today. All the more reason to squeeze it onto today's docket and not give a whole lot of extra time and notice for more attorneys to ooze out of the woodwork, am I right?

Sherry's smile broadened. "You're not wrong, Ms. Winter," she allowed. "I'll let Judge Harvey know there's a matter to be heard." Her gaze shifted over Talon's shoulder. "And it looks like the prosecutor is here as well now. I'll let the judge know you're ready."

"Ready for what?" Cobb demanded, even as the bailiff stood up to walk back to the judge's chambers. "What's going on? Why does the judge want to see us on this? Nothing has happened."

Talon grinned and poked Cobb with a single finger on the center of his tie. "Not yet it hasn't."

Sherry returned a few moments later and a few moments after that, Judge Harvey entered the courtroom. "All rise!" Sherry called out. "The Pierce County Superior Court is now in session, the Honorable Robert Harvey presiding."

"You may be seated," Judge Harvey announced as he did

the same. "Is there a matter ready?"

Talon stepped forward. "Yes, Your Honor. It's the matter of State of Washington versus Karim Jackson." She glanced at the guard standing by the door to the holding cells. "If we could have Mr. Jackson brought in?"

Judge Harvey sighed—there was always one more thing to do—but nodded to the guard. "Bring in Mr. Jackson."

"I still don't know why we're here," Cobb complained in a half whisper. It was loud enough for Harvey to hear, but quiet enough for him to ignore, which he did.

Talon took her normal spot at the defense table and waited for her client to enter. Cobb slunk to his spot opposite her, and after a few more moments, Karim was escorted into the courtroom and to the chair next to Talon.

"All right, Ms. Winter," Judge Harvey said, "your client is here. Now, what are we doing?"

"I wanted to provide the court with the results of the court's ruling regarding the independent forensic examination of the decedent.," Talon explained.

"The what now?" Judge Harvey's face scrunched up at her.

"Yeah, what?" Cobb interjected.

"Your Honor authorized Dr. Evangelopoulos's independent forensic examination of the remains of Mr. Dank," Talon reminded everyone, quite unnecessarily, "and I wanted to inform the Court that the examination took place, as ordered."

"Um, okay," Judge Harvey allowed. "You don't really need to do that."

"Yeah," Cobb interjected again. "Is that really why you dragged me in here?"

"Well, Your Honor," again Talon ignored Cobb and directed her comments to Judge Harvey, "when the police execute a search warrant signed by a judge, they are required to file a list of all the items they seized. I thought this would be similar."

"It's not very similar, Ms. Winter," Judge Harvey opined, "but I'm glad everyone followed my order. Is there anything else?"

"Yeah." Cobb again. "Anything else?"

"Well, yes, Your Honor, of course," Talon answered.

"Of course," Harvey sighed. "Go on, then, Ms. Winter. Out with it. What are you playing at?"

"Playing?" Talon clutched her chest dramatically. "Oh, no, Your Honor. I'm not playing. None of us are playing, I hope. I'm sure Mr. Cobb isn't playing. He honestly, if wrongly, believes he is seeking justice for a dead man. And I know Your Honor isn't playing. You are seeking to ensure justice for all who come before you, even those accused of the worst humans can do to each other. From the outside, it may look like a game, the players dressed in suits and robes instead of jerseys and helmets, but one look at Mr. Jackson," she gestured to her seated client, "and we are all reminded this is the furthest thing from a game. This is life and death. Literally."

"Mm-hmm." Judge Harvey just nodded. It wasn't that Talon's flowery words weren't moving; it was that a judge's job was to be not moved by flowery words. "And?"

"And," Talon finally got to it, "based on the results of that independent forensic examination, and specifically the finding that the decedent had bruising on his right knuckles consistent with striking Mr. Jackson before Mr. Jackson was forced to defend himself with the least amount of force possible, simply breaking away from his attacker, I am asking the Court, once again, to release Mr. Jackson on his own personal recognizance."

"What?!" Cobb didn't whisper that time. "You're making a bail motion? You didn't give me any notice. Your Honor," he complained to the bench, "I was given no notice."

"Or," Talon continued, and also continued to ignore Cobb, "to lower bail to an amount Mr. Jackson could reasonably be expected to post. Such a reduced amount would help ensure the Court's concerns about his reappearance for future court dates while allowing him to better assist me in his defense by being out of custody."

"Again, Your Honor," Cobb whined. "No notice."

Judge Harvey frowned and glanced down sideways at the prosecutor. "You didn't know Ms. Winter wants her client released on a P.R.?"

"Well, I mean, I knew that," Cobb admitted, shifting his weight uncomfortably, "but I didn't know she was going to ask again today."

Judge Harvey pursed his lips and nodded again, the specifics of his thoughts hidden even as their existence was obvious from his expression. "So, this is new information, Ms. Winter?"

"You're actually considering hearing this motion?" Cobb blurted out.

Harvey glared down at Cobb. "If I wasn't before, Mr. Cobb, I am now. You will get your chance to speak. You always do. Until then, I strongly advise you not to interrupt me again. I can hold prosecutors in contempt, too."

The judge returned his gaze to Talon. "New information?" he prompted.

"Yes, Your Honor," Talon confirmed. She fell back into a formal posture and delivery, answering just the question posed. She'd noticed Harvey was both quick to anger and angry at being quick to anger. Her mistake before had been to provoke that anger. Cobb had managed to avoid it by being in control of the previous hearings, initiating the case, deciding the charges, filing the paperwork, even scheduling the hearings. Prosecutors were used to running the show. But put them in a position where not only were they not running things, where they didn't even know what was happening, and they were bound to react badly. Piss off the judge. Hand the advantage to the other side. To Talon.

"Explain to me how it's relevant to a bail determination," Harvey invited. "It seems like that sort of information is more relevant to a determination of guilt or innocence, and that's what the trial is for."

Talon actually agreed with him. In fact, that's what she had tried to argue at the first bail hearing—when Harvey had let slip that he was treating Karim as a murderer rather than an accused murderer. He had looked to that and ignored the actual standard for bail: is the defendant a flight risk, and is the defendant likely to reoffend and endanger others? From that hearing, Talon knew her only chance of getting Karim out was to shake Harvey's confidence in the State's allegations. If she could make Harvey think Karim might actually be innocent, and not just pay lip service to that whole 'presumed innocent' thing, she might be able to guide him back to those actual bail standards. Not that she could say any of that. Persuasion involved meeting people where they were, but it was rarely helpful to tell them where they were, especially when they didn't know where they were, and doubly so when they really shouldn't be there in the first place.

"Thank you, Your Honor," Talon began her reply. Formal and deferential. Judges ate that shit up. "I believe this new information goes to the issue of whether the defendant is likely to reoffend and whether, by doing so, he would be a danger to the community or a specific member of the community. It is, of course, difficult for a court to make that sort of subjective determination with the limited information available at the time of charging. The facts available to the Court at arraignment are usually quite limited, and that was certainly the case here."

Talon knew to take a moment to justify Harvey's earlier, terrible decision. It was a bit of a tightrope. She wanted him to change his prior ruling, which meant she thought his prior ruling was wrong. But calling out a judge for making a wrong decision was the surest way to get them to dig in on that decision. So rather than condemn that prior decision, she needed to praise it.

"The Court looked at what was presented to it by the State," a head nod toward Cobb, "and reasonably concluded that Mr. Jackson might be a general risk to the community. If he were the sort of person who would react violently to the slightest provocation, who would push an old man to the ground for getting too close to him, then yes, it was conceivable he might do the same to others who got too close to him or otherwise provoked him. The Court has to balance several competing factors, and not least among them is the safety of the community."

And having praised his earlier decision, she needed to give him a way out of it.

"But this new information, Your Honor, allows the Court to have a fuller picture of what may have transpired that day," Talon said. "More importantly, it allows the Court to have a fuller picture of what may transpire in the future. Or more correctly, what will likely not occur in the future. Mr. Jackson did not lash out at a stranger who got too close to him. Mr. Jackson reacted to a person who punched him. This is not a situation where Mr. Jackson's response was disproportionately overreactive, but rather, if anything, was an underreaction.

"The State told the Court that Mr. Jackson shoved a man to the ground after that man yelled in his face," Talon continued. "But this new information tells the Court that the man punched Mr.

Jackson, and rather than punch back, Mr. Jackson simply pushed him away. That was a de-escalation of the conflict. And it allows the Court to conclude, reasonably and confidently, that Mr. Jackson does not, in fact, pose any threat to the community. He is not a loose cannon waiting to go off again. He is a man who, when assaulted himself, did not respond in kind, but rather did the absolute minimum to protect himself from further assault. Quite honestly, Your Honor, he did less than most of us would do. He poses less of a threat to the community than most of us. And for that reason, Your Honor can and should reconsider the bail you previously set, based as it was on the earlier but incomplete information you had at the time. Thank you."

When Talon finished her argument, she sat down next to her client. Karim tried to talk to her, probably to thank her or ask what was happening all of a sudden, but Talon shushed him. It wasn't about him. Maybe in the larger scheme of things it was, but right there, right then, it was about Judge Harvey and how he felt he might be perceived. Talon understood that. She was pretty confident Cobb did not.

"Mr. Cobb," the judge invited, "any response?"

Cobb bolted up out of his seat. "Absolutely, Your Honor. Absolutely." He stormed around to stand in front of the prosecutor's table. A little aggressive, but Talon was okay with that. Judges didn't like being aggressed against.

"I would start," Cobb started, "by pointing out, again, that I had no notice of the defense's intent on ambushing me with a motion to reduce bail."

"Having an intent to ambush," Judge Harvey observed, "would preclude giving notice, I would think."

That staggered Cobb a bit; he likely expected sympathy, not derision. "Yes, well, I suppose that's so, Your Honor."

"So, I take it," Judge Harvey put a point on it, "you're objecting to a release on personal recognizance?"

"Of course, I'm objecting," the prosecutor practically stammered. "The State charged this man with murder. Obviously, we believe he is a danger to the community. I wouldn't be doing my job if I agreed to a personal recognizance release."

Harvey nodded. "Okay." He raised an eyebrow at Cobb. "Anything else?"

"Well, yes, of course," Cobb blundered forward. "Nothing has changed since the Court made its original, and if I may say so, very sound decision to set bail at one million dollars."

"You may say so," Harvey confirmed. "But what about what Ms. Winter has just reported? That there were offensive injuries on the alleged victim's knuckles. Isn't that new information?"

Talon smiled, just a bit, at the fact that she didn't have to remind Judge Harvey to use the word 'alleged'.

"I don't know, Your Honor, is it?" Cobb was doing a bad job hiding his exasperation. "I mean, I haven't seen any reports, have you? I haven't seen any photographs, have you? All we have is Ms. Winter's representation that they exist, but—"

"Be careful," Judge Harvey interrupted. "Ms. Winter is a member of the bar and an officer of this court. I will not have you cast aspersions on her honesty or candor."

Cobb's mouth twisted as he tried to simultaneously bite his tongue and grit his teeth. "Of course not, Your Honor," he managed to growl after a moment. "I only meant to say that the Court should want more information, more verification, before making a decision as weighty as this. This is the reason we have a five-day notice requirement."

"For my benefit?" Judge Harvey coaxed.

"Exactly," Cobb agreed. "For the Court's benefit."

Harvey frowned in thought for a moment. "Then I feel comfortable waiving it. I made my original decision based on nothing more than assertions of fact by one lawyer—that's you, Mr. Cobb—so I see no reason why I cannot reconsider that decision based on assertions by the other lawyer. Anything further. Mr. Cobb, before I make my decision?"

Cobb blinked at the judge. Lawyers didn't always know when they're going to win an argument, but they usually knew when they were going to lose. "I guess not, Your Honor. I just hope no one else dies because of the Court's decision."

Talon's eyebrows shot up at that, but she managed, just barely, to keep her jaw from dropping. If Cobb really did think he was going to lose, he had just guaranteed it. Self-fulfilling advocacy.

"Thank you, Mr. Cobb," the judge replied with a tone that was anything but grateful. "The Court is ready to make its ruling."

Talon finally looked at her client. He had been looking at her the whole time. There wasn't anything to say really, and she certainly didn't want to interrupt or otherwise irritate the judge at that exact moment with overly loud whispering. So, she just reached out and gave Karim's hand a squeeze.

"I am not going to release an alleged murderer on his own recognizance," Judge Harvey announced. Talon's heart dropped a bit, but she knew to hang on. "However, neither am I going to set bail based solely on the nature and severity of the accusations. Ms. Winter made several good points at the original bail hearing, and I still believe I was correct to consider but ultimately reject those arguments at the time. However, times change and circumstances change. And while facts, by their nature, do not change, they may reveal themselves after being previously unknown. Bail is meant to ensure two things: the appearance of the accused at future court dates, lest he lose the money posted; and the safety of the community, to keep incarcerated those whom the Court deems likely to reoffend pending resolution of the current charges. In this case, the new information brought forth by Ms. Winter convinces me that bail should be, and hereby is, reduced to the amount of one hundred thousand dollars."

Karim lowered his head and began to shake it. But Talon knew better.

"Stop shaking your head," Talon whispered to him. "That's a huge change. It changes everything. You're getting out."

"How?" Karim whispered back. "I don't have a hundred grand."

"You don't need it," Talon explained. "No bonding company will put up a million for a murder defendant, even if you had the ten percent to pay them. But plenty of them will put up a hundred grand. Your family just needs to come up with ten K and you're out."

Karim thought for a moment. Then that head-shaking turned into head-nodding. "Yeah, we can do that. So, really? I'm getting out?"

Talon returned the nod and squeezed his hand again. "You're getting out."

CHAPTER 19

It took another day before Karim actually got out of jail. First, Shayla had to find a bail bond company willing to post the $100,000. Second, she had to access the funds to pay them the standard ten percent. Third, the bonding company had to deposit the money with the court. And finally, the court had to notify the jail to release the defendant. None of that should have really taken that long; it was all electronic. No one was walking into the jail with a bag full of cash. But no one was hurrying to get an accused murderer out of custody either.

It meant one fewer night of freedom for Karim, but he looked none the worse for it when he showed up the next afternoon at Talon's new office, showered, fed, and dressed in his own clothes. And smiling. He couldn't stop smiling.

"Thank you, Talon." He also couldn't stop shaking Talon's hand after she greeted him and his sister in the lobby. "Thank you so much. When I yelled at you to get me out, I didn't mean, get me out right then. I didn't think you could do it right then. But you did it. You did it right then. Man, that was awesome. Thank you. Thank you for doing that. Thank you."

Talon extracted her hand from Karim's grip. "I was happy to

do it right then. Anything to beat that jackass Cobb." She took a moment, then remembered to add, "And get you out of jail, of course."

Karim looked sideways at Shayla, but she just grinned and shrugged her shoulders. "What can I say? She likes to win. That's why we hired her."

Talon smiled at that herself. She couldn't disagree. But she could move the conversation along from topics other than herself and her motivations. "Come on. Curt's waiting for us in the conference room."

Jailhouse visits were all well and good—actually, they were neither—but Talon wanted to have a nice long sit-down strategy session with the entire defense team, even Shayla. It was overdue, in fact. Another impact of incarcerating the accused pending trial was damaging their ability to fully prepare a robust defense. But Karim's release and Talon's conference room offered them that opportunity. Plus, a view of the bay.

"Nice place you've got here," Shayla admired. "I wondered why you moved offices, but now I get it."

"Yes, but no," Talon replied. "I got kicked out of my old office because I took this case. The company that owns the private jail Dank was running also owns my old building. Guess whose lease didn't get renewed?"

"That's bullshit." Shayla's jaw dropped. "You should fight back."

But Talon shrugged. "Pick your battles. Discretion is the better part of valor. Chaos equals opportunity. Difficult times reveal true friends. Water view." She spread her arms. "It's all good."

"Plus, I got an office here too," Curt put in.

"Yeah, that." Talon's arms dropped. "But all in all, still a good move."

Curt cocked his head at her, but then just shook it.

"Grab a seat, everyone," Talon announced. "We've got a lot of work to do."

Karim and Shayla joined Curt at the table, but Talon ignored her own directive and instead took a spot at the whiteboard affixed to the wall opposite the window. She wrote the word 'STRATEGY' at the top.

"First things first," she said. "We have a decision to make."

"What decision?" Karim asked. He was leaning forward, fully engaged. Almost like his life depended on it—which, of course, it did.

Talon wrote three more words on the board: 'FIGHT – BEG - RUN.'

"Run?" Shayla questioned.

"I'll get to that in a minute," Talon said. "Not my top choice. But let's go through them in order. We can't know what specific steps to take if we don't know what our goal is."

"Fight," Karim prompted with a nod at the board. "What's that mean?"

"It means trial," Talon answered. "It means we prepare for war. One hundred percent. All in. Every decision is made through the lens of 'how does this impact our chances to win at trial?' If it helps, we do it. If it doesn't, we don't."

"I like that," Karim nodded. "What does 'beg' mean?"

"It means plea bargaining," Talon explained. "We can't knock the charges down ourselves. Only the prosecutor can do that. So, it means we beg him for the best deal we can get. If we get good information, information that makes our case stronger, we don't hold it back to spring at trial. We show it to the prosecutor, and we hope it makes him cut us a deal."

Shayla crossed her arms and pushed back in her chair. "I

don't like that option. A guilty plea to a reduced charge is still a guilty plea. It's still a conviction. It's still prison time."

Karim nodded at the last word on the whiteboard. "What's run?"

"Run is run," Talon said. "It means you fill up your car with gas and drive three hours north. Canada."

"Flee?" Shayla exclaimed. "You can't advise him to flee. You just told the Court he wasn't a flight risk."

"Why would I go to Canada?" Karim asked, but evenly. He wasn't challenging her. He wanted to know why it was on the board. "Won't they extradite me?"

"They will," Talon confirmed. "But it will take a while. Plus, they won't do it on the felony murder charge. That's the one where you're charged with intentionally assaulting Dank, then accidentally killing him. We call that Murder Two. The Canadians call that an accident. They don't have felony murder in Canada, and you can't extradite on a crime unless both countries criminalize it. So, they could extradite on the underlying assault, but the prosecutor here would have to agree not to pursue the felony murder charge."

"So, the murder charge just goes away?" Karim seemed intrigued.

"Probably not," Talon shook her head. "They can just amend it to intentional murder. That's definitely a crime in Canada too. Then you come back to face that charge."

Karim nodded. "Plus, it's cowardly to run. And I'm not a coward."

"It's not cowardly to do something smart," Curt chimed in. "If Talon thinks this is a legitimate option, then it's smart."

Talon smiled at him. "Thanks, Curt." She looked again at her handwriting. "It's legitimate, but again, it's not my top choice. You will get arrested, you will spend months in a Canadian jail while the paperwork gets done, and you will never get your bail lowered again. So, really, it just delays Option One or Option Two."

"Option One," Karim said. "I'm not running, and I'm not begging. We fight."

Talon allowed herself a grin. "Good." She turned and crossed out 'BEG' and 'RUN', then circled 'FIGHT'.

"We fight." She turned back to her audience. "Now, what's the most important thing about fighting?"

"Winning," Karim answered.

Talon pointed the dry erase marker at him. "Yes. I like your enthusiasm. But what else? What comes before that?"

"Know who your opponent is."

All heads turned to the door to the conference room, and the source of the answer Talon had been seeking.

"Hi," said the man carrying a tray of coffee. "I'm Paul. I hope I'm not interrupting. More importantly, I hope I'm not wrong."

"You are definitely not wrong," Talon answered.

"And if that coffee is for us," Shayla put in, "you're not interrupting."

Paul smiled. He was wearing a white dress shirt, but with the collar open and the sleeves rolled up. It looked like maybe he'd been in a meeting earlier in the day and hadn't had the time to change back into something more casual.

"This coffee is most definitely for you," Paul answered. "For my two newest tenants and their guests." He set the tray down on the conference table. "I'd offer to pour but I don't know how everyone takes their coffee. Also, I don't want to."

Shayla laughed a little too hard at the joke. She flashed Talon a knowing glance, but Talon flashed one back that assured she did not know. Although she didn't know that she didn't want to know.

"You own the building?" Shayla asked as she stood up to pour herself some coffee.

"Not exactly," Paul answered. "I manage it. It's, well, complicated."

"Mysterious, he means," Talon put in. "Paul is very mysterious, but in an understated kind of way."

"And a very helpful way," Curt added as he accepted the coffee carafe from Shayla. "My office is already set up with full wi-fi and a welcome basket of gift cards to all the nearby businesses."

Paul gave a small bow of his head. "First rule of business is to make your customers feel valued." He glanced at Talon's whiteboard. "Just like the first rule of fighting is knowing who your opponent is. Sometimes it's obvious. Most of the time it isn't. At least, that's been my experience."

"What is your experience?" Shayla asked, looking up at him over her coffee cup.

"Focus, people," Talon cut in. She tapped the whiteboard with her marker. "Who's our opponent here?"

Talon looked back to Paul. She felt like he probably knew the answer, even if he didn't know the case. But his expression let her know he wouldn't blurt out the answer and ruin her Socratic strategy session.

"The prosecutor," Shayla answered. "Cobb. That ass."

Karim nodded. "Seemed like the judge was against us too. I mean, until he wasn't. But I don't know, it seems like the whole system is the enemy."

Talon nodded at their responses. She pointed to her investigator. "Curt? What do you think? Is it the prosecutor?"

Curt shook his head. "No. He's a distraction. He's the bureaucrat they put in front of the real enemy."

"True enough," Talon agreed. "So, who is Karim fighting in the courtroom?"

"The same person he was fighting in front of that jail," Curt knew. "James Dank."

Talon smiled. A glance at Paul confirmed he was smiling too.

"Exactly," Talon confirmed. "The jury isn't going to decide between me and Cobb. They know we're hired guns. Nobody believes what a lawyer says. They're going to decide between Karim and Dank."

Karim shook his head and frowned. "They're going to choose between a rich middle-aged white guy who's part of the system and an angry young Black man?" He pushed back in his chair and crossed his arms. "I'm screwed."

"You are if that's the choice they get," Paul spoke up again.

"We need to give them a different choice," Talon added. "Same people, but different labels. We need to repackage you into a peaceful social justice advocate and repackage him as a worthless piece of shit who fed off others' misery."

Shayla cocked her head and smirked. "We should work on that definition a bit. I don't think the jury will like that particular phrasing."

"We can work on the exact words," Talon allowed. "But that's what he is. We just need proof."

"I've got a start," Curt announced. "I finally tracked down some cell phone videos from a couple of the other protesters who were there that day." He pulled out his phone and held it up. "They don't show everything and they're not the best quality, but they show at least part of the fight."

"Attack," Talon corrected. "Fights are mutual. Attacks are unilateral and unjustified."

"Okay," Curt went along, "they show part of the attack."

He placed his phone down on the conference table and started tapping the screen to queue up the first video. "This one is from kind of far away, so it's sort of hard to see, but—"

"Here." Paul leaned over and picked up Curt's phone. "Let me help." He stepped over to a control panel on the wall and began tapping buttons there and on Curt's phone. The lights dimmed, a projector descended from a recess in the ceiling, and the video was blown up to a three-foot-tall image on the wall next to Talon. He handed the phone back to Curt. "Here you go."

"Awesome," Curt said. Then he pressed play.

The clip was a wide angle shot of the entire protest. It panned slowly from left to right. The jail was visible in the background, behind the fence, which in turn was behind the protestors. There didn't seem to be any particular focus of the video; it was more to capture the entire feel of the event. Karim was visible, standing slightly above the protestors nearest him, but his form glided from one side of the shot to the other just like everyone else.

"Okay, here's where Dank shows up." Curt pointed at the image on the wall. "Far left."

As the camera continued to pan, the jail guards could suddenly be seen through the crowd, appearing on the left edge of the scene, with Dank right behind them. At first the cameraperson didn't seem to notice, because the shot continued to pan away, but after a moment, it jerked back and centered on Karim and Dank. There was an attempt to zoom in, but it mostly just made the people standing in front of the confrontation even bigger and more in the way. Then Karim stepped down and became even more difficult to see through the crowd. A few moments later, the crowd suddenly parted and Dank was visible on the ground, motionless. Another moment and the guards were pouncing on Karim.

"Not very helpful," Talon observed.

Curt shrugged. "I know, but at least it shows the protest was peaceful up to that point."

Talon frowned slightly. "I suppose," she conceded. "I hope the next one's better."

"Yeah, it is," Curt assured. He tapped on his phone a few times, and the next video started.

Karim was perfectly centered in the frame, about ten or twenty feet away from the camera. He was standing above the crowd, chanting through the bullhorn, and generally looking pretty damn awesome.

"Who took this video?" Shayla asked.

"She said her name was Monica," Curt answered. "I forget her last name right now. She goes to school with Karim, I guess."

Shayla looked over at Karim with a raised eyebrow. "Monica?"

Karim shook his head. "I don't know who that is," he insisted.

Shayla crossed her arms and cocked her head at him. "Mm-hmm. Well, Monica sure knows who you are."

Karim just smiled and leaned back in his chair.

But his satisfaction was short-lived as the event that resulted in his arrest and incarceration unfolded before them.

Again, the guards could be seen appearing first, with Dank behind them. Dank started yelling at Karim. Karim tried to ignore him, but eventually stepped down to engage him. There are definitely people in the way, but Monica moved and was able to keep Karim and Dank mostly centered and mostly unobscured. Dank grabbed for the bullhorn, there was a struggle, and then Karim pushes him away. It was pretty much exactly how Talon remembered it, except from a slightly different angle. The bad news was, when Dank stumbled backward, he went off screen, as Monica kept her shot on Karim. It would have been nice to have seen exactly how Dank managed to lose his balance; maybe he tripped on an uneven sidewalk joint. But it didn't show that. It also didn't show any punches.

"Did I miss it?" Talon asked. "Did I miss the punch? I just told Judge Harvey that Dank punched you. Did he punch you? He punched you, right?"

Karim shrugged. "I don't know. He grabbed me. He was all over me. He might have punched me too. I don't know. It happened really fast."

Talon frowned. "Rewind it," she told Curt.

Curt complied and they watched it again. And again.

"There's no punch," Curt said.

"The video doesn't show the punch," Talon reframed it.

"Yes, it doesn't show it," Shayla agreed. "Right, Karim?"

"Sure," he agreed. "Whatever you say."

"Okay, well, maybe Karim and I should have this particular conversation alone," Talon advised. "There's no attorney-client privilege with all of you in the room with us."

"I'm an attorney," Shayla pointed out.

"You're not his attorney," Talon reminded her. "And anyway, the rest of us have other things we can talk about. For example, does this video help us make Dank the bad guy?"

"Nope," Paul knew.

"Agreed," Shayla said. "It needs to show more. He was the aggressor. The jury needs to see that."

Talon pursed her lips. She pointed at Curt. "What do you think, Curt? You're the one who got these videos. Can you get more? Will they be more helpful?"

Curt thought for a moment. "I don't think it matters how many videos we get or how good they are. We could have a perfect view, and it would still only show this one interaction. It will show two men fighting. Maybe one was the aggressor, maybe one pushed too hard, maybe the good guy, maybe the bad guy."

"Whose side are you on?" Karim asked.

"Oh, I'm on your side," Curt assured. "But that's because I know the whole story."

"And you're getting paid," Talon half-joked.

"And I'm getting paid," Curt didn't disagree. "I'm on Team Karim. But there are going to be people on Team Dank. We're like the entourage before the big fight, following the fighters onto the arena floor and up into the ring. There's music blasting and lights flashing, and the crowd is cheering and booing and going crazy. But the actual fight is only a small part of it all. And you don't pick who you want to win based on what happens in the ring. You've already decided that. Based on everything you learned beforehand. All the pre-fight publicity. All the weigh-ins and the trash talk and backstory. You pick a favorite, and then you root for them. And that's boxing. In wrestling, they don't mess around: they tell you exactly who the bad guy is, *before* the fight. There's a whole storyline set up way before anybody steps into the ring. That's what we need to do here. By the time the jury finally sees whatever videos we can scratch up, they will have already decided who they're rooting for. The scrappy young protestor or the protector of law and order."

"The Black guy or the White guy," Shayla grumbled.

"Maybe," Talon admitted with a frown. "Probably. But that's why Curt is right. We need to define it differently, up front, before they see what happened. They need to know Karim is the hero. But more importantly—"

"They need to know Dank is the villain," Paul finished, "before they see the fight."

The corner of his mouth curled into a smile. "I can help with that." Then, "Let me help with that."

Talon smiled. She gestured at the others assembled in the conference room. "You want in on this?"

Paul shrugged. He pointed at the paused video on the far wall. "I want in on that. I know people like Dank. I know the kind of things they've done in their lives and I know what they do to try to hide it. More importantly, I know how to find it and uncover it. And I can give it to you."

Talon liked the sound of that. She looked to her client. It was his life on the line after all. "What do you think, Karim?"

"I may not be a hero, but I'm not a villain," he answered. "I don't know if that other guy is the bad guy, but I know I'm not. So, if you can prove he's the bad guy, he's the kind of guy who would come out and start a fight, even if I'm the one who finished it, then hell yeah, let's do that."

Talon nodded. "Yeah, let's do that." But she narrowed her eyes at Paul. "So, how are you going to do that?"

"I can't do it all. That's not my thing," Paul answered. He looked to Curt. "You already have an investigator. He can dig up the basics. Criminal history, lawsuits, bastard kids three states over. Public record stuff. My expertise is more, let's say, nuanced. I can find the stuff other people can't. Stuff that's buried, and buried deep. And a guy like Dank? A guy who runs a prison for a private company? A guy who walks out with a half dozen armed guards and attacks a guy who would kick his ass three ways to Sunday in a fair fight? That's one entitled asshole. He's got stuff buried, and I'm betting it's very, very deep."

"Too deep for you?" Talon questioned.

Paul smiled and actually winked at her. "Nothing's too deep for me. But it might take a little longer to get it uncovered."

Talon decided to ignore the wink, for the moment anyway. "One week. I want to meet again in one week. Find out everything we can about James Dank and throw it on the table. Then we'll figure out how to construct our villain. I want that crowd, that jury, booing when they watch him step into the ring against our hero."

CHAPTER 20

With everyone tasked with their assignments, and the rendezvous scheduled a week out, Talon figured it would be a few days before she saw Paul again. She figured wrong. It was less than four hours later. After five, but before 'quitting time'—a concept that changed depending on the day and the needs thereof.

"Working late?" Paul said from the spot where he suddenly appeared in Talon's doorway. It was one of those phrases that was meant as a question, but obviously wasn't. There was no question she was working late. It was more of a statement, an observation, and a painfully obvious, pedestrian one at that. It was a conversation starter. But Talon never felt like talking when she had work to do.

"Is that a question?" She looked away from her computer only long enough to react to the unexpected voice in her door jamb before returning her gaze to her screen.

"I suppose not," Paul admitted. "How's this: want to stop working late? There's a pretty good bar across the street. Not the best I've ever been to, but the bartender who's there tonight makes a pretty damn good Hemingway daquiri."

Talon sighed and pushed back from her keyboard. "First, I

drink whiskey. Second, I don't drink whiskey when I have work to do. Third, I don't drink whiskey with my landlord."

"Technically, I'm the property manager," Paul defended, "not the landlord."

"I feel like that's a distinction without a difference," Talon replied.

"Come on, there's precedent for that sort of thing," Paul tried.

"Yeah," Talon agreed. "It's a porn category."

Paul's eyebrows shot up. "How do—?" he started to ask, then thought better of it. He pulled out his phone. "Look, just give me your number and I can—"

"Yeah, no," Talon interrupted. "I don't give out my personal number."

Paul sighed and ran a hand through his thick, dark hair. "Okay, fine. Never mind. I was just trying to be friendly. But you're busy, you don't drink rum, you don't give your number out, and I'm gonna leave now."

"And you're going to get that dirt on Dank by next week," Talon reminded him. "Right?"

Paul laughed, and shook his head. "Always business, aren't you? Smart, beautiful, domineering. Pretty sure that's a category too."

Talon let herself smile at that. It wasn't that she didn't find Paul attractive. Just the opposite. But she wasn't going to let something as fleeting as that endanger her case. Again, just the opposite. She knew how to use it to help her win the case.

"Then impress your mistress, young man," she purred under lidded eyes, "and see what reward awaits you."

CHAPTER 21

Talon's own reward was more bullshit from Helen Hampton Montclair. The next morning, when Talon went into her office, there was a process server waiting for her in the lobby. She knew not to get mad at him—he was just some skinny, scraggly Gen Z'er wearing a bike helmet and a messenger bag—but she was, nevertheless, pissed as he presented her with a raft of documents and stated the cliched, "You've been served."

Talon only hesitated for a moment before snatching them out of the bike messenger's hand. There was never much point in trying to avoid service—not unless she was willing to move to another state, maybe even country. And if she did that, then Helen Hampton Montclair would have accomplished her goal of scaring Talon off the case. Talon glanced down long enough to confirm the name of her old firm at the bottom right corner of the pleading, then looked up at the process server, who was still standing there, just staring at her.

"What, you want a tip?" Talon demanded. "People don't give tips after they get served, do they? That can't be a thing, right?"

"No, it's just, um," he rubbed the back of his unshaven and sweaty neck, "well, like, you're really pretty."

Talon's eyes rolled so far back into her head she could have seen her own brain. "Are you kidding me? You're hitting on me after you serve me with legal papers?" She shook them at him. "These could be divorce papers."

The young man shrugged. "Then you'd be available."

Talon frowned, although she appreciated both his effort and his sense of opportunity. But she was less than interested. "Nice try, bike boy, but not interested. Now, go on. Get. Go ruin someone else's day."

Bike Boy shrugged again. "That's what I do, ma'am. All day long."

Talon stared at him for a moment, fists clenched. "'Ma'am'? Did you just call me 'ma'am'?" She jabbed a finger at the exit. "Get the fuck out."

The Gen Z just shrugged. "Whatever. Have a nice day." And he made his exit.

Talon watched after him, her anger melting first into ambivalence, then indifference. She turned her attention back to the papers in her hand. She experienced a moment of cognitive dissonance as she first confirmed the pleading was definitely on her old firm's pleading paper, then that the case caption was definitely the criminal case of *The State of Washington v. Karim Jackson*. Talon had half expected to get sued, delivering on the promise of the cease and desist letter, but the case would have been something like *The Estate of James Dank v. Talon Winter, Extraordinaire*. Hampton Montclair didn't represent anyone in the criminal case; she couldn't file anything under that case number. Talon's dissonance turned to curiosity. She dropped into a lobby chair and began reading.

COMES NOW the Estate of James Dank, decedent and named victim in the above-captioned case, by and through its attorney, Helen Hampton Montclair of the Law Firm of

Gardelli, High & Steinmetz, and moves this Court for an
Order enjoining the Defendant, personally or through his
attorneys, from making any derogatory or negative
statements and/or committing any further acts of
defamation, including but not limited to slander and libel,
against James Dank, his Family, or his Estate, in the
furtherance of the litigation herein, during the pendency of
said litigation, or in any other forum or manner, whether
orally, electronically, in writing, or otherwise, unless and
until the termination of said litigation, to include any
appeals that may arise from the likely result of a
conviction(s) for the crimes charged.

"Wow," Talon breathed, after finishing just the first,
paragraph-long sentence. "What a bitch."

The motion went on, and was attached to a lengthy brief, but
the basic gist was that Hampton Montclair wanted the judge in the
criminal case to prevent Talon from bad-mouthing Dank in any way
during the trial. It would have been laughable if it hadn't been so
potentially dangerous to Talon's ability to defend Karim. A few
more 100-word sentences later, the exact danger presented itself in
so many words:

Specifically, the Court should prevent the Defendant and
his Attorney from presenting any statements, arguments,
questions, documents, or other potential evidence or
advocacy which purports to show that the Defendant was
acting in self-defense and/or that James Dank was in any
way the aggressor in the incident or was anything other
than the innocent victim of the intentional and murderous
actions of the Defendant.

So, if granted, Hampton Montclair's motion would prevent
Talon from arguing self-defense. The jury would hear Karim

pushed Dank for no reason, Dank fell and hit his head, and Dank died as a result. The judge might as well just order the jury to convict.

Talon sighed. One more damned thing to do.

It was a bullshit motion, brought by a lawyer who didn't even have standing to bring motions, and obviously flew in the face of her client's constitutional right to present a defense to the criminal charges against him. But she couldn't ignore it. Ignoring it would mean relying on the prosecutor and judge to do the right thing. And that would be even stupider than Hampton Montclair's motion.

CHAPTER 22

The motion, somehow, had been scheduled for argument by the court, despite the fact that neither she nor Cobb had filed it. The saving grace was that whichever clerk had docketed the hearing had also followed the court rules and given Talon five days' notice of the hearing, not including weekends. That gave her a week before she would have to go in and make sure a stupid motion wasn't granted by a stupid judge. Cobb was stupid, too, but he wasn't really part of the equation.

That week gave Talon time to prepare her response. It also gave her time to do some of the other things she had been putting off, like cleaning out her old office. She'd moved most of the equipment over to her new locale already, but there were still those last things that always straggle behind in a move. The kind of things that clutter up the bottoms of desk drawers and file cabinets, and lay haphazardly across the flat surfaces behind where the aforementioned equipment had been. Most of it couldn't have been that important, or it would have been moved already. But there was something final about taking out the last of what was wanted, throwing what wasn't in the trash can, and dropping off the keys with the receptionist.

"We're gonna miss you," Hannah said as she accepted the keys from Talon. She frowned. "Well, I am, anyway."

Talon returned the frown, then looked sideways down the hallway. "Is he here?"

Hannah nodded. "Yeah. I told him you were coming by to drop off the keys. I think he made sure to be here. In case you wanted to say anything to him."

Talon wanted to be angry with Olsen. She had every right to be. But she didn't want to put in the effort. He wasn't worth it. People suck. Olsen was no exception. Neither was she, she knew. Eventually everyone lets everyone else down. It wasn't a question of if, just when. Or rather, when will you let yourself notice it? It happened all the time, every day. You just agree to overlook it. So, when will you notice it, admit it, and move on? People were worth what they were worth until they weren't worth it anymore. Meanwhile, other people arrive, and they suck too. Eventually.

"Are you going to say goodbye to him?" Hannah asked.

Talon turned her frown upside down, but only because she didn't want to let Hannah down right then. "No, I don't think so. But I'll say goodbye to you. Good luck with everything."

Hannah managed a smile too. "I'll miss you."

Talon nodded, but didn't return the sentiment. Maybe that was a letdown for Hannah. But lying was a lot of effort too.

* * *

Talon threw the box of the last of the stuff from her old office onto the desk of her new office. She could sort through it tomorrow. Or after that. Or never. She plopped down in her chair and, despite herself, began contemplating the futility of human existence.

Then Paul walked in.

"Hey, I've got some good news," he announced.

Talon took a beat to decide whether to engage with humanity or continue her retreat from it. She wasn't one to wallow—and there would be time for that later anyway, if she was still feeling it—so she leaned forward and rested an elbow on her desk, then her chin on her fist. "Oh, yeah? What's the good news?"

"It's about Dank," Paul began.

Talon figured as much, although there was a chance it had something to do with a rent reduction, or new items in the vending machine.

"Cool," she said. "Don't tell me."

Paul cocked his head at her. "What? Why not?"

"It's dirt on him, right?" Talon leaned back in her chair again. She recalled the language from Hampton Montclair's motion. "Is it derogatory or negative statements and/or defamation, including but not limited to slander and libel?"

Paul took a moment. "It's only slander or libel if it isn't true," he narrowed his eyes at her for confirmation, "right?"

Talon nodded. "Right. Truth is a defense. But I'm guessing it's still derogatory or negative. In fact, it better be. That's what I'm paying you to find. I just don't want it yet."

"Why not?" Paul was clearly not only puzzled, but disappointed.

"Because I have to argue a motion next week," Talon explained, "about precisely this sort of information and whether it should be admitted at the trial. In addition to arguing that the motion is stupid, and the Court should deny it out of hand, I'd also like to be able to say I don't have any such information anyway."

Paul stuck out his bottom lip a bit and nodded. "Smart."

"Of course." Talon was offended he might have thought anything else. "Then, after the hearing is over, you can tell me all about whatever you've found."

"Okay," Paul replied.

"Over that drink," Talon added with a smile. It was important to throw your pets a bone once in a while.

Paul's face lit up. "You've got yourself a deal."

CHAPTER 23

Five days' notice (not counting weekends) might have seemed like a long time when they wrote the court rules, but those five days (not counting weekends) usually flew by and certainly did in this case, so five days later (not counting weekends), Talon found herself once again in the Criminal Presiding courtroom waiting for the other attorneys to arrive and for Judge Harvey to emerge from his chambers.

It was the first hearing where Karim was out of custody. Rather than be dragged in by a jail guard after another jail guard bellowed his name into the bowels of the holding cells behind the courtroom, Karim had met Talon in the lobby, dressed in a sharp suit and muted tie, and walked into the courtroom with his head held high. He looked more like a lawyer than Cobb did, especially when Cobb scrambled in, furtively avoiding Talon's gaze.

Cobb ignored her completely, hurrying to the prosecutor table and busying himself with his file and notepad. Talon found that strange. Cobb usually liked to say something jackassy to her as he strutted in, totally unprepared but confident in his imminent victory, which usually came, even if just because the playing field was always tilted so far in the prosecution's favor.

Talon stepped over to Cobb. "This should be quick, right?" she just wanted to confirm. "You agree that Hampton Montclair has no standing to bring any motions in our criminal case."

Cobb offered an ambivalent shrug and avoided eye contact. "I don't know. Maybe not. But the logic behind them makes sense. So, we're going to join in her motions."

Talon dropped her head to one side. "Really? That's what I'm up against?"

She wasn't really surprised. She wasn't even disappointed— the bar for Cobb was already exceedingly low. She had just let herself hope the patent stupidity of the situation might actually carry the day. But that wasn't how The System worked.

"You're up against the family of a murder victim and the government charged with holding the murderer responsible," Cobb replied, still avoiding Talon's gaze. "Next time, don't kill anyone."

"Well, I personally didn't kill anyone," Talon replied. "But there's always a first time."

Cobb finally looked at her, to confirm it was a threat. Talon held his gaze just long enough to do so, then turned and stormed back to join Karim at their table. Again, she wasn't surprised, or even disappointed. And she sure as hell wasn't unprepared.

Hampton Montclair arrived next, attended by a younger version of Talon from back in the day: a brand new attorney, identifiable as such by her dark suit and bright eyes. That shine would wear off, Talon knew. In the meantime, though, she was literally carrying Hampton Montclair's briefcase, but doing so with her chin up and her long brown hair pulled back in a tight ponytail. Talon remembered that early stage of her career. Pretending to be a badass to impress the partner. Then she became the badass and realized the partner wasn't worth impressing.

"Ms. Winter," Hampton Montclair greeted Talon as she

stepped forward to the prosecution table as well. She ignored Karim. Her assistant placed the briefcase on the table next to Cobb's materials and began extracting files and notepads and pens and such.

"Helen," Talon returned with a nod. "Who's the sherpa?"

Hampton Montclair's nostrils flared in irritation. Talon wasn't sure if it was at being addressed by her first name like an equal or acknowledging the presence of her underling. Talon hoped it was both.

"This is Erin Vandergraben," Hampton Montclair gestured vaguely behind her, but didn't turn around. "She's an associate in our litigation department."

"Hey, Erin Vandergraben." Talon craned her neck around Hampton Montclair and waved.

Erin Vandergraben's eyes widened at the greeting. She didn't reply. Instead, she avoided eye contact and redoubled her efforts at emptying her superior's briefcase.

Talon considered pushing more, just for the fun of it, but it also would have been distracting too, and she didn't need that. In any event, it was time to start the hearing.

"All rise!" the bailiff called out as Judge Harvey once again entered the courtroom.

Harvey pulled up short for a moment when he saw Talon, Cobb, and Hampton Montclair all assembled before him yet again, but then picked up his gait and took his seat on the bench.

"Be seated," he instructed. It was intended for everyone in the courtroom but seemed especially directed to Talon and her opponents. "This case keeps turning up on my docket. Like a bad penny, I believe the phrase is."

No one uses cash anymore, Talon thought, *but okay.*

"Ms. Winter. Mr. Cobb." Harvey nodded down to the

attorneys who were actually on the case. Then, "And I see Ms. Hampton Montclair is here as well."

"Yes, Your Honor. Thank you," Hampton Montclair stood up and replied.

"Don't thank me yet, counsel," Harvey said. "I believe we have a threshold issue to address before I hear from you, if I hear from you at all."

Hampton Montclair's nostrils flared again, and she stood up a little straighter, but she didn't say anything. Instead, Cobb jumped up to make things messy. Of course.

"The State will be joining in Ms. Hampton's motions, Your Honor," he announced.

"Hampton *Montclair*," she hissed at him.

Judge Harvey took a moment before responding. His mouth twisted into a bit of a knot on one side. Then he relaxed it again and addressed Talon. "Were you aware of that, Ms. Winter?"

"I was made aware a few minutes ago, Your Honor," Talon acknowledged, also standing to address the Court. "And I'm not surprised. I considered asking the Court to strike Ms. Hampton Montclair's motions, and I believe the Court could still do that. Mr. Cobb really should be required to file his own motions. He is the prosecutor after all, and his charge is to seek justice, in case he's forgotten, not simply to advocate for whatever the wishes of the family are."

She took a moment to glance over at Cobb. He was looking at her now. More of a scowl, really. But she had his attention.

"But I'm not going to do that, Your Honor," Talon continued, "I am not going to ask the Court to strike the motions. I am going to ask the court to *deny* the motions, in full, on the merits. Trial is approaching quickly, and I don't want to have to come back again in a week after Mr. Cobb has cut-and-pasted Ms. Hampton

Montclair's work onto the prosecutor's pleading paper."

Judge Harvey nodded. "Alright then. If that's how you want to proceed, we'll do the hearing now." He sighed, then swiveled his head to the prosecution table. "But there will be rules. Mr. Cobb, this is your motion. You will make the arguments. And Ms. Hampton Montclair?"

"Yes, Your Honor?" She flashed an eager expression.

"You will not address the Court," Judge Harvey instructed. "At all. You have no standing. This is a case between the State of Washington on the one side and Karim Jackson, a private individual, on the other. Your clients, the family and estate of the decedent, while certainly important to and affected by this case, are not parties to it. Accordingly, you will not address the Court. Is that entirely understood?"

How entirely understood it was, was made clear by the several long seconds it took Hampton Montclair to finally say, through gritted teeth, "Yes, Your Honor."

Talon looked over at Erin Vandergraben, who couldn't help her instinct to return the glance just long enough for Talon to wink at her.

"I don't care if you want to consult with Mr. Cobb briefly before he presents the State's arguments," Judge Harvey threw her a bone, "but he will need to articulate those arguments to the Court on his own."

"Understood." Hampton Montclair's response was immediate that time. She'd recovered.

Cobb followed it up with a less convincing, "Of course, Your Honor."

Harvey sighed again. The sigh of someone weighted down by a job that was somehow both important, but tedious. And speaking of tedious: "Mr. Cobb, you may begin whenever you're ready."

Cobb offered a nod to the judge, but his brain was too full of whatever Hampton Montclair was fervently whispering into his ear at the moment for him to form any actual words for the judge. Harvey leaned back patiently, and Talon sat down and followed suit. She glanced again at Erin Vandergraben, but the young associate had locked her head into a forward-facing position lest she accidentally make eye contact again with the enemy.

Talon leaned over to her client. "How are you doing?" she whispered.

Karim offered a slight shrug and even slighter nod. "I'm glad to be out of handcuffs. But this whole thing seems ridiculous to me. They really want the judge to prevent us from telling the jury the whole story? The truth? I thought the courts were about justice."

Talon took a moment to look at her client. A young Black man charged with the murder of someone who attacked him. "Do you really think that?"

Karim took a moment, then frowned. "I think that's how it should be."

"Shoulda, woulda, coulda," Talon replied. "That and five bucks will get you a cup of coffee. Well, maybe seven bucks."

Karim shook his head again, fully. "That's messed up."

Talon put a hand on his shoulder. "Look, the system may be screwed up, but there's a weakness."

"Oh yeah?" Karim asked. "What?"

"Me." Talon answered. "I'm their weakness. It's my job to take their system, turn it around on them, and plunge it into their throats. It's my job to stand over them, boot on their chest, and listen to the blood gurgle in their throats—until the gurgling stops."

"Damn." Karim laughed, a little nervously. "I'm glad you're on my side."

Talon grinned, then glanced over again at Cobb, Hampton Montclair, and Erin Vandergraben. "Yeah." She nodded. "Me too."

"The State is ready, Your Honor," Cobb finally announced.

Harvey leaned forward again. He rolled his wrist at the prosecutor. "Then, by all means, Mr. Cobb, proceed."

Cobb cleared his throat and rubbed his hands together. Tells that he was uncomfortable and unprepared. "Yes, Your Honor. Thank you. So, yes."

Excellent introduction, Talon thought. She had to remind herself to not be overconfident. Cobb might not be able to articulate the arguments well, but Harvey would understand them anyway, and he wasn't going to rule in her favor just because Cobb was a putz. Especially if she failed to address whatever points he might accidentally bump into while making his oral argument.

"The Court is to protect the rights of everyone involved in a matter brought before it," Cobb settled into his presentation. "That includes the defendant, obviously," he conceded with a diffident wave at the defense table, "but it is not limited to him. There are others involved and one of those others is the victim. And in a murder case, the family of the victim.

"As the saying goes, 'Your right to smell and at my nose', and the defendant's right to make arguments about what happened on the day in question ends at the victim's right not to be slandered."

Hampton Montclair, who was seated next to Cobb, pulled on his jacket. He leaned down for her to whisper into his ear, then stood up again and added, "Or libeled, Your Honor. Um, slandered if Ms. Winter says it out loud to the jury and libel if she puts it in a pleading, Your Honor."

"I'm familiar with the distinction," Judge Harvey muttered.

"Yes, of course you are," Cobb stammered. "Right. Well, as I was saying, um, Ms. Winter should not be allowed to make baseless and defamatory claims about the victim—"

Another tug on his coat and another harsh whisper from Hampton Montclair.

"Uh, Mr. Dank," Cobb corrected himself. "I will use his name, of course, because, uh, he's a real person—*was* a real person—and the Court should treat him as such. And his family; they are real persons, too. People. Real people."

Cobb took a moment to gather himself. He closed his eyes, took a deep breath, then looked up again at the Court. "What I'm trying to say, Your Honor, is that the State expects Ms. Winter to attack Mr. Dank and blame him for what happened. To blame Mr. Dank for the incident, even though it was the defendant and his cohorts who came to Mr. Dank's place of employment. To blame Mr. Dank for the altercation, even though it was the defendant who pushed Mr. Dank. To blame Mr. Dank for his own death, even though it was the defendant who killed him.

"So, what I'm saying, Your Honor," Cobb continued, "is that the Court shouldn't allow that. The Court shouldn't allow Ms. Winter to violate Mr. Dank's rights. His right against being slandered. His right against being libeled. His right against being defamed. His right against being lied about. Mr. Dank is the victim here. Mr. Dank is the dead person here. But Mr. Dank has no voice here, thanks to the criminal acts of the defendant. And so, the Court should safeguard that voice and silence those who would use their voices to attack someone who has no voice to respond. Thank you."

That was a lot of voices, Talon thought with a frown. Cobb seemed to be on a roll for a moment, but he kind of lost it there at the end. The result of arguing someone else's motion, she supposed.

Cobb sat down, only to be met with a whispery onslaught from Hampton Montclair, who grabbed his arm and pulled his ear practically into her mouth.

"Ms. Winter," Judge Harvey invited from the bench, "your response?"

Talon stood up and tugged on her coat to straighten it. It would be the only movement she would make until she was done delivering her remarks. She wasn't about to let unconscious gestures distract from her arguments, and she knew the conscious gestures she used to help sway jurors would be useless on an experienced, and increasingly impatient, judge.

"Truth," she began, "is a defense. It is a defense against any claim of defamation, whether slander or libel or whatever else Ms. Hampton Montclair whispers into Mr. Cobb's ear. And while I think it's important to note that truth is a defense, and to submit to the Court, which I do now, that any claim by the defense that Mr. Dank was the primary aggressor, that my client acted lawfully in self-defense, and that his actions were not the proximate cause of Mr. Dank's death are very much the truth, I believe it is even more important to note that threats of civil litigation against a criminal defendant and his defense attorney are not only inappropriate and unprofessional, but are, in fact, an abhorrent attack on the very foundations of our criminal justice system."

System, meet throat.

"As a criminal defendant, charged with any crime, let alone murder, Mr. Jackson has several very important rights. So important, in fact, that they have been enshrined in both the United States and Washington Constitutions. Among those rights is the right to present a vigorous defense and to confront any and all witnesses against him. These rights are constitutional and will not bow to threats of common law torts like slander and libel. Not only does Mr. Jackson have the right to present whatever information may help defend him against the charges brought by the government, the Court—*this* Court—has an absolute and honor-bound duty to defend that right. Not only to permit it, but to clear away any challenges to it, to make a safe place where that vigorous defense may be presented, and presented in the most effective and powerful way possible."

Talon did allow one gesture. She pointed up to the judge.

"This Court is not neutral, Your Honor. It cannot be. Neutrality means indifference, and this Court cannot be indifferent to the constitutional rights of anyone, but especially not a criminal defendant. Especially not a man charged with murder. Especially not a man who was defending himself against an attack from one member of the prion industrial complex only to find himself then attacked tenfold by those who support and profit from that complex.

Talon retracted her hand slightly and curled it into a fist in front of her chest. "Indeed, Your Honor, I would submit this motion is an allegory for the private prison system Mr. Karim was protesting in the first place. A private entity is attempting to insert itself and profit from what should be a public governmental function. In the case of P.R.I.C.E., a private corporation with a board of directors and stockholders and other investments, like, oh, I don't know, real estate, that feeds itself off what should be the public charge of punishing and rehabilitating criminal offenders. Likewise, here we have a private law firm, with partners and shareholders and its own commercial real estate division, I'm sure, billing time and profiting off what should be a public and impartial search for justice."

Talon didn't bother glancing at Hampton Montclair, but she sure noticed that Judge Harvey did, however briefly, before returning his stone-faced gaze to Talon.

"In both cases, Your Honor," Talon continued, "a private

entity is using its private resources to tip the scales even more in favor of the government. This is all the more alarming where the entire weight and mass of the government is already being pressed down onto a single citizen. Mr. Jackson has almost no ability to counter such power, Your Honor. The only thing he has is the power of the truth, and the solemn duty of this Court—of you, Judge Robert Harvey—to safeguard his right to present that truth, and to fight off any challenges to that right, whether from the State's attorney or a high-priced attorney from the city's biggest law firm. None of them matter. What matters is the constitution. What matters is the truth. What matters is justice. The prosecutor knows that. I know that. But most importantly, Your Honor knows that. And that is why we ask you to deny these motions and permit us to make the arguments we need to make to ensure that due process, a fair trial, and justice, sweet justice, prevails. Thank you."

Talon took a moment to nod at her own stirring words, then started to sit down. But Judge Harvey wasn't quite done with her.

"Stirring, counsel," he remarked flatly, "and I appreciate the advocacy. Can you also help me out with some actual citation to actual authority? Maybe a court rule or something?"

Talon straightened back up and smiled. Harvey hadn't asked for any authority from Cobb, but that wasn't necessarily a bad thing. First, expectations were lower for Cobb, especially when arguing someone else's motion, but also just generally. Second, decisions were supposed to be grounded in legal authority. If Harvey was asking for her citations, it could be a signal that he planned to ground his decision in her authority.

"Of course, Your Honor," Talon answered. "United States Constitution, Amendments One, Five, Six, and Fourteen. Washington State Constitution, Article One, Sections Four, Five, Seven, Nine and Twenty-Two. Revised Code of Washington,

Section 9A.16. Evidence Rules 401, 402, 404(a). Does the Court want case law as well? I provided a table of cases at the front of my written response."

Harvey offered a discreet grin. "No need, counsel. I just wanted something on the record."

"May I reply?" Cobb interjected.

Harvey swung his head toward the prosecution table. It was customary to allow the moving party a short reply to the other party's argument. It was also usually a waste of everyone's time. "Briefly," Judge Harvey instructed.

"Thank you, Your Honor." Cobb stood up again. "Ms. Winter went on and on about the truth, but the truth in this case is that the defendant murdered Mr. Dank. To say anything else is false, and therefore not a defense to slander." A tug from Hampton Montclair. "Or libel," he added.

"The truth, Mr. Cobb," Judge Harvey responded, "is rarely what either side thinks it is. It's also not usually exactly what the jury ultimately thinks, but, in my experience, they are usually the ones who get closest to it. They will be the ones who decide what happened that day, and they will be the ones who decide what legal consequences, if any, flow from that, at least as it pertains to the criminal charges brought by the State. I am not going to prevent either side from presenting their version of the truth to the jury, except insomuch as such presentation violates the evidence rules. I expect the verdict in this case will have an impact on any possible civil actions which might be brought at a later time by the decedent's family estate, but those potential claims are not before the Court, and indeed couldn't be, because no such defamation has yet been filed."

Talon winced slightly at that. *Don't give them any ideas.*

"My job is to ensure the defendant receives a fair trial,"

Judge Harvey continued. "The authority cited by Ms. Winter, the law on self-defense and the rules regarding admissibility of evidence, have all been designed by people far smarter than me to ensure every criminal defendant receives that fair trial. I will follow those rules, and we will have a fair trial. The State's motion to prevent the defense from arguing their version of the facts of this case is denied."

Talon allowed herself an exhale. She looked down at Karim and placed a hand on his shoulder.

"However," the judge added, "I will not allow this trial to turn into a policy debate about the wisdom or desirability of contracting corrections services to private corporations. This case will be about what happened that day in front of that detention center, but it will not be about that detention center. Is that understood, Ms. Winter?"

Talon offered her sweetest, most professional smile. "Understood." *But not agreed to.*

Judge Harvey didn't ask Cobb whether he understood, probably to avoid giving him, or very possibly Hampton Montclair, the opportunity to argue with his ruling. Instead, he called out, "Next case!" and a pair of different attorneys stepped forward to push Talon and the rest of them from their spots at the counsel tables.

"I'll meet you outside," Talon instructed Karim, and she took a moment to gather her things and her thoughts before exiting the courtroom.

Cobb hurried out, nearly pushing past Karim on his rush to the door, but Hampton Montclair lingered. She stepped over to Talon, Erin Vandergraben trailing behind, but definitely still behind.

"You heard what he said," Hampton Montclair taunted in a

lowered voice, as the next hearing began.

"I heard he denied your motions," Talon answered.

"Only because we haven't filed our defamation suit yet," Hampton Montclair responded. "I can remedy that very quickly. So maybe you should think twice about pursuing your slander of—"

"And libel," Talon interrupted. "I plan to libel him too."

Hampton Montclair sneered. "If you're smart, you won't do either. If you're smart, you'll talk your client into pleading guilty and accepting his punishment for murdering a good man in cold blood."

Talon rolled her eyes. "There are so many things wrong with what you just said, I don't even know where to start. Maybe with the warden of a for-profit prison being a 'good man'…"

Hampton Montclair interrupted her. "If you don't want to get sued, I advise you to comply with our demands."

Talon took a moment, then unfurled a broad, hateful smile. "And if you don't want to get your bleached teeth knocked down your wrinkled throat, I would advise you to fuck off."

Talon craned her neck again to look past the stunned Helen Hampton Montclair. "Nice to meet you, Erin Vandergraben. Bye."

CHAPTER 24

Talon walked into Paul's office.

"You ready for that drink?"

Paul looked up from his monitor, then to the clock. "It's noon."

Talon nodded. She wasn't going to ask twice.

"Um, yeah, sure," Paul stammered. He made a few mouse clicks to close whatever he was working on and stood up. "I'm not even sure the bar across the street is open yet."

Talon gave him a wink. "I know a place."

* * *

The name of the place in question was simply 'The Bar' and it was tucked under the freeway on-ramps and off-ramps where Interstate 5 intersected with State Route 7, Interstate 705, the Tacoma Dome, and the Port of Tacoma. It was the location that gave the place its unique charm—part nautical, part run down, all Tacoma.

"I have never been here," Paul practically admitted as they walked into the dimly lit establishment. It was a sunny enough day, but little of that sunlight permeated the thick glass of the front windows, the only windows in the bar. "I'm disappointed in myself."

"Well, let's hope I don't end up disappointed too," Talon responded. She pulled out a stool at the bar. "Or you may have to pay for your own drink."

Paul sat down on the stool next to her. "I can manage that. But I would hate to disappoint you. Although, I have to say, you seem like you might be easy to disappoint."

Talon acknowledged the comment with a shrug. "I start every relationship already disappointed in the other person. It saves time. But my mind can be changed."

"Everyone is presumed disappointing, huh?"

"Precisely." Talon nodded. "I'm glad we understand each other."

"So, how did your hearing go?" Paul asked as the bartender, the only employee in the place, approached.

But Talon shook her head and her finger at him. "Nope. We're not here to discuss that. It went great, of course, but no small talk."

She glanced at the bartender. "Old fashioned, please."

Paul turned to him as well. "Um, do you have any craft—?" He glanced around. "You know what? Never mind. I'll just have an old fashioned too. No twist. Thanks."

The bartender nodded and left to make the drinks.

"The twist is the best part," Talon chastised.

"Okay, then how about this twist?" Paul threw a broad smile and dramatic hand flourish at her. "Dank was a Russian spy who was also a double agent for the Chinese, and he was selling national security secrets to the highest bidder."

Talon blinked at him. "That's bullshit, right?"

Paul laughed. "Yeah, totally made that up."

"Would have been a good segue way, though," Talon

complimented.

"I know, right?" Paul nodded. "I couldn't resist."

"You probably could have," Talon opined. "Now my expectations are raised. Whatever you do have, it better be at least as good as that."

The bartender returned with their drinks. Talon thanked him and took a sip. "So, what do you have for me?"

"I have," Paul pulled his glass over and prepared to take a drink, "the beginning of wisdom."

"Christ." Talon rolled her eyes and took a longer drink. "I'm not really looking for more clever words today. I know the guy was an asshole. I know his family are assholes, and they hired an asshole attorney. Don't be an asshole too. Just tell me what you have without the Lord of the Rings riddles."

Paul's expression lit up. "Are you into Lord of the Rings?"

Talon shook her head. "I don't even know if they have riddles. There was like a quest or something, right? Weren't there riddles along the way or something?"

"That was Monty Python and the Holy Grail," Paul corrected.

"Oh yeah," Talon laughed. "Something about pigeons."

"Swallows."

Talon raised an eyebrow. "Excuse me?"

"The riddles were about swallows," Paul explained. "The type of bird?"

"Oh, right." Talon nodded slowly. "The bird. Right. I thought—You know what? Never mind." Another gulp. Her drink was already almost gone. "What do you have for me? I shouldn't have to ask three times."

Paul took a patient sip and grinned at her over his glass. "I doubt you ever have to ask a man more than once."

Talon grimaced and set down her glass. "This isn't going well. In case you were thinking maybe this was going well, it's not going well. Tell me what you have on Dank. Now." She stood up. "Or I'm done, and you can walk back to the office."

"Okay, okay." Paul raised his hands at her. "You're right. He's an asshole. But he's a documented asshole. In his twenty-three years at American Correctional Enterprises, he's had seventeen documented complaints against him, including five allegations of physical force on subordinates."

Talon took a beat, then sat down again. "That's good."

"Right?" Paul agreed.

"What happened with them?" Talon followed up.

"Well, judging by the fact that he was still working for A.C.E. when he died," Paul surmised, "nothing happened, I imagine."

"You imagine?" Talon squinted at him. "Aren't you supposed to know?"

Paul shrugged. "I know some of them. Most were investigated internally and found to be unfounded."

"Including the physical force ones?"

"Those were harder," Paul admitted. "I was able to confirm one of them was ruled unfounded, three were unsubstantiated. The difference between unfounded and unsubstantiated is—"

"I know the difference," Talon interrupted. "What about the fifth one?"

Paul grinned and took another sip of his old-fashioned, then tipped the glass toward his companion. "Exactly."

Talon threw her head back and ran exasperated fingers through her hair. "Oh, my god, Delgado. You're killing me. I'm not a patient person."

Paul laughed. "I can see that, but I enjoy a little theater.

Sorry. That last case?" He shrugged. "I don't know."

"You don't know?" Talon raised a disappointed eyebrow.

"No," Paul confirmed. "And that's how I know it's so important. You know?"

Talon closed her eyes and pinched the bridge of her nose. She opened them again and called out to the bartender. "Another old fashioned, please."

She turned back to Paul. "This isn't going to get any better, is it?"

"I'm having a good time," Paul said.

"Well, that's the important thing." Talon rolled her eyes again. "I'll tell you what, Paul. You like a little theater? Great. Put on your play. I'll just sit here, drinking the drink that I really, really hope shows up soon, and you can take however long you want to tell me whatever the hell it is you're taking so damn long to tell me."

Paul nodded. "You swear a lot."

"I'm a trial lawyer," Talon responded. "Sue me."

Paul narrowed his eyes at her. "Is that a joke?"

The bartender arrived with Talon's second drink.

"Thank God," she breathed. Then, to the bartender, "And thank you." She raised the glass to her lips and rolled her wrist at Paul. "Proceed, Sir Playwright. Entertain me."

Paul offered an exaggerated nod, but then did, in fact, proceed. Finally. Talon just needed to find the right motivation for him. And filed it away for later.

"I can access every other record on the complaints against Dank," Paul started. "Don't ask me how. I just can."

"I wasn't going to ask," Talon assured him.

"Right. Good. So, anyway," Paul continued, "the fact that I can't access that one record shows just how important it is. I was able to find the initial complaint, but it was redacted. The name of the complainant was blacked out and all of their personal identifiers too. There was a brief summary narrative of the complaint, and a lot of that was also blacked out, but the gist of it was Dank broke the person's arm."

"Damn." Talon nodded appreciatively. "Broken bones are where the money's at in civil litigation. Well, where it starts anyway. The real money is in damage to reproductive organs, but broken bones are good too. Not that soft tissue injury bullshit from people in car accidents claiming whiplash."

"Right," Paul agreed. "Exactly."

"How'd he break it?" Talon asked.

"According to the complaint, he grabbed the person's wrist, and twisted," Paul said. "Broke the elbow and dislocated the shoulder."

"Fuck," Talon said over her glass.

"Yeah," Paul said, "you do swear a lot."

Talon frowned at him.

"But also, yes, fuck," Paul agreed. "That is a fucked up way to hurt someone."

"Probably why you can't find the records," Talon surmised. "It was probably easy enough for A.C.E. to dismiss all the other claims as unsubstantiated, but those kinds of injuries would make it hard to sweep that one under the rug."

"So, they swept it off the servers," Paul said. "That's why I can't find it. There's no digital trace of what happened or why."

"Or how much or to whom," Talon added. "Somebody got paid off."

"But payoffs require paperwork," Paul said what they both knew. "At a minimum, a release of liability and a non-disclosure agreement."

"And that's what you couldn't find," Talon nodded. "An absence of a record can be evidence of the destruction of that record. Evidence rule 803."

"Really?" Paul questioned. "That's cool."

"No, Talon admitted. "Actually, the rule says absence of a record for an event which would normally produce a record is evidence the event never happened," Talon admitted, "but that's bad for us. My version is better, so we're going with that."

Paul offered an appraising frown. "Good idea."

"A better idea is to get those records," Talon knew. She clicked a scheming fingernail against her glass. "It's one thing to suspect a payoff and hush money, it's another thing to show the jury the receipts." She frowned and shook her head. "There must be some way to get those records."

"I'm sure there is," Paul answered. "Just not digitally."

"Then how?"

"Analog," Paul flashed that mischievous grin again. "I have a plan to get our hands on those records—literally. But we're going to need a team."

"Great," Talon sighed. "Witnesses. Just what we'll need when we get caught."

CHAPTER 25

Conference rooms were fine if you had a large group and wanted to impress with free coffee and a view of the water, but some meetings needed to be more intimate, behind closed doors, in Talon's office, jammed around that small conference table she ordered and where no one in the lobby might overhear plans to commit a burglary.

"Burglary?" Shayla threw up your hands. "Are you crazy?"

"Think of it more as trespassing," Paul suggested.

"Still a crime," Shalya pointed out. "And Trespassing plus theft inside where your trespassing equals burglary."

"It doesn't even have to be theft," Curt put in. "Any crime will do. Like in Pirates of Penzance."

"Right," Shayla agreed.

But Talon couldn't let it pass. She raised her eyebrows. "Pirates of Penzance?"

Curt grinned. "Yeah. There's this scene when the pirates are on their way to break into the Major General's house and assault him and they sing a song about committing," he placed a hand over his chest and sang the last word in a surprisingly solid baritone, "burg-lar-ee!"

Talon's eyebrows didn't drop.

"So, you know," Curt continued, "trespassing plus assault is also burglary, but most people don't know that. At least not if they aren't Gilbert and Sullivan fans."

"Or criminal defense lawyers," Talon added, finally relaxing her face.

"I suppose," Curt agreed.

"Which we are, by the way," Shayla picked up. "If anyone should know better, we should. Is that why Karim isn't here?"

"That's exactly why Karim isn't here," Talon confirmed.

It was just the four of them. Talon, Shayla, Curt, and Paul. Planning a little burg-lar-ee.

"Karim can't get so much as a speeding ticket," Talon said, "or he'll be back in jail until the trial is over."

"Or longer," Curt pointed out, "if we lose."

Talon frowned. "Or longer," she admitted, "if we lose."

"Even just this conversation could be a crime," Shayla complained. "Conspiracy to commit burglary is a crime too."

Talon shrugged. "We can talk about it. It's only conspiracy if we actually agree to do it and then one of us takes a substantial step. So, let's not do that. Yet."

"Yet," Curt agreed.

"Can I say something?" Paul finally put in.

"You better," Talon answered. "This is your idea."

"We don't have to do this," Paul said. "There are always at least two options, and one of those is always to do nothing."

Talon waited a beat, to see if there was more. Apparently, there wasn't. "Nice pep talk, coach."

Curt laughed. Paul did too. Shayla did not.

"It's not meant to be a pep talk," Paul defended. "It's an assessment. Any course of action should be thoroughly assessed. In this case, there is always the option to do nothing, but if we do that you will miss out on obtaining information important to your case."

"We will miss out on information vital to our defense," Talon sharpened Paul's statement. "Information that shows who Dank really was."

"The villain," Curt said.

"Exactly." Talon pointed at him.

"Information that will be completely inadmissible," Shayla complained. "How are you going to authenticate it? Put Paul on the stand and have him testify we know it's authentic because he stole it from Dank's office himself?"

Talon offered an appraising frown. "Actually, we could probably do that, but—"

"I'd go to prison," Paul finished.

"Right. That," Talon agreed. "But we may not need to authenticate the actual documents. They might lead us to other evidence we can authenticate. Like, if we can get the name of whose arm Dank broke, we can find that person and they can just testify from memory."

"If they remember," Shayla doubted.

"I'd remember if my boss broke my arm," Curt said.

"Especially if I got a fat settlement out of it," Paul added.

"See?" Talon smiled. "Nothing to worry about."

Shayla crossed her arms and frowned. She seemed to be worrying about quite a lot.

"So, where is the corporate headquarters or whatever?" Curt asked. "Downtown? Up in Seattle? Are we taking a road trip?"

"We're taking a road trip," Talon confirmed, "but not to Seattle."

"And not to a corporate headquarters," Paul expanded. "Corporate headquarters are for shareholder meetings and conference calls. Records are stored off site. Especially old, paper records."

"So, where are we headed?" Curt asked.

"A storage warehouse in Sumner," Talon answered.

"Sumner?" Curt asked. Sumner was a tiny town east of Tacoma, right on the county line with King County. Its main claim to fame was a bridge over the Puyallup River that people used when they were already in the valley and wanted to avoid the traffic on Interstate 5. "There's nothing in Sumner."

"There's one of those storage places," Talon contradicted. "That's not nothing."

Curt thought for a moment. "I stand by my previous comment."

Shayla spoke up again, uncrossing her arms so she could hold her shaking head with both hands. "Explain to me again how any of this would be relevant or admissible?"

"Come on, Shayla," Talon chided. "You know the evidence rules. Once we put self-defense into play, we can attack the victim's credibility." She reached over and pulled her book of court rules off her desk. She couldn't quite remember the exact wording, but she wanted to get it right to make sure she won the legal argument. She had to win every legal argument, even with a friend. "Here it is. Evidence Rule 404(a): 'Evidence of a person's character or a trait of character is not admissible for the purpose of proving action in conformity therewith on a particular occasion, except evidence of a pertinent trait of character of the victim of the crime offered by an accused."

Shayla snatched the book out of Talon's hands and read the rest of the rule, "'Or by the prosecution to rebut the same, or evidence of a character trait of peacefulness of the victim offered by the prosecution in a homicide case to rebut evidence that the victim was the first aggressor.' So, they will just introduce all the times Dank wasn't a violent asshole."

"All the more reason to have evidence of the time he was," Talon returned.

"So, you're going to risk your entire career," Shayla challenged, "to break into a storage facility to maybe get some information that maybe will get you more information that maybe a judge will allow into evidence because one evidence rule will maybe let you do that."

Talon smirked. "Maybe."

The truth behind that smile was more complex. Talon wasn't about to risk her career for any defendant. There was a saying among the criminal defense bar: 'Bar card first.' Representing criminals—*accused* criminals—it was only a matter of time until one of them would ask you to do something that would help the case, but which was definitely illegal. It might be tempting, but the answer had to be no. No one defendant was worth being disbarred. Bar card first.

Getting caught burglarizing a storage unit would probably be enough to get disbarred. Doing it to help a particular defendant in a particular case would definitely be enough to get disbarred. She knew that. Shayla knew it too. Talon suspected Curt had a vague feeling in that general direction. But Paul? Paul must have known it too. He wasn't a vague feeling kind of guy. He was exact and informed and prepared. He wasn't the type to hatch some crazy half-baked scheme that could endanger everyone's freedom and livelihood.

That meant his plan wasn't crazy or half-baked. It was exact and informed. He had a goal in mind, but it couldn't be the stated goal of helping Karim. Because that would be crazy and half-baked. The only conclusion was that Paul had another goal in mind. And

Talon was going to find out what it was.

Shayla threw up her hands and stood up to leave. "I'm out."

Paul frowned slightly but looked to Talon. "What about you? Are you out?"

"Me?" Talon grinned. She stood up, too, but only to grab her keys off her desk. "I'm driving."

CHAPTER 26

Sumner wasn't actually in the middle of nowhere. It was more like in the middle of other somewhere. A small town of some ten thousand residents, tucked between Tacoma on the water and the city of Puyallup, a sort of suburb, named for the Native American tribe whose land was taken to settle it. Sumner had a quaint little downtown about two blocks long, and that bridge to travel over the Puyallup River from Pierce to King County. But once you got outside of the downtown, past the few blocks of craftsmans and ranches that housed those ten thousand residents, it was pretty empty. There were a couple of car dealerships on the way out of town and then right at the edge of the city limits, truly in the middle of nowhere, surrounded by nothing but fields and more fields, stood a single sprawling complex of two-story buildings, its perimeter marked by an eight-foot tall iron-bar fence and a single understated sign that read, 'Corporate Archiving and Storage House.'

"Subtle," Talon remarked when she saw the sign. The words were stacked on top of each other, so the first letter of each word could be read downward. In case anyone missed the intent of acronym, the 'S' for 'Storage' was actually a dollar sign. 'CA$H.'

The middle-of-nowhere feel was enhanced by arriving there at the middle of nowhen—or just after 2:00 a.m. Talon drove, Paul navigated, and Curt sat in the back, uncharacteristically quiet. They had all been mostly silent on the ride over, each lost in their own thoughts, save the occasional directions from Paul to 'Turn here', 'Take the next left', and 'Kill the headlights.' Talon rolled her car to a stop past the main gate, and parked across the very empty street, half in the bushes that rose up from the ditch next to the road.

There were no streetlights—there hadn't been for miles— and Talon had in fact turned off her headlights, so the only light in the entire area came from the spotlights affixed to the tops of the buildings at the CA$H complex.

And the interior dome light of Talon's car when she opened the door to get out.

"Shit, shit, shit," she hissed, and reached up to switch the dome light off. She exhaled loudly. "Sorry about that."

Paul waved it away and gestured for them all to get out of the car. They were dressed all in black. Paul and Curt wore their black ski masks rolled up onto the top of their heads. Talon held hers in her hand. They each had a mini flashlight and Paul carried a small black bag of what he described simply as 'tools.' They convened on the far side of her car to confirm their plan, and their intentions, one more time.

"Are we really doing this?" Curt whispered. There was a chill in the air, and he hugged himself against the cold.

Talon looked to Paul. "Are we?"

Paul seemed to frown slightly, his face mostly untouched by the distant lights behind him. "Do you want those documents or not?"

Talon didn't say anything. She took a moment to study what she could make out of Paul's face, then nodded.

Paul nodded back, then turned toward the main gate.

Talon looked at Curt, his worried expression fully visible as he faced the storage facility and its lights. She shrugged. Curt returned the gesture. They followed Paul.

Paul was ducking low, hunched over as he hurried along the perimeter fence. Talon and Curt followed, trying to catch up, but not quite running. Curt mimicked Paul's crouch. Talon did not. They caught up to Paul at the main entrance, the large 'CA$H' sign blocking the floodlights and casting the three of them into a dark shadow.

Paul pulled down his ski mask and opened his tool bag. "Ready?" he whispered.

Talon didn't respond. She looked to Curt but couldn't make out his face in the dark. Paul extracted something from his bag and took a step toward the lock on the main gate.

Talon grabbed his arm and spun him back around. "Seriously? You were really going to do this?"

Paul took a moment, his face equally inscrutable in the darkness. "You're not?"

"Of course not," Talon laughed.

"Oh, thank God," Curt gasped. "This is a terrible idea."

"The worst idea," Talon confirmed. "Burglarize a corporate document archive? The one used by the business my victim worked for? The private prison business? I might as well just call them directly and ask for a cell. Or a job, at least, because I'd be disbarred before we got back outside the perimeter fence again. There must be a hundred cameras. We'd be surrounded by security guards and Dobermans within five minutes."

"But, but," Paul stammered, "we talked about this."

"I'm a lawyer, Paul, not a spy," Talon said. "None of us are." Then she thought better of that comment. "Well, Curt and I aren't. I don't know about you."

"What do you mean?" Paul's shoulders drooped.

"I mean maybe you're a plant," Talon explained. "Maybe Dank's bosses own your building too. I don't know."

"The ownership is pretty opaque," Curt offered.

"You investigated me?" Paul questioned. Then he nodded. "Counterintelligence. Respect."

"That was a pretty sweet deal on the rent," Talon continued. "You were also pretty quick to butt into our meeting and offer your services, without explaining precisely what those services were. Then you provided just enough information to pique my interest, but not enough to actually be useful. The useful stuff was conveniently hidden—and only accessible through a criminal act! One that would undoubtedly fail and lead to my arrest and removal from the case."

"It's a pretty good plan," Curt opined. "If that was your plan, I mean."

"That wasn't my plan," Paul answered.

"What was it then?" Talon demanded.

"This." Paul gestured at their surroundings, the dark road and waiting storage complex. "Get the records. They're here. They're right in there. That was the plan. I promise."

"That's a terrible plan," Talon shook her head. "Even if you're not a plant, it's a terrible plan."

"I'm not a plant," Paul insisted. "And I'm not a spy."

"I don't know what you are," Talon shrugged, "but I know what I am. I'm a lawyer. I don't need to burglarize someone's business to get documents I want. I just subpoena that shit."

CHAPTER 27

The problem with subpoenas, and really anything lawyers did, was that everything takes so long. Talon had bulled her way through a bail hearing with no notice, but that wasn't going to happen twice, and certainly not when she was dealing with boring paper instead of clever words.

The first thing she had to do was to draft the subpoena. Technically it was a subpoena duces tecum, which Talon surmised was Latin for something like, 'show up, and bring stuff with you.' In her case, the stuff in question was any documents A.C.E. had, whether in its archives or not, related to the allegation that Dank broke an employee's arm seven years earlier. It was addressed generically to the 'Business Records Custodian' and needed to be served on the 'agent of service' that A.C.E. provided the Washington Secretary of State when it applied to do business in The Evergreen State. So, after drafting it, Talon had to drive 30 miles south from Tacoma to Olympia to deliver to said agent of service, which was really just a storefront business that would act as the registered agent for any corporation willing to pay a small fee.

In theory, A.C.E. could choose to comply with the subpoena, send its records custodian to her office on the date and time indicated thereon, and have such person deliver the requested records to Talon. The subpoena duces tecum even allowed for the personal appearance to be waived if the requested materials were provided in advance. Talon had to provide at least five days' notice (not counting weekends) for the appearance date, which would have burned another week, except she knew as well as anyone that there was no way A.C.E. was going to comply with her little subpoena duces tecum.

She knew they were going to fight it, by filing a formal Motion to Quash with the court. She also strongly suspected who would actually be drafting and filing said Motion to Quash, but she didn't for sure until it arrived via the same Gen Z courier on the same GH&S pleading paper, signed by none other than Helen Hampton Montclair herself.

"So," Talon muttered to herself after waving off the bike messenger again and walking, eyes cast down on the pleadings, across the lobby to the elevator, "Ms. Hampton Montclair represents not just the Estate of James Dickhead Dank, but also American Correctile Dysfunction, Incorporated."

She wasn't surprised. She wasn't even disappointed. But she was curious.

Her curiosity would have to wait, however. Five days (not counting weekends) to be exact, for the properly noted and duly noticed Hearing on Motion to Quash Subpoena Duces Tecum. Since the subpoena had issued under the criminal case, Cobb was there as well. And because it was a motion under a criminal case, the judge was once again The Honorable Robert Harvey.

"You three again," he grumbled as he took the bench above the advocates. It wasn't a question. It was a complaint. Definitely a complaint. "It seems you all keep coming up with new things to argue about in this case."

"Not me, Your Honor," Cobb replied first. "The State is ready for trial. This," he waved a hand generally toward where Talon and Karim were seated at the defense table, "is all her."

Talon stood up. "I'll gladly take responsibility, Your Honor. Extremism in the defense of liberty is no vice, and moderation in the pursuit of justice is no virtue."

Harvey rolled his middle-aged white eyes. "This is not going to devolve into another pollical speech, Ms. Winter. This is a motion to quash a subpoena duces tecum. It is a very specific and very limited inquiry, and I will be allowing only very limited and very specific argument. Is that understood?"

Talon took a moment, then nodded. "Yes, Your Honor. Of course."

Harvey pointed to the other two attorneys in turn.

"Understood, Mr. Cobb?"

"Yes, Your Honor."

"Understood, Ms. Hampton Montclair?"

"Yes, Your Honor."

"What about Ms. Vandergraben?" Talon whispered to Hampton Montclair. "I don't want her to feel left out. Do you think she feels left out?"

Erin Vandergraben had again accompanied Hampton Montclair, although again only to carry and empty her briefcase before taking a seat in the gallery. The second row of the gallery.

Hampton Montclair ignored Talon, but Talon knew Harvey could see the whispering even if he couldn't hear it.

"That's enough, Ms. Winter," he admonished. "I have spent more than enough time on this case and trial isn't even scheduled to commence for another two weeks. I will hear this motion, but this will be the last pretrial matter I will allow to be docketed. Any remaining matters can be dealt with on the day of trial."

He didn't finish with his usual, 'Is that understood?' He was getting smarter; that question only invited more argument. But it also left an awkward pause as there was no actual question for the attorneys to respond to, just the implied one the judge held back.

So, Judge Harvey continued. "This is a motion to quash a subpoena. The subpoena was issued by Ms. Winter and Ms. Hampton Montclair wants the Court to quash it. That means it's Ms. Hampton Montclair's motion and she goes first."

Talon nodded. That was legit.

Hampton Montclair didn't say anything at first, also nodding.

But Judge Harvey was in an impatient mood. "Go, Ms. Hampton Montclair. Go!"

Hampton Montclair shook her head slightly in surprise, then opened her mouth and spat out the first words that came to mind, lest she get barked at again.

"Um, yes, Your Honor, thank you. Yes. Right. Well, so, um, as the Court just said, this is a motion to quash the subpoena duces tecum purportedly issued by Ms. Winter for purported records of a purported investigation of a purported incident purportedly involving the murder of, in this case, Mr. James Dank."

"Purported victim," Talon whispered at her.

Hampton Montclair frowned, and continued. "I say purported, Your Honor, because Ms. Winter presents, and indeed cannot present, any information to substantiate that any of the records she seeks even exist, let alone whether they would be reachable by an overbroad subpoena in a criminal case wholly unrelated to my client."

"Isn't your client Mr. Dank?" Judge Harvey interjected. "He's the named victim. I wouldn't call that 'wholly unrelated'."

"Ah, yes," Hampton Montclair raised a finger of

clarification. "I do also represent the estate of Mr. Dank, but I am here today retained by American Correctional Enterprises, Incorporated, the target of Ms. Winter's unlawful subpoena."

"And that's not a conflict of interest?" Judge Harvey questioned.

"Not in the least, Your Honor," Hampton Montclair responded. "The interests of A.C.E. and Mr. Dank's estate are perfectly aligned. It is simply that Mr. Dank's estate would have no standing to challenge a subpoena duces tecum issued to a third-party corporation, and I therefore stand before you representing that third party rather than Mr. Dank."

Harvey nodded along with the explanation. "All right. I'll leave that to you. So, can we get to why you think I should quash the subpoena duces tecum?"

"Well, Your Honor," Hampton Montclair put a fist on her hip, "I think the real question is, can Ms. Winter explain why the subpoena shouldn't be quashed?"

Judge Harvey's eyes narrowed slightly. He took a beat, then frowned. "I don't think that's how this works. It's your motion. You bear the burden of persuasion."

"Do I, though, Your Honor?" Hampton Montclair returned. "Do I really?"

Harvey took another moment to consider, then answered, "Yes. Yes, you do." He pointed at Talon. "She's a real attorney, not a purported attorney. She issued a real subpoena duces tecum, not a purported subpoena. And she has the authority to do that under the real court rules, not purported court rules. If you don't want to honor it, then you need to make a real argument to me as to why you shouldn't have to. That's what lawyers do. They argue things. Then when they're done, judges decide things. So, this is your chance, your one chance before I decide whether to grant your motion. Please do not waste my time with any further rhetorical questions or the word 'purported'. Just tell me why Ms. Winter shouldn't get the documents she's asking for."

"Because they don't exist," Hampton Montclair answered. But then she clarified her assertion. "Or, to whatever extent potentially responsive documents may exist, they would be highly sensitive, and disclosure thereof would be injurious to all involved, not just A.C.E. Before such confidential documents can be obtained, Ms. Winter should be required to establish what exactly she expects to find and how such information could be in any way relevant and admissible in the criminal case under which she has issued the subpoena."

Harvey ran a hand over his mouth in thought. "So, you're kind of admitting they exist, but you're claiming some sort of privacy concern? Is that what I'm hearing?"

Hampton Montclair stood up straight and spoke slightly off to the side for some reason. "I can neither confirm nor deny the existence of the purported documents."

Judge Harvey was unable to suppress his eye roll at hearing the word 'purported' again. He sighed. "Fine. Anything further, then?"

Hampton Montclair took a moment to consider, then smiled confidently up at the judge. "No, Your Honor. We look forward to the Court quashing the subpoena duces tecum. Thank you."

Judge Harvey suppressed that eye roll, but nodded to Hampton Montclair, then pivoted to Talon.

"Tell me why you should get these documents, Ms. Winter," he directed. "And focus on how they would be admissible at trial if you were to obtain them. Even if you might generally be entitled to them, why should you get them now if they won't be admissible at trial?"

Talon stood up to respond even as the judge was asking his questions and Hampton Montclair was sitting back down next to Cobb. Cobb wasn't going to get to speak. That seemed to be okay with everyone assembled, including Cobb, and especially Judge Harvey.

"Thank you, Your Honor," Talon began. "The documents in question pertain to an incident which the defense believes is sufficiently similar to the facts of the instant case as to be admissible under Evidence Rule 404(a) as a specific incident to prove the character of the victim, which will be relevant for the jury to consider when presented with the option of acquittal by reason of self-defense."

Harvey frowned. "How long ago was it?" Then he grinned and added, "Purportedly?"

Talon fought back her own grin and admitted, "Almost seven years, I believe."

"That's an awful long time, Ms. Winter," Judge Harvey observed. "It could be identical, and it might still be too remote in time to be admissible."

"Perhaps," Talon shrugged. "But we can't know that until we see the records."

Harvey frowned. "We might be able to, if only because of the age," he mused. "And how is it that you've come to believe these records even exist? Ms. Hampton Montclair has suggested they might not, although the manner in which she suggested it leads me to believe they do exist."

"Me, too, Your Honor," Talon agreed. Then, to answer the judge's question, or not, she added, "I'd prefer not to reveal my sources, Your Honor. Doing so would compromise my client's constitutional rights to effective counsel and could violate attorney-client privilege."

Harvey sighed yet again. "I doubt that," he opined. He took a moment, then posited, "If you get these records, is that the end of it? Or could they lead to additional documents, or additional witnesses, or most importantly, additional motions? I really do not want to hear any more motions on this matter. This case needs to proceed to trial as soon as possible."

Talon offered a shrug. "I don't know, Your Honor. I won't know until I receive and review the records. At a minimum, I believe they would identify several potential new witnesses who would then need to be interviewed, which could lead to further information—all of which would be relevant and admissible, of course. So, no, I can't promise there wouldn't be additional motions."

Judge Harvey frowned at that.

"But if I might, Your Honor," Talon continued, "my client and I would be willing to agree to a delay in the trial in order to accommodate production of the requested materials and acquisition of any further information which might arise out of such production."

"I'm sure you would, Ms. Winter," Harvey almost chuckled, "now that your client has posted bail and is out of custody. He'd probably be fine with an indefinite delay, rather than face the possibility of a conviction for murder."

"We fully expect an acquittal, Your Honor," Talon assured the judge.

"Good for you," Judge Harvey responded. "That's your job. And to work for it. But I have a different job. And one part of that job is to make sure that cases are brought to trial in a prompt and timely manner."

Crap, Talon thought. She didn't mind losing on the merits— well, that wasn't exactly true, she always hated losing—but she didn't want to lose on a scheduling issue.

She raised a finger at the judge, "Your Honor, could I—?"

But it was too late. "No, Ms. Winter, I think I've heard enough," Judge Harvey said. "I do think there may be potentially relevant information in the materials you are seeking. I also think the information therein might lead to additional potentially relevant information. But I am not convinced any of that potentially relevant information would necessarily be admissible some seven years later. While we could wait to see how that all plays out, I do not believe a first degree murder trial should be delayed for ifs and maybes."

He pointed at Karim, who had been sitting quietly while the lawyers made their arguments. "Your client has the right to a speedy trial," Judge Harvey said, "but the family of the alleged victim also has a right to a speedy disposition of the case, one way or the other."

Talon lowered her head slightly and nodded to herself, her mind already moving on from the imminent ruling and shifting to its next task: trial prep. She almost wasn't listening when the judge finally stated his ruling formally.

"Therefore," Judge Harvey announced, "I am going to grant the motion to quash the subpoena. That concludes the pretrial motions which may be docketed in this case. The parties will return to this courtroom a week from Friday to confirm for trial the following Monday, at which time any last scheduling issues shall be resolved and the trial judge will be assigned. This matter is adjourned."

Talon nodded again. She was disappointed, but she didn't have time to wallow in it. Hampton Montclair, however, definitely wanted to take the time to gloat in it.

"Oh my, you lost, Talon," she announced, unnecessarily.

"You should get used to that, I think."

Talon took a moment to extract herself from her thoughts and look Hampton Montclair in the eye. "Did I, though, Helen. Did I?"

Hampton Montclair was taken aback for a moment. "Why, yes. Yes, you did."

Talon scrunched her mouth into a thoughtful pucker. "All right then. Well, we'll just see what happens next. Nice to see you again. Give my love to Erin."

"Aren't you upset?" Hampton Montclair complained. She clearly wanted Talon to be upset.

That was the main reason Talon refused to be upset. "Of course not, Helen. You'd know that if you were a real trial attorney. A real trial attorney doesn't get upset by a loss. A real trial attorney gets motivated."

CHAPTER 28

In truth, Talon was absolutely upset that Judge Harvey had quashed her subpoena, to the extent that angry is a form of upset. There was relevant information there, even Hampton Montclair admitted it, but Talon had lost the motion over a scheduling issue. Justice delayed is justice denied, they say, but so is justice hurried.

Regardless, Talon was also absolutely motivated. She could appeal Judge Harvey's ruling, but there would only be an appeal if she lost. The prosecution can't appeal an acquittal. So, her goal was to win anyway. She didn't want to be pursuing a years-long appeal while Karim sat in prison for a crime he didn't commit.

She pushed back from her computer and gazed out her window at the bay, its dark waters glistening from the last rays of the day's sun. Friday night in T-Town. She'd spent the week locked in her office and buried in the case file, both digital and paper— 'analog', as Paul would have said. She'd closed her door to discourage Curt, and especially Paul, from bothering her. She wasn't sure where she stood with Paul, but she knew Curt would both try to bother her and also honor her closed door.

Harvey had a point, although one of his own making. Her suggestion to delay the trial having been denied, trial was fast approaching. She needed to get ready. She needed to get organized. She looked at the clock. She needed to get a drink.

It was well past quitting time again. She smiled ruefully and shook her head at the concept of quitting time. When she was in trial, there was no quitting time, just small breaks for things like food, sleep, or a quick drink to mark the transition between working all day at the office and working all night at home.

She stood up, stretched her back with a couple of louder than expected pops, then looked down at her desk, paper strewn across it, illuminated by the glow of her computer monitor. It would only take a few minutes to shut everything down and pack everything into her bag. She'd leave her office door closed until that was completed, then she'd hurry to the stairwell and exit directly into the parking lot, in case Curt was surveilling the elevators again.

Talon saved what needed to be saved, emailed herself a few documents so she could easily open them up on her home laptop, then stuck her case file in her briefcase and stepped to her office door. She turned the light off before opening the door, in part, to get a good look at the last golden ripples fading from the top of Commencement Bay, and in part, to make sure no light spilled into the hallway when she did open it. Which, after one last deep breath, she did.

The hallway was silent. It was even later than she probably realized. It was well past her non-trial quitting time, and that was already well past most other people's normal quitting time. She pulled the door closed as quietly as she could, although it still clicked rather loudly when the latch caught, but she wasn't going to leave her office open and unlocked. She left the echo of the click behind and hurried for the door to the stairwell at the end of the hall. She neither saw nor heard anyone on the brief traverse down the corridor and didn't bother to quiet the slam of the stairwell door as she raced down the steps. She hadn't been seen and in a few moments she'd be pushing open the stairwell door on the first floor and stepping directly out into the parking lot and the night air. She did so, hurried to her car, and jumped in. As she pulled out of the parking stall and drove past the front of the building, she chanced a quick glance into the lobby to see if she might spy Curt standing behind a potted plant, but it seemed to be as empty as the third floor hallway and the stairwell. She let out a sigh of relief and turned south onto Schuster Parkway, toward home.

It was a short drive, and there weren't any other cars on the road. Those were the perfect conditions to let her thoughts return to the case. And also to notice a pair of headlights suddenly bearing down on her in her rearview mirror.

It was probably just some jerk in a rush to get to the freeway, Talon told herself. Luckily, the next street was her turnoff, into Tacoma's Old Town neighborhood, so she slowed a little less than usual and turned right onto McCarver Street, expecting to see the other car race past her on Schuster. Instead, the car turned onto McCarver as well and accelerated toward her again.

Talon frowned. She quickly considered her options, then took a hard left onto N. 30th Street, having almost already passed it. She was watching her rearview mirror more than the road in front of her to see what the other car would do. It turned onto 30th too.

"Damn it," Talon hissed.

Not only was someone following her, but she was now heading in the exact wrong direction, toward downtown and away from both her home and her office.

She accelerated, but so did her pursuer. N. 30th was little more than a feeder street from Old Town to downtown. In fact, it merged back into Schuster Parkway, leading Talon back onto the main road with no cross streets or other turnoffs for at least a mile.

All she could do was try to get to downtown as fast as possible and look for a place to stop and confront whoever it was in her rearview mirror. Right behind her. So close, Talon could barely see the headlights anymore.

She took the exit off Schuster onto Pacific and accelerated up the hill. There would be a stop light at 9th, but she forgot about the stop sign at the top of the hill and blew through it before she realized it was there. Luckily, no one was in the crosswalk. A glance in her rearview mirror showed her pursuer slow but also drive through the stop sign. Talon looked around and turned a sharp left onto 8th, then another onto Court A. The car behind her followed each turn. But it wouldn't follow any more. Court A was a dead end.

Talon screeched to a halt at the end of the alleyway. To her left were the backs of the shops facing Pacific. To her right was a steep hill down to Schuster Parkway and Commencement Bay beyond. There were no other cars there. No other people. She reached over and pulled out the handgun she kept in her glove box. You don't spend a career defending criminals—and pissing off cops—and not own a gun. Then she threw open her car door and jumped out.

The other car had stopped, too, about twenty feet back. Its headlights were still on, so Talon couldn't see into the vehicle from the glare. But she could see the driver's side door open slowly, and a large figure emerge from behind the wheel.

Talon leveled her handgun at the figure. "Get back in the car, asshole! And get the fuck out of here! I will shoot you!"

The figure paused—almost hesitated, Talon thought, or maybe just hoped. She looked to his hands to see if he was also armed. The glare from the headlights right next to him made it hard to see for sure, but his hands looked empty, even more so when he spread out his fingers, then raised his hands over his head and called out, "Talon! Don't shoot! It's me, Paul!"

Talon squinted at the figure, but kept the gun pointed at its center mass. "Paul?" She recognized the voice.

"I've got something for you," he called out.

"I bet you do," Talon called back with a nervous laugh. "Is this how it ends? You couldn't trick me into getting arrested, so now you're gonna kill me in some back alley?"

"Kill you?" Paul repeated. "No, no, of course not." He lowered his hands and leaned toward the interior of the car.

"Stay out of the car!" Talon ordered. She took a step toward him. "Keep your hands where I can see them."

Paul straightened up and raised his hands again. "This is crazy Talon. Put the gun away. You're gonna hurt someone."

"You," Talon clarified. "I'm going to hurt you. At least I'm damned well not going to let you hurt me."

Paul just stood there for a moment, silent.

"Move away from the car," Talon ordered. "I don't want you lunging in and grabbing something out of there."

"I won't lunge," Paul answered, without moving away from the car. "But I do want to grab something out of there. It's for you."

Talon took a step toward him, gun still raised. "Move. Away. From. The. Car."

Paul took a moment, then shrugged and took a few steps away from his car. Out of the immediate glare of the headlights, Paul's face was visible in the ambient light from the streetlights a block over on Pacific. He looked...annoyed.

"Can you please lower the gun?" he asked again. "I'm not armed. I'm not here to kill you or anything ridiculous like that."

Talon took another step toward Paul. She lowered the gun slightly so that it was pointed at his legs rather than his chest and narrowed her eyes at him. "Who are you really?"

"I'm nobody," Paul insisted. "I'm just Paul Delgado."

"Paul Delgado, industrial spy," Talon countered. "Working for American Correctional Enterprises, I'm guessing." She shook her head. "I should have known. Everything just a little too convenient. Great office. Sweet deal on the rent. An offer to help with the case. You learn the inside scoop on our defense. You try to set me up for a felony burglary. And when that doesn't work, you chase me down and corner me after dark. It's all too much, mystery man. Just too much."

Paul shook his head. No chuckle this time. "No, no, it's not like that," he insisted. "Look, please, just lower the gun. You're not going to shoot me."

Talon tilted her head at him and raised the gun again.

"Okay, maybe you are," Paul conceded. "But don't. You think I set you up to get arrested for a burglary? What do you think will happen if you shoot me one block off of Pacific Avenue?"

Talon frowned. He had a point.

"Look, I got some intel for you." Paul pointed at his open car door. "That's it. Really. You've been locked in your office all week, and I didn't want to bother you, so I was going to tell you when you left for the day. But you snuck out the back."

Talon let the gun lower an inch or so. She wanted to believe him. But she knew he could probably tell that.

"I saw your car leaving," Paul went on, "but I don't have your phone number—we should fix that, by the way…"

"Move along," Talon shook the barrel of the gun at him.

"Right," Paul responded. "Anyway, I didn't have a way to call you and you were leaving for the weekend and I thought you would want the info I got, so I figured I would just follow you to wherever you were going and give it to you there." He looked around at their surroundings and circumstances. "Terrible idea, I guess."

Talon tried to process his story as quickly as she could. "This information, it's that important? Important enough to scare the living shit out of me?"

"Yes," Paul assured her. "Well, I mean, I didn't know I was going to scare the living shit out of you. But yeah, it's important. It's what we've been looking for."

She tilted her head at him again.

"You," he corrected himself. "It's what you've been looking for."

"What is it?" Talon demanded.

Paul's hand started to lower, just a bit. Probably because they were getting tired. Talon was more interested in hearing what he had to say, so she let it slide, for the moment.

"I felt bad about how things went down at the archive place," Paul started.

"The ridiculous attempted burglary you proposed?"

"Yeah, that." Paul grimaced. "So, I decided to see if I couldn't find that stuff online after all. I decided to just monitor everything. When you sent them that subpoena, they moved some electronic files, and then when you lost the hearing and the judge threw the subpoena out, they moved them back. I wouldn't have known they were related to the case, but the timing was too much to be coincidental."

"How'd you know I lost the hearing?" Talon challenged.

"Apart from you slamming every door in the building and locking yourself away for four days?" Paul asked. "Curt told me."

Talon considered. That checked out.

"So, what, you noticed some digital files moving back and forth," Talon said. "So what?"

Paul pointed at his car. "So, I got them. And I was right. It's that file against Dank we wanted—you wanted. It's everything. The initial complaint. The investigation. Witness statements. You name it."

"The ruling?" Talon named.

"There was no ruling," Paul explained. "It was a settlement, remember?"

She did remember. She just didn't know if Paul did.

"So, you have all that?" Talon asked.

"Yes," Paul answered. "It's in the car. I was just going to give it to you."

"That's all?" Talon narrowed her eyes again.

Paul hesitated. "I mean, I was going to ask you out again. I thought maybe you'd be grateful." He laughed and gestured at the gun. "But it's cool. This doesn't feel like the right time somehow."

Talon glanced toward his car. "It's in there? Really? That's all this is? You don't have a gun in there?"

"I do have a gun in there," Paul answered, "but it's locked in the center console. If I'd wanted to pull a gun on you, I would have gotten out of the car with it."

Fair point, Talon thought to herself.

"Can I get the info?" Paul asked. "It's in a large envelope."

"Paper?" She found that suspicious. Paul wasn't a paper guy.

"There's a USB drive in there too," Paul explained. "But I know you lawyers are dinosaurs and want everything printed out. I was just trying to be nice."

"And ask me out," Talon added.

"Yeah, and ask you out," Paul agreed. "I thought being nice would help. I guess not."

"Being nice always helps," Talon answered. "Being stupid

doesn't."

Paul nodded, but didn't say anything. He'd lowered his arms most of the way by then. Talon had let him.

"Where's the envelope?" Talon asked.

"On the passenger seat," Paul answered. "I'll stay here, right?"

"Right," Talon confirmed. She circled to the far side of Paul's car, keeping her gun in a ready position. Paul made no effort to do anything except stand there and watch her.

There was indeed an envelope on the front passenger seat. There was also no gun in sight. Talon opened the car door and extracted the envelope.

"This better be what you said it was," Talon warned.

"What else would it be?" Paul shrugged.

Talon nodded. She had to lower the gun completely to open the envelope, but she had the car between them, so she went ahead and took that risk.

When Paul saw that she was momentarily distracted and had lowered her weapon, he just stood there.

Talon extracted the papers quickly. The USB drive came flying out, too, and clattered on the pavement. She ignored the thumb drive and scanned the top page of the documents.

"You were telling the truth," she said, after a moment.

"Yes," Paul exhaled. "Yes."

"You weren't going to kill me," Talon said.

"No," Paul assured her. "And you weren't going to kill me either, right?"

"Oh, no, I definitely would have killed you," Talon responded evenly. "You're just lucky you did everything I told you to."

Paul nodded to himself. "Okay. Well, are we good then?

You've got your stuff. I'm not going to get shot. Friends again?"

Talon examined a few more pages and let the whole pointing-a-gun-at-Paul situation recede from its precedence in her mind. She tucked the gun into the back of her waistband so she could more easily rummage through the papers. "Sure. Whatever."

Paul allowed another chuckle, and finally stepped over toward Talon, although not close enough to spook her. He kept the car between them.

"This is remarkably similar to Karim's case," Talon said, absorbing the information. "The employee he assaulted —"

"Donald Weathers," Paul interjected the name he'd gleaned from his own review of the file.

"Right," Talon confirmed. "Weathers was trying to organize a union. Dank broke his arm, but claimed Weathers attacked him first."

"Dank even had witnesses," Paul expounded, "at first. A couple of the other managers. But then they came forward and said they were pressured by Dank to lie."

"So, the company settled," Talon surmised.

"Exactly. And everything is in there," Paul assured her. "Names, addresses, medical records, check stubs. Even the non-disclosure agreement between Weathers and A.C.E., so no one can ever talk about it."

Talon looked up and smiled. "I can."

CHAPTER 29

Talon appreciated Paul's discovery, and how chill he seemed to be with her holding him at gunpoint, but she was going to task Curt with actually locating Donald Weathers. It wasn't that Paul couldn't have done it; it was just that she still didn't completely trust him. And she wanted Curt to feel like he was valuable, too, although she resisted any deep reflection on why she even cared about Curt's feelings. She told herself it was simply that happy minions made helpful minions.

Weathers's whereabouts, availability, and willingness to cooperate all being unknown, Talon busied herself with preparing the things she did know. She printed out (she hated that Paul was right about that) and organized all of the reports by witness, printing extra copies where the same report might be used by more than one witness. She made clean copies of every exhibit, from the crime scene photographs to the two autopsy reports. She double- and triple-checked that the videos worked on her laptop and that her laptop would be able to connect to the courtroom's projector. And she mapped out every point she wanted to make on every cross-examination of every potential State's witness. It was a lot.

And it took all week. But when the following Friday arrived and she found herself, for one last time, standing before Judge Harvey and opposite Cobb at the prosecutor table and Hampton Montclair in the gallery, she knew she was as prepared as she could be.

"Are the parties ready for trial?" Judge Harvey asked. It was actually a rhetorical question. He'd already made it entirely clear he wasn't about to let the case be delayed. "The answer had better be yes."

"Yes, Your Honor." Cobb stood up first to address the Court. "The State is ready."

Talon followed suit, rising to stand next to her still seated client. "The defense is ready."

Talon half expected Hampton Montclair to stand up and answer 'ready' as well. Cobb even started to glance over his shoulder. But the Attorney for the Estate of the (Alleged) Victim remained seated and silent. Judge Harvey seemed relieved.

"Good," the judge accepted the attorneys' responses. "Now, this is normally the time when I would assign this matter from the criminal presiding department, where it has been bumping along with a remarkably large number of pretrial motions and hearings, to a particular trial department and a particular trial judge. As you know, we judges rotate into the presiding department for six months at a time, conducting arraignments, accepting pleas, and hearing the aforementioned pretrial motions. It is not a particularly glamorous rotation, and it is not particularly interesting or enjoyable. But we each do it, mostly as a favor to the other judges, who are then free to preside, uninterrupted, over the actual trials of those cases which are ready to be decided."

Talon nodded along, interested not in the content—which she already knew—but in where Judge Harvey might be headed. She had a suspicion. She wasn't sure if she liked it.

"As I said," Judge Harvey continued, "we do this as a favor to the other judges, and it is with that in mind that I now face the task of assigning this case out to another judge for trial. I note that I have made several rulings on this case already. I also note that for each of these rulings, there is at least one attorney, and possibly two," a nod to Hampton Montclair, "who disagreed with my ruling, and who, I fear, might take the opportunity of appearing before a new, and less informed, judge to move for reconsideration of those rulings, in the hopes of gaining a more favorable result."

Talon tried to keep a staid expression, but she could feel her features stretching toward a look of 'Who me?'

The truth was, though, that Talon no longer needed that delay. Paul had gotten her the information she needed. But she wasn't about to say that in open court. It wasn't her business how he got it—illegally, almost certainly—but she knew there'd be a fight over it and accusations that she had participated in the illegal acquisition. That was a lot to fight about when she didn't even know yet whether Curt would be able to find Donald Weathers, let alone whether the judge, any judge, would allow testimony from him anyway. So, Talon remained quiet and let Judge Harvey talk himself into what he was about to talk himself into.

"I would not be doing any of my brethren a favor by inflicting this case on them," Judge Harvey continued. "So instead, I will do them all a favor by inflicting myself on you. I have made arrangements for Judge Kerkorian to take over my duties in criminal presiding while I preside over this trial in my own courtroom. The case is hereby assigned to me for trial. The parties are ordered to appear Monday in Courtroom 215 at nine a.m. sharp to begin trial. I plan to conduct this trial quickly and efficiently, with no reconsideration of prior rulings, and argument limited both in time and to the attorneys actually assigned to the case. In other words, rest up this weekend and bring your running shoes. Case adjourned."

Talon looked at Cobb, who offered a friendly enough shrug in return, then started packing up his stuff. Talon didn't bother looking back at Hampton Montclair. Judge Harvey had warned her he wouldn't hear from her, but everyone, including the judge, knew none of them believed him. The person Talon really wanted to talk with was Karim, who had appeared again in a suit and tie and sat patiently and silently while the lawyers discussed the details hovering at the edge of his fate.

"How are you doing?" she asked as he stood up to make room for the next litigants at the counsel table.

He just nodded at first. No words, just a long, sustained nodding. "I'm not sure," he finally admitted. "I'm not sure how I'm supposed to be feeling. This is surreal."

Talon nodded too. "Yeah, it is," she agreed. "And that's pretty much how you should be feeling."

She grabbed his arm and pointed to the courtroom door. "Come on. Let's grab one of the attorney-client conference rooms. We don't want to talk in here. Too many ears."

She led him out into the hallway and down the corridor to the row of small rooms attorneys could use to speak with their out-of-custody clients. They were considerably larger than the closets permitted for in-custody client consultations, with a small table and room for three chairs. Talon took the one farthest from the door. Karim dropped into the closest one.

"Are we gonna win, Talon?" he asked. "Tell me we're gonna win. We have to win."

Talon hated that question. They all asked it. 'Are we going to win?' If she were a coach, or teammate, or a cheerleader, the answer would be simple: 'You betcha!' But she wasn't any of those things. She was a lawyer, and there was only one answer she was allowed to give.

"I can't promise anything," she said, "except to do my absolute best to make sure we do win. But when the last word of closing argument is finished, and the jurors go back to the jury room to start deliberating, there's no way to know what they're going to do. Not really. Anyone who tells you different is lying."

Karim sighed. "Will that be enough? Your best, will that be enough?"

Talon smiled at him. "Same question, different packaging. I can't promise the result. I can only promise the fight."

"But we should win, right?" Karim pressed. "I didn't do anything wrong. I didn't mean to kill him. I didn't mean to do anything except push him away. It was self-defense. I'm innocent. That should count for something."

Talon nodded. "You are innocent," she agreed, "but there are lots of innocent people in prison. It doesn't hurt, but it's not enough."

"What about justice?' Karim asked, almost pleading. "Isn't this called the criminal justice system? Aren't we supposed to find justice? Doesn't anyone care about justice?"

Talon took a moment. Karim was nervous, and that was normal, good even. It meant he understood the stakes. But she needed him calm. She needed him to wear those suits and stand up when the judge came in and look like a man who was wrongfully accused but trusted in The System, and especially in the jurors who would decide his fate. If they sensed he didn't trust them, they wouldn't feel the need to honor that trust. She wanted to tell him all that, but then he would have started behaving like he was acting, pretending. If the jury sensed that, if they intuited any form of artifice from the defense side, that would also seal Karim's fate.

They were supposed to be listening to the evidence, but Talon knew they'd spend at least as much time judging her clothes and scrutinizing Karim's body language. So, instead of telling him all that, she simply reached out and put a hand on his forearm. "I do."

She cared about it. She just didn't have any faith in it.

CHAPTER 30

When 9:00 a.m. Monday finally came around, Judge Harvey's courtroom was full of attorneys and spectators, and the one man whose life would actually be determined by the outcome of the trial.

Cobb had arrived about fifteen minutes early. Enough to make sure he wasn't late, but not so early as to suggest he was putting any extra effort in. Hampton Montclair and Erin Vandergraben had arrived twenty minutes early, taking a prime seat directly behind Cobb. Jurors noticed that sort of thing: how many people were sitting on each side of the gallery, like it was a damn wedding or something. But again, jurors paid attention, so Shayla had arrived twenty-five minutes early, with Karim and several other relatives, to fill the seats behind the defense table. And Talon—Talon was there at 8:30 when the bailiff unlocked the courtroom door. She was going to be the first one there and last one gone every day until the jury came back with their verdict. Karim deserved no less.

When 9:01 a.m. arrived, Judge Harvey emerged from his chambers. It was a little disorienting to see him out of the cramped quarters of the criminal presiding courtroom. Instead of a stuffy crowded mini-courtroom, with attorneys and jailors perpetually milling about at the edges, this new courtroom was large and spacious, with no one but the present litigants and the people in the gallery, everyone focused on one and only one case.

"The State of Washington versus Karim Jackson," Judge Harvey called the case as he took the bench and those assembled sat down again after the bailiff's initial cry of, "All rise!" He looked down at the lawyers set up at the counsel tables in the front of the courtroom, the empty jury box filling up one side wall, the other taken up by rows and rows of stately lawbooks on built-in bookshelves. His shoulders were flanked by the United States and Washington State flags, and his head was haloed by the Seal of the State of Washington, Ol' George's head blocked out by that of the judge. "Are the parties ready to proceed? Good. Let's start with motions *in limine*. Mr. Cobb?"

So much for the nicety of asking the parties whether they were ready to proceed. *Running shoes*, Talon supposed. What if she'd broken a rib over the weekend? She would probably still be ready to proceed, sucking back the pain and using it as inspiration. But what about Cobb—he was weak sauce. Maybe he needed a potty break or something.

"Um, oh," Cobb stammered. "Right. Motions *in limine*. Limiting motions. Evidentiary limiting motions." He swung his hands together and apart. "Yeah, I don't really have any of those."

"You have no motions to limit potential evidence?" Judge Harvey raised an incredulous eyebrow. "Nothing you think should be excluded up front, to avoid having to make an objection in front of the jury?"

Cobb considered for a few seconds, his hand still swinging, popping a palm over a fist when they came together in front of him. "Nope. We're the State, Your Honor. We have nothing to hide. This case is what it is. Ms. Winter can have at it. I can deal with whatever she tries."

It sounded confident, but really it was lazy. In order for Cobb to have motions *in limine* ready, he would have had to have given thought to what Talon might try to do. He would have had to anticipate her defenses and what evidence she might try to introduce through cross-examination of his witnesses and direct examination of her own witnesses. That was a lot of steps ahead. Or he could just object in the moment, interrupt the trial, and waste everyone's time with something that should have and could have been handled in advance. Lazy.

Harvey knew it was lazy, too, and that it was highly unlikely Cobb would really just let things slide once the trial got underway. But he couldn't force Cobb to raise anything in advance, and he wouldn't be able to prevent Cobb from objecting later. So, he exhaled loudly through his nose and turned to Talon. "Ms. Winter, any motions *in limine?*"

"But of course, Your Honor." Talon smiled. "Our first motion is to prevent the State from referring to the facility where this took place as a 'jail'. It is not a county or city jail; it is a private detention center. To the extent there may be members of the jury who consider themselves more of 'law and order' types, they would probably have a greater sympathy for public employees of a publicly run institution than they would for private profiteers."

Judge Harvey just stared at Talon for several moments. "Are you really planning on going there?"

Talon shrugged. "You know I have to, Your Honor."

Harvey nodded. He looked to Cobb. "Any response?"

"It's a jail, Your Honor." Cobb waved a hand dismissively at Talon. "If anything, we shouldn't tell the jury how it's funded or who owns it. It's a lawful place to lawfully incarcerate criminals.

Criminals like the defendant in this case, I might add. So, I guess I would make a motion to exclude any mention of the fact that the jail is private."

Harvey sighed again. "So, now you have a motion *in limine?*"

"Yes, Your Honor," Cobb answered. "I may have more as we go through Ms. Winter's."

"I suspect so," Harvey agreed. Then his ruling, "This one is easy. We will be honest and accurate with the jury. That seems like a good guiding principal, but maybe that's just me. In any event, Ms. Winter, you can refer to it as a private detention center, and Mr. Cobb, you can refer to it as a jail. As far as I can tell, it's both. I don't know how either of those labels might impact any given juror, and so I'm not going to limit such labels to one side or the other. So, both motions are denied. Next motion?"

"Thank you, Your Honor," Talon answered. "Our next motion is to exclude any prior bad acts under Evidence Rule 404(b)."

A glance at Cobb revealed a confused expression. He stood up to respond. "Um, I'm not sure what Ms. Winter is referring to exactly, Your Honor. I don't believe Mr. Jackson has any prior criminal history. I mean, I could check again, but—"

"No, that's correct," Talon interjected. "He has no prior criminal history."

"Right." Cobb pointed at her, "Okay. So, um, I'm not sure what exactly she's getting at, Your Honor, so I guess I'm going to object."

"You object?" Judge Harvey asked. "You want to allow evidence of prior bad acts?"

"I object to her motion, Your Honor, yes" Cobb answered.

Harvey looked down at Talon, who made every effort not to

reveal in her expression or manner that it was fully her intent to introduce prior bad acts of the alleged victim, and she had just tricked Cobb into asking the Court to allow just that. "Ms. Winter?"

"I have nothing to add, Your Honor," she said. "Mr. Cobb has been quite persuasive. I understand the Court will deny my motion."

"Do you now?"

"Yes, Your Honor."

"What if I grant it?"

Talon shrugged. She had a way around that too.

"Fine then," Harvey said. "I'm curious where this might go. Okay, based on Mr. Cobb's argument, I will deny Ms. Winter's motion to exclude prior bad acts offered to prove actions in conformity therewith."

Cobb could hear Judge Harvey's condescending tone as well as anyone; he just didn't care. He'd won that skirmish, and gotten a tie out of the one before it. He was doing great for someone who had obviously spent the weekend doing anything other than preparing for the trial.

Judge Harvey looked again to Talon. He opened his mouth, presumably to ask for her next motion *in limine*, but then closed it again and raised a hand to his chin. After a few moments, he finally spoke, but it was to both sides, not just Talon.

"I think perhaps we don't need to run through any more motions *in limine* after all," he said.

"But I have more," Talon offered.

"I'm sure you do, Ms. Winter," the judge replied with a grin, "I'm sure you do. But in the interests of getting this trial moving, and avoiding any further rulings by me which might be reviewed poorly in the event of an appeal, I believe we should move ahead with the other preliminary matters."

"Whatever the Court wants, Your Honor," Talon replied. "I can certainly make my objections during the course of the trial."

"Me too," Cobb put in. "I'm ready to move on as well."

Harvey nodded, a bit longer than he probably should have. "Wonderful. All right then. Have all witnesses been disclosed and all discovery exchanged?"

Cobb was quick to answer, almost as if he were prepared for that question. "The State has provided all of the police reports to the defense and any witnesses we intend to call at trial are fully disclosed, referenced, and identified therein, Your Honor."

Talon looked sideways at him. That was a weirdly rehearsed response. She made a mental note to make sure she hadn't overlooked any potential witnesses in the reports. Maybe some guy who only gave his first name and said he didn't see anything.

But Judge Harvey simply accepted Cobb's answer, then followed up with Talon. "What about the defense, Ms. Winter? Have you disclosed all of your potential witnesses?"

"She hasn't disclosed any witnesses, Your Honor," Cobb complained. "I mean, I know about that one doctor, but that's it."

"Is that accurate, Ms. Winter?" Harvey raised an eyebrow at her. "Do you intend to only call Dr. Evangelopoulos?"

"Right now," Talon answered, "I don't intend to call any witnesses, Your Honor. My client is presumed innocent. We don't have to prove anything, so we don't need any witnesses. I will wait and see what evidence, if any, the State is able to put on, and then, but only then will I be able to say whether the defense plans to call any witnesses."

Judge Harvey sighed. "Really?"

"Really," Talon confirmed.

"Didn't you say," the judge asked, "and more than once as I recall, that this is a self-defense case? Doesn't that require you to at least put the defendant on the stand?"

"My client has an absolute right to remain silent and not testify," Talon returned, an edge to her voice. "Even inquiring into whether he will testify or not before the State has put on even a scintilla of evidence has a chilling effect on his Fifth and Sixth Amendment rights, and the Court knows that. I am sure the Court is not asking me to divulge whether my client intends on testifying. Am I right?"

Harvey sighed again, but then sat up and assumed a more formal posture than the one he had let himself slouch into as he spoke with the attorneys. "I am not asking you to divulge whether your client intends to testify. There is ample case law on that issue. You don't have to make that decision right now, and I am not asking you to do so or to divulge your current thoughts on the topic."

"And so, too, for the remainder of the defense case," Talon pressed the point, "if any."

"If any," Judge Harvey repeated. "Fine." He turned to Cobb. "Are you really ready to deal with whatever Ms. Winter has in store for you?"

Cobb took a moment to answer. Talon supposed he was weighing answering 'Yes' against answering 'No' and having to do additional work. He straightened himself to his full, abnormally large height, and pronounced, "Yes, I'm ready."

"Great," Judge Harvey responded. "I'm looking forward to that already. All right, let's discuss jury selection."

Talon raised her hand, about to make an inquiry, but Judge Harvey waved her off.

"Perhaps 'discuss' was the wrong word," he said. "Let me tell you how jury selection will proceed."

Ah, Talon thought. She lowered her hand. Then she sat

down again to listen to Judge Harvey. She didn't need to stand if she wasn't going to be speaking. Cobb sat down too.

"We will, of course, seat twelve jurors," Judge Harvey began. "In addition, we will seat two alternate jurors, in the event any of the regular jurors are unable to sit for the length of the entire trial. I am not going to let the case end in a mistrial because we lost too many jurors to unexpected illness or hardship."

Talon was fine with that. She was also fine with a mistrial, honestly, because it was better than a conviction, and the State usually lost interest in prosecuting after one trial fell apart. She glanced over at Cobb. It was hard to imagine him being less interested.

"Challenges for cause will be made at the time the basis for cause becomes known," Judge Harvey continued. "If a potential juror says they can't be fair because they hate the police, then make your challenge right then and there. Do not pocket it for argument later. The other side, and the Court, get the opportunity to inquire further and see if the potential juror can be rehabilitated and remain on the panel."

Just once, Talon would have loved to hear a potential juror say they couldn't be fair because they hated the police. In her experience, it was always the other way around. Jurors who said they would believe a cop over a lay witness, and judges who refused to excuse a juror like that for cause, despite their openly admitted bias.

"Per the court rule, each side will get six peremptory challenges, plus one each for each alternate juror spot," Judge Harvey said.

That was where the real juice in jury selection was: peremptory challenges. Each side could kick off six potential jurors without giving any reason at all. Just boot them for any reason.

Well, almost any reason. It was pretty well established in case law—regrettably recent case law, but still—that neither side could strike potential jurors for things like race or gender. Apparently, Judge Harvey wanted to make that a part of the record.

"Studies have shown that prosecutors have historically stricken minority jurors, particularly when the defendant is also a minority," Judge Harvey proclaimed, accurately. "Accordingly, Mr. Cobb, you will not use your peremptory challenges against minorities."

Talon appreciated the directive, even as she cringed at the somewhat outdated word 'minorities'.

"And Ms. Winter," Judge Harvey turned to her.

Uh-oh.

"I am aware of a prevailing belief among the criminal bar," he said, "that men are more likely to excuse physical altercations as mere fisticuffs, especially when self-defense is at issue, while women are more likely to find any sort of physical violence unacceptable. Accordingly, you will not use your peremptory challenges against any female potential jurors."

'Fisticuffs'? Maybe Harvey was older than she thought.

In any event, Talon didn't argue the directives. They were overly proscriptive, but she felt like she got the better of the bargain. She didn't necessarily agree that women were less likely to approve of self-defense, but she definitely expected Cobb to try to strike all the Black jurors.

Jury selection ended up taking the better part of two days. Monday afternoon they dealt with hardships: potential jurors who couldn't sit on a murder jury for weeks on end because of things like losing their jobs, not being paid while away from their jobs, children or parents to care for, and even pre-paid vacation plans. Judges could be jerks, but they took vacations too. That left Tuesday morning and afternoon to question those potential jurors who basically had nothing better to do than sit in a courtroom eight hours a day, five days a week. The resultant pool skewed toward the retired and those with government jobs that would still pay them while they were playing hooky on jury duty. Not the best demographics for Talon, but at least Cobb didn't strike any of the 'minorities'.

So, at the end of the second day of trial, Judge Harvey swore in a jury of twelve, plus two alternates, mostly but not completely white, with two more women than men. They all said they could be fair. Talon hoped they were telling the truth.

Harvey excused everyone for the night and ordered them to return Wednesday morning at 9:00 a.m. sharp. When they did, and everyone—jurors, attorneys, clients, and interested members of the public—was assembled in the courtroom, it was time for the trial to begin in earnest. Judge Harvey took the bench and spoke.

"Ladies and gentlemen of the jury, please give your attention to Mr. Cobb who will deliver the opening statement on behalf of the State of Washington."

CHAPTER 31

Cobb stood up, buttoned his suit coat, and stepped out from behind the prosecution table to stand directly in front of the jury box. It was a short walk—the defense always sat farther from the jury so any whispered conversations could remain confidential— and Cobb was a tall man, so it was noticeable as the heads of all the seated jurors raised in unison to look at the attorney for the People of the Great State of Washington as he began his opening statement.

"When you kill someone, that's homicide. When you do it by assaulting them, that's murder. If you do it with an extreme indifference to that person's life, then it's murder in the first degree. And that's what the defendant in this case did." He pointed at Karim but didn't say his name, following an infamous, and judicially disfavored but not quite unethical, prosecution tradition of dehumanizing criminal defendants by never speaking their actual names. "Murder in the first degree."

Talon looked over at Karim, in part to see how he was doing, but in part because she knew the jurors would all look over at their table when Cobb called Karim out like that. She wanted to look caring, because the jurors would be looking at her as much as at Karim. If she seemed distant, that would be a sign he might be a killer. But if she put a hand on his arm and whispered something reassuring, it showed she cared—and how could you care about a killer?

"Don't look up," she whispered. "You're doing great. I'm just trying to look like I care."

"You don't care?" Karim whispered back, his expression changing automatically with the sentiment he was expressing.

"Of course, I care," Talon replied quickly, with a squeeze of his arm. "Now try not to look worried. Well, not too worried. Don't look like a murderer worried that he got caught. Look like an innocent man worried he might go to prison for a crime he didn't commit."

"I am an innocent man worried about going to prison for a crime he didn't commit," Karim pointed out.

Talon smiled ever so slightly. "Then it should be easy for you. Now, hush. I have to pay attention."

Cobb returned his gaze to the jurors although even Talon could tell from where she was sitting that he was sort of looking past them as he spoke.

"It really is that simple," he continued. "This is actually a very simple case. The facts are pretty much undisputed. The only thing in dispute is the legal import of said facts."

Talon smiled inside. 'Legal import of said facts.' Jurors hated lawyer speak. Jurors were regular people and most regular people already hated lawyers, so it was never a good idea to draw attention to it. Especially by using phrases that made you think you were smarter than other people—the main reason people hated lawyers.

"But like I said, it's pretty simple what happened out there that day." Cobb opened his hands and began pacing in front of the jury box. It was a casual enough move at the beginning, but if he kept pacing back and forth, it would become annoying and thereby distracting. "This all took place out in front of the new jail they're building down near the water. The defendant and some other troublemakers decided to go down and protest the new jail. I guess they don't want criminals locked up. I guess they just want them to be able to walk the streets of your neighborhood."

He looked over his shoulder again at Karim. "I guess I can see why."

Talon considered objecting. Cobb was giving her a lot of grounds for it. He was playing on the jurors' fears and prejudices by suggesting criminals would stalk their neighborhoods, and he was attacking Karim personally for what were essentially his political beliefs. But she decided against it. She found Cobb mostly overbearing and tiring. She calculated the jury would too.

"So, there he is, the defendant, leading a protest against a facility vital to the safety of our community. He's jumping and dancing and chanting and yelling and just whooping the crowd up into a frenzy. It's starting to become a very dangerous situation."

Talon was almost deafened by the racist dog whistle of a Black man jumping and dancing and 'whooping' the crowd into frenzy. But again, she was going to have to rely on the jurors to do the right thing, and part of that might be hearing those dog whistles themselves and being turned off by them without having to be told so by the defense attorney.

"Here's this jail," Cobb continued. He was still pacing, even accelerating a little as he told the story. Definitely distracting. "And here's this protest which is starting to get out of control. Now, the people who run this jail, they can't just let it get vandalized. And who knows what kind of violence might happen if these rioters start scaling the walls and jumping the gate. You would have a very dangerous, very explosive situation on your hands, and ladies and gentlemen, you just can't have that. You can't let that happen. And you really can't let that happen right outside of a jail. So, the next thing that happened was the authorities in charge of the jail came out to ask the protesters, the rioters, to leave the premises."

Cobb finally stopped pacing. He had been doing it so long and at such an increasing pace that it was a bit jarring when he suddenly stopped to point at Karim.

"Because remember, ladies and gentlemen, the defendant didn't get permission to be there. He didn't get any kind of permit or anything, and he certainly wasn't invited onto the jail property. They were trespassing and threatening property damage and probably physical violence as well. Someone had to ask them to stop. That someone was James Dank, the warden of the jail."

Talon leaned forward, ever so slightly, to see whether Cobb would follow their own plan of defining the combatants as Hero and Villain before showing—or describing—the actual fight. She thought he might, in which case there would be a preliminary battle over the competing Hero/Villain narrative before there was the battle over, as Cobb called it, 'the import of said facts' that led to Dank's death. But she had a suspicion Cobb might fall into a trap a lot of prosecutors fell into, namely focusing too much on the defendant. Victims could become afterthoughts, especially murder victims who were literally not around to make themselves be seen and heard. The case name (*State v. Jackson*) referenced the defendant, but not the victim. And the focus of any criminal trial was the conduct of the defendant. Talon was about to see whether Cobb could step back from that narrow focus. She guessed, and hoped, not.

"Mr. Dank came out right through the front gate," Cobb began pacing again, "and walked up to the defendant. There were a couple of uniformed jail guards with him, but only for protection, and it turned out he needed that protection. The defendant," Cobb tried to point at Karim again, but he was still pacing, just a little too fast, so it made for just a weird knot of tall gangly body parts as he tried to keep speaking while somehow looking at both Karim and the jurors simultaneously, "attacked Mr. Dank. Like I said, he was hooting and hollering and getting everyone all worked up. Well, I guess he got himself worked up, too, because when Mr. Dank approached him and asked him to leave the jail property before anything or anyone got hurt, the defendant reacted by shoving Mr. Dank as hard as he could."

Cobb stopped pacing again, and it was jarring again. He took a moment to look over and size up Karim, expecting the jurors to do the same, which they mostly did once he said, "Now, the defendant is a strapping young man, in the prime of his life, big and strong and able to take care of himself." He looked back to the jury. "But Mr. Dank was not. He was an older man, not in the best physical shape, and certainly no match for the defendant in a physical fight. So, when the defendant, young and strong, pushed Mr. Dank as hard as he could, Mr. Dank went flying backward, off of his feet, and landed on the cold, hard cement."

Cobb mimed an exaggerated push in the air. Again, kind of an awkward motion at 6′4″. "The push was so strong and so unexpected, Mr. Dank didn't have time to break his fall. He landed directly on the back of his skull. And the medical examiner is going to tell you that Mr. Dank died from the injuries he suffered when the defendant pushed him onto the ground and smashed his skull against the pavement."

Tripped and fell, Talon thought. *To-may-to, to-mah-to.*

"And so." Cobb took a large step and centered himself in front of the jury again. He opened his long arms wide and fanned out his big hands. "Like I said at the beginning. When you kill someone, it's homicide. When you do it by assaulting them, it's murder. And when you do it with extreme indifference to that person's life, it's murder in the first degree. The defendant is guilty of murder in the first degree. At the end of this trial, I am going to stand up again and ask you, based on all of the evidence you are about to hear, to return a verdict of guilty to murder in the first degree. Thank you."

Cobb turned on his heel and marched back to his seat at the prosecution table. Talon watched him a bit, then turned her attention back to Karim. Not that she really needed to talk to him, but again, she wanted the jury to see that she cared about, maybe even liked, him.

And why shouldn't she? As she was about to explain, Karim was the Hero.

"Now, ladies and gentlemen," Judge Harvey announced, "please give your attention to Ms. Winter who will deliver the opening statement on behalf of the defense."

CHAPTER 32

Talon stood and nodded to the judge. She was going to go ahead and do the whole formal ritual. "Thank you, Your Honor," she looked to Cobb, "Counsel," then the jurors, "Ladies and gentlemen of the jury." She stepped out from behind her table, but not up to the jury box. "May it please the Court, I am Talon Winter." She paused, then stepped to the front of her counsel table and gestured with an open hand at her client, "And this is Karim Jackson."

Karim obviously wasn't expecting that. He smiled awkwardly, then turned to the jury and offered a stilted wave. A couple of the jurors reflexively waved back.

Good, Talon thought.

"I mention his name," Talon began a slow, not awkward stroll, to her usual spot directly in front of the jury box, close enough to be heard, far enough away not to be weird, "because the prosecutor didn't. He wouldn't. And he won't. He doesn't want you to think of Karim as a person. He wants you to think of Karim as a thing, a label. A defendant is what he said. A criminal is what he implied."

She gestured again toward him but kept her eyes on the

jurors. "Go ahead, take a look at him again. Mr. Cobb was right about one thing: he's a strong, young man in the prime of his life. He's also a Black man. He's exactly the type of person—he looks like the type of person—a lot people would cross the street to avoid. Just in case."

It was uncomfortable, especially for the white jurors, but it was also true. And anyway, Cobb had started it.

"Mr. Cobb suggested as much when he warned you just now that Karim was a criminal, or consorted with them anyway, and that if you weren't careful, he'd be walking the streets of your neighborhood. Well, let me tell you what I think about that kind of talk. It's regressive. It's bigoted. Honestly, it's disgraceful and has no place in a courtroom. But perhaps most importantly, it's untrue. Karim is exactly the sort of person you would want walking the streets of your neighborhood. Because Karim cares about making those streets safer and making that neighborhood better."

She did take a moment then to look back at her client, and she smiled. Then she turned back. "Let me give you a little more detail about that so-called riot Mr. Cobb just tried to describe. And a little more information about that so-called jail. Because, you see, it's not exactly a jail, and what Karim and several dozen other concerned citizens were doing there that day was not a riot."

Talon paused then. They say in jazz, it's not the notes you play, it's the notes you don't play. Rests and silences are their own types of sounds, and when speaking to a group, especially a group of people you're trying to persuade, pauses are important, and powerful when used properly. One obvious use is just for everyone to catch their breath, and Talon certainly didn't mind a moment for that. But in persuasive speaking, the most important function of a pause is to force the listener to live with whatever you just said. Sit with it, without something new pushing it out of the way so quickly it can be forgotten. Sometimes it was to let the point drive itself home. Other times, like then, it was to build suspense, to spark curiosity, to move the listeners just a little bit toward the edge of their seats, to get those jurors to lean forward and listen to the answer of the question they weren't allowed to ask: 'What do you mean it wasn't a jail?'

Cobb had said it was a jail. Talon just said it wasn't. So, which was it, and why? And only Talon had the floor to answer the question.

"You see, a jail," she explained, "is something the community builds together to house people duly convicted of crimes. It is funded by the government, run by the government, and its administration is answerable to the people directly through that government. It's the county jail. Just like the county morgue or the county fair. It's ours, together. Funded with our dollars, staffed by our employees, responsible to us." She pulled a fist to her chest to emphasize 'us'.

"But that building down by the water where Karim was that afternoon? That was no jail. That, ladies and gentlemen, was a private business. It's a private business with a CEO, a board of directors, and shareholders who care about one thing and one thing only: money."

Talon took a moment to scan the eyes of her audience. Some of them probably were repulsed, or at least a little discomfited by hearing that. Some of them were probably fine with it and thought she was being overly dramatic. She thought she saw both types in the jury box, along with more than a few who were encountering the idea of a private prison for the first time. They were curious for more. She was happy to oblige.

"The private detention center," she raised a cautionary finger, "not a jail," she reminded them. "The private detention center is called the Pierce Regional Institute for Correctional Endeavors, or P.R.I.C.E., and it was built and is owned and operated by American Correctional Enterprises, a private business. You see, a few of the smaller cities here didn't like having to pay the county so much to house their criminals at the county jail, so they got together and hired a private company to build a cheaper jail. They pay less per inmate, and American Correctional Enterprises uses the money they get from those cities to build walls, buy cots, pay private guards, and, of course, the main reason they're in business: to profit off of the misery of other human beings."

That was being a bit dramatic, Talon knew, but it wasn't entirely wrong, Anyway, every Hero needed a corrupt System to fight against. Speaking of which...

"Now, there some people who will argue that contracting out jail services to a private corporation is simply a way to increase efficiencies and save taxpayer dollars. Those people are on the city councils of the places that hired A.C.E. to build their private cages on our waterfront. They are elected officials, they get to make that decision, and that is part of our political process.

"But you know what else is part of our political process? Peaceful protest. We have a long and storied tradition in this country of protesting against things we find unjust with the goal of making our country better. We were founded on protest and almost every major social advancement has come from people who took to the street, showed the strength of their numbers, and demanded that we do better. The Boston Tea Party. The Women's Suffrage Parade. The United Mine Workers. Selma. Stonewall. The Million Man March. The list goes on and on.

"In fact, the right to protest is so fundamental to what it means to be an American—a good patriotic American—they put it in the Bill of Rights, in the very First Amendment, right next to freedom of religion, freedom of speech, and freedom of the press. Under the First Amendment, we, as Americans, have the right to peaceably assemble and to petition our government for the redress of grievances. In fact, I would go so far as to say we don't just have the right, we have the duty."

Talon raised her arms and glanced around the courtroom. "Our country has always been a promise, but that promise has always been and is still unfulfilled. To fulfill that promise, it will take patriots—dare I say heroes—to peaceably assemble, to petition for the redress of grievances, to stand up for what is right and just and demand better. Better for all of us. Better for our streets. Better for our neighborhoods. It takes people like Karim Jackson."

Everyone looked at Karim again. Talon hoped, for some of the jurors anyway, it was in a slightly different light. Maybe even a heroic light. But she had a long road ahead of her still. She wasn't at a political convention and Karim wasn't running for president. He was still a murder defendant.

"So, let me tell you a little more about Karim," she segues into his personal story. The one thing they stress at the defense attorney trial seminars is to make your client human, likeable even, if possible. Luckily, with Karim, it was very possible. "Karim was born and raised right here in Tacoma. His parents were teachers. His dad taught at Franklin Elementary, and his mom was a science teacher at Stadium High School. He is one of two children. His older sister is actually an attorney here in town. And Karim is a student at U.W. Tacoma, just up the street here, studying philosophy and criminal justice."

Talon paused again. This time to give the jurors another chance to glance at Karim, just before she reminded them. "He's not a criminal looking to stalk the streets of your neighborhood. He's a hard-working young man looking to make those streets better."

Talon took a single step to one side. In part just to keep her circulation going, but also as a nonverbal cue that she was shifting topics slightly as well.

"But it's one thing to study justice in a classroom," she said. "It's another to show up in person and put words into action. And that's exactly what Karim was doing that afternoon in front of that privately owned and operated detention facility. He was there with several dozen other people, trying to bring attention to a matter that he felt was both unjust and unknown. He was trying to raise awareness about an issue where he thought we could do better. And despite what Mr. Cobb just said, he wasn't the leader. But he wasn't alone.

"It was a hot afternoon, and the protest had been going on for a while. There was nothing violent or dangerous about it. There was no property damage. No one was trying to break open the gates. It was just a group of like-minded, motivated people getting together for a cause they believed in. So, they were passing the bullhorn around. By the time the bullhorn landed in Karim's hand, the protest had been going on for some time. It was almost over, in fact. But I guess it didn't end quite soon enough for the people who made their living off of that private detention center and others like it. It didn't end soon enough for people used to telling other people what to do, and punishing those who didn't comply. It didn't end soon enough for James Dank, the director of that private detention center."

Talon knew she had to be careful. It wasn't good form to speak ill of the dead. That was even more true when the dead was also the murdered. But she needed a Villain. And Cobb had left her space to define him. She couldn't pass that up.

Sometimes the best way to do something that was distasteful was to acknowledge it and label it, then do it anyway.

"I don't want to speak ill of the dead," she said. "Especially not someone who died prematurely from a freak accident. But that's what happened here, and you deserve to know the truth if you're going to be asked to make a decision as significant as the one that will be placed in your hands at the end of this trial."

She also needed to undersell it, just a bit. It was a way of showing respect for the dead. She didn't need to go overboard. The jurors could fill in the rest, and they would appreciate her letting them be the ones to do so.

"James Dank spent most of his career with American Correctional Enterprises. He didn't start as a guard and work his way up or anything, though. He was a middle manager at a company that sold equipment to A.C.E., mostly furniture and kitchen supplies, and one day they offered him a job and he took it. From then on, he worked his way up from middle manager to supervising manager and finally to director. He had a knack for running a detention center. And by had a knack for it, I mean he maximized profits for the company. He didn't get promoted for treating inmates with extra dignity or making sure that conditions were as humane as possible. He got promoted for cutting costs and dealing with the constant lawsuits filed against A.C.E. for the way they treated those entrusted to their care."

So, not evil. But not a great guy either.

"On the day in question here," Talon continued, "Mr. Dank was at P.R.I.C.E., and for the same reason Karim was there. They were about to open the jail. Mr. Dank wanted to get everything ready. Karim wanted to stop him."

Talon smiled, the smile of a teacher who appreciates her student's hard work but knows it won't amount to anything. "Now, Karim and his friends weren't actually going to succeed in shutting down that detention facility. The city councils had voted, the contracts had been signed, the police departments had the directions and phone numbers downloaded into their patrol vehicles. They were just making noise, and eventually they would go away. All Mr. Dank had to do was ignore them. Go about his business that day. Make sure every cell had four beds crammed into it. Make sure the industrial sized bags of oatmeal and instant mashed potatoes were in the kitchen. Sanitize the toothbrushes and wipe down the seatless toilets.

"But no."

Talon shook her head. "No, James Dank, director of the Pierce Regional Institute for Correctional Endeavors, was not someone who let other people tell him what to do. He told other people what to do. And they had to listen to him. Literally. Because they were inmates. Criminals. And that made him better than them."

Talon suppressed a glance at Cobb, but she noticed at least one juror take a glimpse at the prosecutor. *Good again.*

"Mr. Dank decided to confront the protestors outside his business. But he didn't do it alone. Oh no. The reason people did what he said wasn't because he convinced anyone of the superior reasoning of his argument. It was because he was backed up by a gang of armed guards. And he made sure he was backed by a gang of armed guards when he went out to confront the protestors. To confront Karim."

Talon took a moment again. She smiled slightly, a rueful grin really. The smile was for what she was about to describe. The pause was to let the setup sink in. Hero vs. Villain. The fight was about to start. They needed to be reminded of who to root for.

"But here's the thing," Talon said. "Karim had every right to be there. He was protesting, but he was acting responsibly. He was acting like an American. He wasn't going to be intimidated by some angry corporate profiteer even if he did have a gang of armed guards behind him. So, when James Dank ordered him to shut up and go away, Karim told him something he wasn't used to hearing. He told him, 'No'."

Talon widened her eyes at that. "Now, be sure about this: James Dank could have taken no for an answer. He could have walked away. Or he could have engaged in a conversation with Karim. He could have tried to explain his point of view, and he could have tried to listen to Karim's. But he didn't do any of that. He resorted to what he was used to. He resorted to what underlies the entire concept of forcing a human being into a jail cell. He resorted to violence."

Talon pantomimed the rest of the confrontation, mimicking the actions of each participant as she described it.

"He grabbed at Karim, trying to take the bullhorn out of his hands. Karim didn't let him and curled his body away to protect it. Mr. Dank then wrapped his arms around Karim. Karim lifted his arms up to break free, and that's when Mr. Dank lost his balance, pushed backwards by Karim defending himself."

Talon paused again. She was about to describe a man dying. Even if he was the Villain, she needed to hit the right tone. She needed to seem like she cared. She didn't, but she needed to seem like it. She assumed a neutral posture, dropped her hands to her sides, and pasted on a slight frown as she explained, "Mr. Dank stumbled away, lost his balance, and fell backward onto the pavement. The back of his skull hit first, cracking the plate beneath his brain. He lost consciousness and blood began to pool under his head. He was taken to Tacoma General Hospital, but they couldn't stop the brain bleed, and the next morning he died."

She paused again. Out of respect. She didn't respect him, but she needed to seem like it.

But back to Our Hero.

"And Karim? Well, when those armed guards saw Mr. Dank bleeding on the pavement, they jumped Karim. Pushed him into the pavement as well, busting his lip and bloodying his nose. They called the real police, and they booked him into a real jail. Then they sent a report to the prosecutor's office and said Karim had killed a jail warden. One of their own." Finally, that glance at Cobb—a cold, accusing glance—and then back to the jury. "And now here we are."

"So, ladies and gentlemen of the jury, that's what really happened. Karim Jackson is a good man who was doing a good thing, and he was forced to defend himself. James Dank is dead now, and that's a tragedy, but it's not murder. Karim Jackson is an innocent man, and at the end of this trial, I will stand up again and ask you not to add to the tragedy of James Dank's unintended death by convicting an innocent man of a crime he didn't commit. I will ask you to return a verdict of not guilty. Thank you."

Talon turned and walked solemnly back to sit down next to Karim.

"That was great, Talon," he whispered. "Thank you."

"Don't thank me yet," she whispered. "We're just getting started."

Judge Harvey looked down at Cobb. "The State may call its first witness."

CHAPTER 33

Cobb stood up. "The State calls Jeremy Little to the stand."

"Who's that?" Karim whispered, as Cobb came out from behind the prosecution table and one of his helpers went out into the hallway to fetch the witness.

"One of the guards who jumped you," Talon answered. She recognized the name from the police reports.

Jeremy Little entered the courtroom and walked toward the witness stand to be sworn in by Judge Harvey. He was in his early twenties, with a short haircut and a boyish face. He was wearing a jacket and tie, not his A.C.E. uniform. Talon wondered why.

After raising his right hand and swearing to tell the truth, the whole truth, and nothing but the truth, Jeremy Little sat down on the witness stand and Cobb began his questioning.

"Could you please state your name for the record?"

"Jeremy Little."

"How are you employed, Mr. Little?"

"I am a correctional specialist for American Correctional Enterprises," Little answered.

"So, you're a jail guard?" Cobb attempted to translate.

Little shifted in his seat a bit. "My job classification is

Correctional Specialist Four. But yeah, I do basically what you think of when you say, 'jail guard'. I monitor the inmates, in person and through video. Sometimes I escort people places, like to the medical facility. Stuff like that."

"Stuff that a jail guard does," Cobb pushed.

"Sure," Little agreed with a small shrug.

"Now, were you working on the day of the incident in this case?" Cobb proceeded.

"The day Mr. Dank died?" Little clarified. "Yeah, I was one of the correctional specialists who went out with him to confront those protesters."

"Ask them to leave?" Cobb suggested.

"Yeah, sure," Little agreed again.

He seemed honest enough, if a little compliant with whatever he thought Cobb wanted him to say. But then again, you don't make Correctional Specialist Four by questioning orders.

"How many guards, or correctional specialists, or whatever," Cobb stumbled through the next question, "how many of you went out with Mr. Dank to ask the protestors to leave?"

Little took a moment to confirm in his own mind. "Six, including me.

"Are you sure?" Cobb followed up.

"Yes," Little answered. "I know because we all had to write reports after that and list every employee who was present. It was me, Harris, Sanchez—"

"I don't need you to list everyone," Cobb interrupted. "So, six of you. Great. Now, please tell the jury what happened when you went out there."

"Uh, sure." Little seemed confused about whether he should talk directly to the jurors or keep looking at Cobb. He elected to start by looking at them, but then turned back almost immediately to Cobb to finish his narrative. "Mr. Dank went out first, but he told us to walk right behind him, in case anything went sideways. If it started to get violent, we were supposed to step in and protect Mr. Dank. But it happened so fast, we didn't get a chance."

"What happened so fast?" Cobb prompted.

"The assault," Little answered. Then he pointed at Karim. "By that guy over there. He pushed Mr. Dank before any of us could do anything to stop it."

Cobb nodded, obviously happy with that answer. "So, the defendant pushed Mr. Dank? You saw that?"

"Oh, yeah, I saw it," Little confirmed. "Mr. Dank went up to him because he was the one with the bullhorn, chanting and stuff."

"What was he chanting?" Cobb inquired.

Little hesitated, throwing a quick glance at the jurors. "Um, I'm not sure I can say it in court. It was like cuss words."

"You can say it," Cobb assured him. "Courtrooms are about truth. If it's true, you can say it, even if it's cuss words."

"Right, okay." Little nodded. "I don't remember it exactly, but it was like 'Fuck this jail' or something."

"Oh, it was way better than that," Karim whispered to Talon.

She hushed him. "You can correct the record later. Now, listen."

"Okay, so something obscene," Cobb summarized, "and that's why Mr. Dank went up to him?"

"Well, I'm not sure it was because it was obscene," Little clarified. "It was more like because he was the one with the bullhorn, so it seemed like he was the leader, I guess."

"And when Mr. Dank walked up to the defendant," Cobb led his witness, "the defendant pushed him."

Little hesitated. He pointed at Karim. "He's the defendant,

right?"

"Right," Cobb confirmed, a bit tersely.

"Yeah, he pushed him," Little said.

"Were any words exchanged before he pushed him?" Cobb probed. "Or did he just push him immediately?"

"Um, well," Little shifted again in his seat, "I mean, I think they exchanged words. I'm not a hundred percent sure. I was kind of watching the crowd too. There were like a lot of people out there, and there were only six of us. I was worried what would happen if they all rushed us at once."

"Did they?" Cobb let the questioning divert for a moment.

"I mean, yeah, kind of," Little answered. "After we apprehended, um, the defendant. You know, for killing Mr. Dank."

"After you detained the defendant, the crowd rushed you?" Cobb asked.

"Well, no, not exactly," Little admitted, "but it looked like they might. That's when I unholstered my weapon and ordered the crowd back."

"You unholstered your gun?" Cobb clarified.

"Yeah, my gun," Little confirmed. "It took a few of us to get control of the defendant, so I cleared the perimeter for officer safety reasons."

"He threatened to shoot everyone," Karim whispered.

"Yeah, I was there," Talon reminded him.

"Did the crowd comply?" Cobb asked.

"After a minute, yeah," Little confirmed. "Then we were able to transport the defendant inside the facility."

"For his own safety?" Cobb suggested.

Little shrugged. "I mean, not really. It was for our safety, while we waited for the police to arrive."

"You called the police?" Cobb asked.

"Yeah, once we were inside, we called Tacoma P.D.," Little explained. "When they arrived, we handed him off to them."

"Okay," Cobb acknowledged. "So, did that end your involvement in the case?"

"Well, I had to write a report," Little answered. "A.C.E. makes us write a lot of reports. Especially when there's something like this."

"Does this sort of thing happen a lot?" Cobb seemed a bit surprised.

"I mean, violence? Yeah," Little answered. "It's a jail or whatever, right? But not murder. That was the first murder I seen since I started."

Cobb nodded and took a moment, to make sure he hadn't forgotten anything before he sat down, Talon knew.

"Thank you, Mr. Little," Cobb finally said. "No further questions."

Judge Harvey looked down to Talon. "Any cross-examination, Ms. Winter?"

Of course, Talon thought. "Yes, Your Honor," she said.

She stood and made her way around the defense table. There was a certain spot to stand when cross-examining a witness. She couldn't stand too far back or she would seem intimidated by him, but she couldn't stand too close or she would seem overly aggressive, and it would make everyone feel weird. But there was a sweet spot where she was close enough to telegraph that she was challenging him, but far enough back to show she was still respecting him, or at least respecting The System. The Damn System.

"Good morning, Mr. Little," she started. "Or should I call you Specialist Little?"

"Mister is fine," Little replied. "I'm not on duty right now."

Talon gestured at his attire. "Is that why you're not wearing your uniform?"

"Um, yeah." Little glanced down at his clothes. "We have to keep our uniforms at the facility, in our locker."

"Just a rule, huh?" Talon commiserated.

"Right."

"I imagine there are lot of rules you have to follow," Talon suggested.

Little shrugged. "I guess so."

"Okay." Talon nodded. "We can come back to that. First, though, let's talk about what you saw that day. Or rather what you didn't see. Did you see Mr. Dank grab at Mr. Jackson at all?"

"Mr. Jackson is the defendant, right?" Little confirmed, pointing yet again at Karim.

"Right."

"Um, no," Little answered. "I did not see that."

"So, I want to take a moment to break that down a bit, okay?" Talon said.

"Okay," Little agreed.

"You said you didn't see Mr. Dank grab at Mr. Jackson," Talon repeated. "Does that mean you were watching them the whole time, and it didn't happen? Or does that mean it might have happened, but you weren't looking at them the whole time?"

"Um…" Little hesitated.

"Do you understand the difference?" Talon asked.

"I think so," Little answered. "I'm just trying to remember. I definitely didn't see anything like that. I think that's because it didn't happen, but I can't say that for sure."

"Because you were also watching the crowd, right?" Talon suggested. "In case they rushed you."

"Um, yeah, I guess," Little admitted.

"You were worried about that?"

"Yes."

"And you were watching them?"

"Uh, yes."

"So, you weren't watching Mr. Dank and Mr. Jackson the entire time they interacted, right?"

"I guess not," Little agreed.

"Okay, good." Talon gave that exchange a verbal check mark. "Now let's back up a little. You said there are a lot of rules at A.C.E. What about Mr. Dank specifically? Was he hard to work for?"

Talon knew there was no way Little was going to bad mouth his late boss. In fact, she was counting on it.

"Oh, no," Little insisted. "He was great to work for. He really cared about all of his employees."

"He did, huh?" Talon gave him a chance to confirm.

"Definitely."

"Did he let his employees form a union?" Talon asked. "Are you in a union?"

"A union? Um, no," Little answered. "But I mean, I never... I mean, I don't know if anyone really wants to be in a union."

"If you were a corrections officer at the county jail, you'd be a member of the police union, right?" Talon asked.

"Um, I'm not sure," Little responded.

"Have you ever applied to be a police officer or a corrections officer?" Talon was breaking one of the cardinal rules of cross-examination: never ask a question you don't already know the answer to. But she knew the answer.

"Um, well, yes," Little admitted.

"And they rejected you, didn't they?"

"I didn't get the job, if that's what you mean," Little said.

"And that's why you're still an at-will corrections specialist at a private detention center, isn't it?"

"It's a good job," Little defended.

"And you don't want to lose it, do you?" Talon pointed out.

"Of course not," Little answered. Then he realized what she was implying. "But I would never—"

"No further questions," Talon interrupted. "Thank you, Mr. Little."

Talon turned back to sit down again as Judge Harvey asked Cobb, "Any redirect examination?"

Cobb thought for a moment. At a minimum he could let Little finish his answer and tell the jury he wouldn't lie on the stand just to save his job. But Cobb shook his head. "No, Your Honor. The witness may be excused."

Normally Talon was infuriated at how lazy some prosecutors were. They didn't do half the work of the defense bar, but they usually won anyway, and chalked it up to their superior trial skills, when really it was just that the cops did all their work for them and jurors wanted to believe innocent people didn't get charged with crimes. She'd heard defense attorneys say more than once that a trained monkey could be a prosecutor. But right then, in that moment, she was grateful for Cobb's hubris and laziness.

Talon knew it wouldn't be the last time in the trial, but she was surprised how quickly it manifested itself again.

CHAPTER 34

There was the burden of proof, then there was the burden of persuasion. The burden of proof was clear: it was the amount of evidence a plaintiff needed to present to be able to win the case, and in a criminal case that level was proof beyond any reasonable doubt. The burden of persuasion was less concrete. It was the nature and quality, and to some extent the quantity, of evidence the plaintiff needed to present to make the jury comfortable in deciding the burden of proof had been met.

It was the difference between a stick figure and a Mona Lisa. They were both images of people, but one was far more convincing. Luckily, when it came to painting a picture in a courtroom, Cobb was no Da Vinci.

Cobb called all the necessary witnesses; he just didn't bother calling any others. Little testified, but Sanchez, Harris and the other 'correctional specialists' didn't. It avoided them telling conflicting stories, and it made sense to call the one who drew a gun on everyone, lest it look like he was trying to hide that person, but it meant Cobb was wasting one of the biggest advantages of being the prosecutor: time of possession. He could have dragged the State's case-in-chief on for weeks, calling every last person who had anything to do with the case. Talon would never be able to call that many witnesses, and it could leave an impression with the jury that the State's evidence, which took so much longer to present, must be overwhelming.

That meant Talon had a chance of putting on as much evidence, timewise, as Cobb. It also meant she was going to have to do it a lot sooner than she'd anticipated. Cobb called just twelve witnesses, instead of the thirty or more Talon would have if she'd been the prosecutor. It didn't take weeks. It took days. And almost before Talon knew it, they were on the State's final witness.

"The State," Cobb stood up to announce, "calls Dr. Michael Smith."

CHAPTER 35

Dr. Smith entered the courtroom and made his way directly to the judge. He didn't need any direction from Cobb; he'd testified hundreds of times. Just like he'd done thousands of autopsies. He was definitely qualified to give his opinion as to how James Dank died. Talon was never going to convince the jury he wasn't qualified. She just needed them to realize even the most qualified people can make mistakes sometimes too.

"Please state your name for the record," Cobb began his examination once Smith was sworn in and seated.

"Michael Smith," he answered.

"How are you employed, sir?"

Smith turned to deliver his answer directly to the jurors, like all of the prosecution's professional witnesses were trained to do. "I am an assistant medical examiner with the Pierce County Medical Examiner's Office."

Ooh, Talon thought sarcastically. But she knew at least some of the jurors were duly impressed.

Cobb delved into Smith's qualifications next. B.S. M.D. Residency in pathology. Years as a medical examiner. Number of autopsies. Again, there was no doubt he was qualified and experienced. The challenge would be using that experience against him. It didn't need to be a knockout blow, just an opening to exploit later.

Cobb moved next to the specific autopsy of James Dank. Smith explained to the jury the same thing Talon had told them in opening: Dank died from swelling to the brain caused by the fracture of the bone under his brain. He just used fancier words: 'blunt force trauma', 'occipital bone', 'cranial hemorrhage'. It all meant the same thing. He died from hitting his head on the concrete.

They agreed on those facts. They just disagreed on the legal import thereof.

"Were you able to determine a manner of death, Dr. Smith?" Cobb began the last section of his direct examination.

"Yes," Smith replied.

"And as a reminder to the jury," Cobb dragged it out, "what are the four possible manners of death again?"

Smith looked again to the jury. "Natural causes, accident, suicide, and homicide."

"And what did you determine was the manner of death for James Dank?"

"James Dank's death," Smith told the jurors, "was a homicide."

"Thank you, Doctor," Cobb gushed. "Thank you very much. No further questions."

Judge Harvey looked down at Talon. By that point in the trial, he had stopped asking her if she had any cross-examination. She always had cross-examination. She stood up and approached the Good Doctor.

"Homicide is not the same as murder," she began. "Correct?"

"Murder is a subset of homicide," Smith answered.

"So, no," Talon translated. "Your answer is, 'No, Ms. Winter', correct?"

Smith clenched his jaw a bit, then surrendered a, "Correct."

"Okay, so go ahead and say that," Talon insisted. "Say, 'No, Ms. Winter. Homicide is not the same as murder.'" She rolled her wrist at him. "Go on."

That jaw clenched a bit more. "No, Ms. Winter. Homicide is not the same as murder."

"Murder is a legal conclusion, correct?" Talon continued. "It's a homicide that's unlawful."

Smith thought for a moment, then nodded slightly. "That sounds right."

"So, a lawful killing, like in self-defense," Talon posited, "that would be homicide, but not murder, correct?"

Smith hesitated. He glanced at Cobb for the tiniest moment; Talon hoped at least one of the jurors noticed. Then, he tried, "I'm not a lawyer."

Talon smiled. "No, you're not. Thank you for that admission." She took a half step toward him. "Now, let's see what kind of doctor you are. Do you have your autopsy report with you there?"

Smith tapped on the copy Cobb had given him during his direct examination. "Yes."

"Good," Talon said. "You documented everything in there, correct?"

"Correct," Smith answered, looking a bit sidelong at her as he tried to figure out where she was going with that.

"Everything?" Talon repeated.

"Everything," Smith confirmed. "I didn't leave anything out."

"So, if it's not in there," Talon pointed at the report, "then it didn't happen, right?"

"Right."

"Or you didn't see it," Talon added. Then, before Smith could answer—because, really, his answer didn't matter—Talon asked her next question, "Mr. Dank didn't die immediately from his injuries, correct? He lingered for a day or so, correct?"

"Um, correct," Smith stammered. He obviously wanted to return to the previous question Talon didn't let him answer. "But—"

"And for that entire day," Talon interrupted. "And I'm sorry, this is going to sound like a ridiculous question, but I need you to say it. If I say it, it's not evidence, but if you say it, it is evidence. That entire day or so when Mr. Dank was still alive, his heart was still beating, correct?"

Smith blinked at her. "Seriously?"

Talon nodded. "Stupid question, right?"

"Kind of," Smith allowed.

"Answer it anyway," Talon instructed.

"Was his heart beating while he was alive?" Smith attempted to clarify Talon's question.

"Yes," Talon confirmed.

"Yes," Smith answered. "His heart was beating while he was alive. That's how that works."

"I know," Talon said. "And you should have too." She turned on her heel and called out, "No further questions."

Cobb stood up, his expression almost as dumbfounded as Smith's.

"Any redirect?" Judge Harvey asked him. He always still asked Cobb.

Cobb took another few moments to answer. "Based on that

line of questioning? No, I don't think so."

Harvey didn't need to hear it twice. He spun to Dr. Smith. "You are excused." Then back to Cobb. "Does the State have any further witnesses?"

Cobb shook the puzzled expression off of his face and stood up straight. "No, Your Honor. The State rests."

Everyone in the courtroom seemed to exhale at once. Talon certainly did. There was a moment of calm whenever the State rested, but it was always immediately followed by the true battle. Or at least the invitation to join it right then.

"Is the defense prepared to proceed at this time?" Judge Harvey asked. He looked at the clock. It was still early in the afternoon, but it was the afternoon nevertheless. "Or shall we adjourn until the morning?"

Everyone also knew what Talon's answer would be. "The defense will be ready to start its case first thing in the morning, Your Honor, thank you."

Harvey nodded approvingly. "So be it. The court stands adjourned until nine o'clock tomorrow morning."

"Just enough time," Talon whispered to herself.

CHAPTER 36

Even as the courtroom was still emptying, Talon raised her cell phone to her ear and motioned at Karim to join her in the hallway.

"Hello?" Curt answered.

Talon stepped out of the courtroom and around the corner, before covering her mouth and half-whispering into the phone. "I need Weathers. Now."

"Done," Curt answered. "We found him."

Talon paused. "We?"

"Paul helped."

Talon rolled her eyes. The whole point of assigning to Curt was… Never mind. "Good. I need him at my office—"

"I can you one better," Curt interrupted. "He's in the courthouse."

"He's in the courthouse?" Talon asked as Karim walked up to her.

"Who's in the courthouse?" Karim asked. Talon hushed him.

"Well, he's in the law library connected to the courthouse," Curt clarified. "He's in one for their conference rooms. Paul just went to buy him some coffee."

"Of course, he did." Talon shook her head. "Well, keep him there," she ordered entirely unnecessarily. "I'll be there in two minutes."

"Who's in the courthouse?" Karim asked again as Talon hung up.

"Our star witness," Talon answered. "I hope."

* * *

Donald Weathers was exactly where Curt said he was, doing exactly what Curt said he would be doing: sitting in a conference room at the law library, sipping coffee. Curt and Paul were keeping him occupied with conversation about something or other Talon couldn't have cared less about.

She stepped into the conference room, hand extended. "Mr. Weathers? I'm Talon Winter. Thank you for coming here today."

Weathers stood up and shook Talon's hand. He was older than she expected. It had only been seven years since his run-in with Dank. He must have already been in his late thirties when it happened. His hair was thinning atop a rosy scalp, and transitioning from a boyish blond to a mature gray. Blue eyes smiled out, flanked by new but unmistakable wrinkles. His grip was dry and firm.

"I never turn down free coffee," Weathers quipped. "But like I told these gentlemen, I don't think I'm going to be able to help you."

Talon didn't like the sound of that. She didn't believe it either. Not yet.

"Why not?" she asked.

"You want to talk to me about what happened when I was working at the private jail down by Olympia, right?"

"Right," Talon confirmed. "The one run by American Correctional Enterprises."

"Exactly," Weathers pointed at her. "That's why I can't talk about it. I signed a non-disclosure agreement as part of the settlement I got. If I talk about it, I have to pay everything back."

"But you came here today anyway?" Talon asked.

Weathers shrugged. "I'm not rude, ma'am. And it's not like I don't want to talk about it. I just can't. I gave my word."

"You're a witness in my case, Mr. Weathers," Talon advised him. "I'm not going to just let you walk away."

"I'm not walking anywhere," Weathers defended. "But I'm not talking either."

"So, you'll show up if subpoenaed?" Talon confirmed.

"Sure." Weathers shrugged. "But sitting on the witness stand is different from talking on the witness stand. Ask whatever you want. That doesn't mean I'll answer."

Talon opened her briefcase and searched through the papers tucked into the pockets—the blank forms she carried around with her, just in case. She extracted a single piece of paper and a pen, then offered Weathers a tight smile and a raised finger. "One sec."

She filled in the case name at the top, Weathers's name in the middle, and the appearance date and time below that. Then she signed at the very bottom and handed the document to Weathers. "That's a subpoena. I'll see you the day after tomorrow. Nine a.m. sharp. Don't be late."

CHAPTER 37

Talon had told Weathers to show up in two days because she knew the next day was going to be filled with other witnesses. Two of them in fact. She had called Weathers the star witness, but really he was one of three co-stars, each with their own indispensable role. Weathers would confirm Dank was the villain, but first Karim had to describe the fight. And before that, there was that unfinished business about Dank's heart beating for twenty-four hours or so after attacking Karim.

"The defense may call its first witness," Judge Harvey announced after everyone was assembled again in his courtroom the next morning.

"Thank you, Your Honor." Talon stood up at counsel table. "The defense calls Dr. Giannina Evangelopoulos to the stand."

Dr. Evangelopoulos was seated in the last row of the gallery. As the first witness of the day, she didn't need to wait out in the hallway to follow the judge's order that witnesses not hear one another's testimony. She stood up and strode to the front of the courtroom to be sworn in by Judge Harvey.

Talon had imagined the moment as she allowed the trial to play out in her head every damn night for the last month, and for some reason, she had always imagined Dr. Evangelopoulos wearing a long white lab coat over something in the teal category, hair pulled back in a pony tail, and a stethoscope around her neck. A doctor. But the reality was much different, and Talon had to admit, much better.

She was dressed in a dark tailored business suit, with a cream shell and a simple gold necklace. Her thick black hair was loose, falling comfortably and confidently onto her shoulders. She may not have looked like a doctor per se, but she definitely looked like an authority, and that was probably even better.

"Could you please state your name for the record?" Talon began.

"Giannina Evangelopoulos," she answered. She smiled at the jury. "It's a lot."

Most of the jurors smiled back. Again, good. If they were going to believe Dr. Evangelopoulos over Dr. Smith, it would help if they liked her.

"How are you employed?" Talon followed up.

"I am a resident medical doctor," Evangelopoulos answered, "at Greater Puget Sound Tahoma Medical Center in Steilacoom."

"You're a medical doctor?" Talon just wanted to say it again.

And let Dr. Evangelopoulos say it again too. "Yes."

"Please tell the jury," Talon prompted, "about your education and experience that allows you to hold the position of a resident medical doctor at Greater Puget Sound Tahoma Medical Center."

So, she did. It sounded about the same as what Smith had said. B.S., M.D., residency, doctor, pathology, blah blah blah. Fancy Doctor Expert Person.

"As part of your duties at Greater Puget Sound Tahoma Medical Center," Talon asked after Evangelopoulos had finished reciting her resume to the jurors, "do you ever conduct postmortem pathology examinations?"

Not exactly autopsies, but in the same neighborhood. Zip code, anyway.

"Yes." Again, to the jury, "Most of the residents at our facility are elderly and many are there for end-of-life care. When a patient passes away, one of my duties is to conduct an examination on the person's remains to confirm the cause and manner of death."

"Doesn't the county medical examiner do all of those?" Talon asked the question more than a few of the jurors were probably wondering about as well.

Dr. Evangelopoulos grinned. "No, definitely not. The county medical examiner only gets involved if the death holds some public interest. For example, if there is a police investigation, or if someone is found outdoors in public, away from any medical facility. But if someone dies in a medical facility, it is normally the pathologists on staff who examine the body. In fact, doctors like me do the vast majority of postmortem examinations not in this county, but every county across the country."

Mic drop.

Except there was more Talon needed her to tell the jury, so Talon picked up the mic again.

"Do you also do consulting work outside your duties at Greater Puget Sound Tahoma Medical Center?" Talon asked the woman she had hired to do consulting work.

"Yes, I do," answered the woman who hadn't done any consulting work before being hired by Talon.

"So, were you hired to do some consulting on this case?" Talon followed up.

"Yes, I was."

"What were you asked to do?"

"I was asked to review the autopsy performed by Dr. Michael Smith."

"Please tell the jury what steps you took to conduct that review," Talon instructed.

Dr. Evangelopoulos turned to the jurors. "I began with a review of the autopsy report. I reviewed the photographs taken at the autopsy. I also reviewed all of the police reports. Finally, I conducted my own external examination of the body to compare my own observations with the observations Dr. Smith documented in his report."

"So, you read everything Dr. Smith did," Talon summarized, "and you examined the body yourself. Is that correct?"

"That's correct."

"What were you looking for?"

"Primarily, I was looking for any inconsistencies," Dr. Evangelopoulos admitted. "Either within Dr. Smith's own work, or, perhaps more importantly, between Dr. Smith's work and my own examination of the body."

"Why would that be important?" Talon asked.

Again, Dr. Evangelopoulos delivered her answer to the jury. "Dr. Smith made a conclusion that the manner of death in this case was homicide. If that conclusion was made based on inaccurate information, then the conclusion itself is unreliable. I wanted to see if I agreed with him."

"Did you?"

"No."

Nice. Talon suppressed a grin. "Why not?" she asked.

"I found some inconsistencies between Dr. Smith's examination and my own," Dr. Evangelopoulos answered.

"Inconsistencies?" Talon prompted.

Dr. Evangelopoulos shrugged and looked to the jury. "He

missed something."

That was a big deal. The jurors seemed to understand that. Dr. Evangelopoulos had their attention.

"What did he miss?' Talon asked. "And why was it important?"

"I'll answer your second question first," Dr. Evangelopoulos replied. "Not every inconsistency is equally important. It depends on what the goal of the autopsy is. If there's no mention of, say, fresh needle tracks on the person's arm, that may or may not be significant. If the cause of death is a drug overdose, it would be very significant to leave it out. If the cause of death was multiple gunshot wounds to the chest, it's probably not as important."

"What about in this case?" Talon asked. "What would be important in this case?"

"Well, as I mentioned, in addition to the autopsy report, I reviewed all of the police reports in the case," Dr. Evangelopoulos said. "I was aware that there was an allegation of a physical altercation and the possibility of criminal charges. Because of that, anything related to offensive or defensive wounds would be of paramount importance."

"That makes sense," Talon agreed, of course. "So, what happened in this case?"

"In this case," Dr. Evangelopoulos told the jury, "Dr. Smith overlooked offensive injuries on the decedent's' hands."

Talon cocked her head. "Can you translate into regular words?"

"He had fresh bruising on his knuckles," Dr. Evangelopoulos explained. Then in case that wasn't clear enough. "He punched someone."

Mic drop two.

But again, Talon had to pick it up.

"And that wasn't in Dr. Smith's report?" Talon wanted to make sure the jury understood that part. "At all?"

"Not at all," Dr. Evangelopoulos confirmed. "It was not in his written report, and there were no photographs taken of the decedent's hands."

"Did he leave it out on purpose?" She had to ask.

"I'm not willing to say that," Dr. Evangelopoulos answered carefully. "I just know I saw them even though Dr. Smith didn't document them in any way."

"Is it possible they weren't there during the autopsy Dr. Smith did," Talon suggested, "but they appeared afterward, before your external examination?"

Dr. Evangelopoulos shook her head. "No. Bruising occurs when blood vessels are broken beneath the skin surface and blood pools under the skin. That can only happen if the heart is beating. In addition, as bruises heal, the blood drains away from where it's been trapped. That's why fresh bruises are dark and purple, but older bruises turn yellow and then fade away. In this case, the color of the bruising suggests they were approximately twenty-four hours old at the time the decedent's heart stopped beating."

"So, right when the physical altercation took place?" Talon wanted to make sure everyone understood that.

"Exactly," Dr. Evangelopoulos confirmed.

Talon used another few moments of silence to let that all sink in, including the fact that she wasn't crazy for asking Dr. Smith about Dank's heart beating between the fight and his death.

"Does this additional information impact, in your opinion," Talon picked up again, "what the manner of death was in this case?"

Dr. Evangelopoulos nodded. "Yes."

"Why?"

"Because," she explained to the jurors, "the fatal injuries themselves would be insufficient to determine a manner of death. Mr. Dank could have suffered the exact same injury and outcome if he had fallen backwards off of his porch accidentally. The only way to conclude this was a homicide is to rely on information from the police report. However, the bruising on the knuckles indicates that there was more to the incident than documented in that report. As a doctor and a scientist, I cannot, or should not, rely on information I know to be incomplete or biased. Without relying on the police report, then, there is no way to determine the manner of death to be homicide."

"In your opinion, Doctor," Talon set up the final answer, "what should have been the manner of death?"

Dr. Evangelopoulos turned one last time to the jury. "The manner of death in this case should have been listed as undetermined."

Talon nodded. "Thank you, Doctor. No further questions."

Cobb stood up and approached Dr. Evangelopoulos before Talon had made it back to her seat or Judge Harvey had invited him to cross-examine.

"You're not a real medical examiner, are you?" he huffed. "You just work in a nursing home and confirm when someone dies of a heart attack or whatever."

Dr. Evangelopoulos thought for a moment. "I'm a pathologist. I'm not any less of a pathologist because I work at a private medical center. You're a prosecutor. Are you not a real lawyer because you don't work at some fancy firm?"

Cobb reflexively glanced back at Hampton Montclair, still in the front row of the gallery. That glance made some of the jurors look too.

"Of course not," Cobb defended.

"Exactly." Dr. Evangelopoulos smiled at him.

"Let me ask it a different way," Cobb tried to reset. "You and Dr. Smith came to different conclusions about the manner of death, is that correct?"

"That is correct," Dr. Evangelopoulos confirmed.

"But he's a career medical examiner who has done thousands of autopsies, especially murder autopsies, and you," Cobb waved his hand toward her, "you have not."

"That's true," Dr. Evangelopoulos allowed.

"So, why should we believe you over Dr. Smith?" Cobb asked the question he didn't know the answer to. *Oops.*

"Because," Dr. Evangelopoulos answered, "he missed something. And I didn't."

Mic drop three.

Cobb didn't know how to pick it up.

"No further questions," he conceded, and stormed back to his table.

That was fun, Talon thought as Dr. Evangelopoulos was excused.

"The defense may call its next witness," Judge Harvey said.

But it was time to get serious.

Talon stood up. "The defense calls Karim Jackson to the stand."

CHAPTER 38

It wasn't every day a defendant took the stand to testify in his own defense. In fact, in most trials, the defendant didn't get anywhere near the witness stand. One reason for that was that most defendants were guilty, of something at least, even if not of exactly what they were charged with. There was no surer way to get convicted than to take the stand and confirm your guilt to the jury. Another reason was that even the innocent defendants could be made to seem guilty by a good cross-examination. Finally, when a witness took the stand, a lot of their prior bad behavior would become admissible, and a lot of defendants had prior criminal history the jury wouldn't hear about if they didn't take the stand. Wrap that all up in repeated warnings from the judge that a criminal defendant has a right to remain silent and the jury may not use a decision not to testify against the defendant in any way, and most defense attorneys advise their clients to sit still, sit quiet, and let them do the talking.

But Karim wasn't guilty, Cobb wasn't good, and Karim didn't have any prior criminal history. Plus, Talon was arguing self-defense and although, legally, she could argue that from the evidence without having Karim actually take the stand, the jury was going to want to hear it from his own mouth: 'I was defending myself.'

The reason judges repeatedly admonished juries not to draw any adverse inferences from a defendant's election not to testify was because, of course, they were going to do that. They wanted to hear the defendant say he didn't do it. And Talon knew to give her audience what they wanted.

Talon stepped out of the way and Karim came out from behind the defense table and walked up to the judge, who already had his right hand raised. Karim followed suit.

"Do you solemnly swear to tell the truth, the whole truth, and nothing but the truth?" Harvey asked.

Karim nodded. "I do, Your Honor."

"Take the stand," Judge Harvey instructed. Then, "Whenever you're ready, Ms. Winter."

Talon took a moment to let Karim settle into the witness chair. Then she jumped in.

"Please state your name for the record."

"Karim Daniel Jackson." He was nervous—and rightly so. He kept his eyes on Talon, but she would eventually encourage him to deliver his answers to the jurors. She was going to let him warm up first. Basic questions, easy answers.

"Are you currently working?"

"No, I'm a student."

"Where?"

"University of Washington-Tacoma."

"What are you studying?"

"I have a double major," he answered. "Philosophy and criminal justice."

Talon grinned and nodded. "So, the philosophy of justice?"

Karim smiled weakly and shrugged. "I guess so. I have an

interest in social justice issues, especially criminal justice reform. I want to be a lawyer someday."

Talon considered making a self-deprecating joke about advising him against it, but decided against diminishing her client's passions. Plus, the jury needed to know Karim had plans and a future. It was easier to throw someone away into prison if you thought he wasn't going to amount to anything anyway.

"Very nice," she said. "I'm sure you'll make an excellent lawyer." *If you get acquitted,* she didn't add.

Karim just nodded in acknowledgement. He was still nervous.

"Have you gotten involved in any social justice efforts here in town?" Talon moved the examination along.

"Yes," Karim nodded. "A few."

"What kinds of things?"

"Um, well, let's see," Karim looked up at the ceiling as he tried to remember. "Some get out the vote rallies. There was a vigil against police brutality. And of course," he sighed, "that protest against the private jail down on the waterfront."

Talon nodded. "Yes. Let's talk about that. Are you ready?"

Karim took a deep breath and sighed. "Sure. Let's do it."

"First of all," Talon began, "were you the organizer, or one of the organizers, of the protest?"

Karim shook his head. "No. It was organized by some friends of mine at school, but I didn't do any of the planning. I just agreed to show up."

"About how many people showed up for the protest?"

"Like twenty or thirty," Karim estimated. "Not more than thirty. It was pretty small, actually." He chuckled a bit. "We looked pretty weak."

Okay, he was starting to relax.

"Where was the protest exactly?" Talon continued.

"Right outside the front gate at the jail—or detention center, or whatever," he tried to track Talon's language. "It's called P.R.I.C.E., but I forget exactly what it stands for."

Talon shrugged. "It doesn't matter. It's a private detention center, and you and twenty or thirty people were there to protest it. Is that right?"

"Yeah, that's right," Karim agreed.

"How was the weather?" Talon knew the answer to that one.

"It was hot," Karim chuckled again. "Really hot."

"Probably no fun to protest in the hot sun, huh?" Talon posited.

"Nope," Karim agreed. "Overcast and mid-seventies is perfect. It was pretty brutal that day."

"Did the heat affect the crowd, do you think?"

Karim nodded. "Yeah, you lose your energy really quick in the sun. We hadn't been there for more than like half an hour when people started talking about leaving."

"Please describe the protest for us." A gesture toward the jury. "Were there scheduled speakers? Signs? Songs? What exactly?"

"Um, no, no speakers." He turned slightly and delivered at least part of his answer to the jurors. "It was just a bunch of us standing out there. A lot of people had signs, like 'No Private Jails' or whatever. And somebody brought a bullhorn, so we were doing some chants too."

"What kind of chants?" Talon asked.

"Um, you know," Karim suppressed a grin. "Just like, 'Hey hey, Ho ho, Private prisons have to go' or something like that."

"Something like that," Talon agreed. "Were you the one leading the chants?"

"No," Karim answered. Then he clarified, "I mean, not at first. People were just passing the bullhorn around."

"Did you get it eventually?"

"Um. Yeah. Right at the end."

"And did you come up with a chant?"

Karim shifted in his seat. "Um, yeah."

It was a bit of a gamble. Some of the jurors were undoubtedly not going to like what Karim had said. But almost as surely, there would be some jurors who saw the humor in it. More importantly, though, they would all appreciate how it could have pissed off James Dank. And she wanted her Villain already angry when he stepped into the ring.

"Tell the jury what the chant was," Talon instructed.

It was embarrassing, but sharing in that embarrassment would actually break down barriers between him and the jurors. They needed to see him as a human being, not just 'the defendant'.

"Um okay." Karim nodded a couple of times, then turned to jurors. "I wanted it to rhyme, you know, so it was, um... 'Fuck court. Fuck bail. Fuck the cops. And fuck this jail.'"

The jurors kept poker faces for the most part. At least none of them seemed visibly offended.

"Very nice," Talon commented. "And you yelled that through the bullhorn?"

"Um, yes."

"Did the crowd repeat it back?"

Karim grimaced. "Yeah."

"So, that's when the warden and the guards came out, isn't it?"

Karim's grimace deepened into a true frown. "Yes."

"What happened then, Karim?" She waited a beat, then clarified, "Tell the jury what happened then, Karim."

Karim nodded and turned to the jury. Talon thought she noticed his eyes glisten, but she couldn't be sure. She sure hoped so, though.

"I was standing on this little plastic milk crate somebody brought," he started. "That's where you stand if you're leading the chant. Everyone was hot and tired, and it was probably going to be the last chant before we packed it in and headed home. But then all of a sudden, the front gate opened up and out walked this man in a shirt and tie and like five or six jail guards behind him. They were in uniform and had guns. The man—I learned later his name was James Dank—Mr. Dank walked right up to me and yelled something like, "Stop this right now'. I just looked at him, then I stepped down and shouted the chant through the bullhorn again, but like right in his face. It was pretty loud, I guess, 'cause he put his hands over his ears, and then got this super angry expression on his face. He grabbed for the bullhorn, but I turned away and blocked him with my body. Then he like hit at me and wrapped his arms around and put me in a bear hug."

"So, what did you do?" Talon interrupted his narrative. In part, because long narrative answers were objectionable. But more because she wanted the jury to hang in that moment a little longer. Karim turned away, protecting his property (or his friend's property anyway), James Dank's arms around him in a bear hug. What was he supposed to do?

"I broke free," Karim answered. He mimed it for the jury. "I lifted my arms up hard and fast and broke his grip on me."

"You were stronger than him?" Talon wanted to confirm.

"Well, yeah," Karim answered. "I was younger, and bigger, and yeah, stronger."

"Did you have any trouble breaking his hold on you?"

"Well, he wasn't super weak either," Karim explained. "He

was a grown man with his arms all the way around me. It took a lot of my strength to be able to break free."

"What happened when you used your strength to lift your arms up and break Mr. Dank's hold on you?"

"I raised my arms up and out," Karim recalled. "He went flying backward. Well, not flying. But stumbling. He was definitely off balance, and was falling backward. I thought he was going to catch himself, or maybe fall onto his butt, but he didn't. He just fell backward like a tree. The back of his head hit first. It was..." Karim paused at the memory. "It was loud. I knew it wasn't right. Everyone did. Everyone just sort of froze for a second. Everyone was looking at him to see if he'd get up again. But he didn't. He didn't even move. Then the blood started to ooze out from under his head. And that's when the guards jumped me. I don't know what happened after that."

"The guards jumped you?" Talon repeated. "How many of them?"

"All of them," Karim answered. "Except one guy drew a gun on the crowd, I guess. But I had like five grown men on top of me. Honestly, I thought they were gonna crush me."

Talon decided not to go down that road. It wasn't about what they did to Karim. It was about what Karim did to Dank. She had questions she had to ask, and she had to ask them in a particular order. They tracked the law on self-defense: when you can defend yourself and how much force you can use.

"I want to back up a moment, Karim," Talon said. "Back to when you made the split-second decision to break free from the bear hug Mr. Dank had on you."

Karim nodded along. "Okay."

"Did you mean to hurt him?"

"No."

"Did you think he was going to hurt you?"

Karim took a moment. "I mean, not seriously. I was bigger than him. I can handle myself. But yeah, he grabbed me. He could have hurt me. I didn't think I had to let him."

"You were right," Talon assured him. "Did you think about retreating? Running away?"

Karim took a moment. "There wasn't really time for that, but no, I guess not. We had every right to be there. We had a right to protest. I felt like I could stand my ground."

Talon nodded. "You're right again."

Cobb probably could have objected to her confirming the law of self-defense for the jury. The judge was supposed to do that. But he was staying quiet. Talon didn't know if it was because he was choosing not to object, he wasn't aware he could object, or he wasn't paying enough attention to know he should object. She didn't glance over to see. She pressed on.

"Finally, Karim. did you use any more force than you needed to in order to break his grasp on you?"

Karim shook his head. "No. I could have grappled with him and tried to get him into a position to punch him, but I just wanted him to let go of me, so I burst my arms up and out. That's it."

And there it was. The battle between the Hero and the Villain. As told, finally, by the Hero. The Villain, of course, wouldn't get a chance to tell his side of the story. That was a rare, and morbid, advantage in a murder trial. But it also resulted in the jury being a little extra skeptical of the one side of the story they did get to hear. So Talon needed to corroborate it.

"Your Honor," she looked up to Judge Harvey, "at this time the defense would ask permission to play the video footage on the CD previously marked as Exhibit 47."

"Any objection?" Harvey asked Cobb.

Cobb could hardly object, not in front of the jury anyway. That would look like he was hiding things. And juries didn't trust prosecutors who hid things.

"Um, no, Your Honor," he responded after a moment's thought. "No objection."

"Very well," Judge Harvey said to Talon. "You may proceed."

She may, but it was going to take a few minutes. Technology wasn't her strongest suit, and interfacing her new laptop with the ancient projecting equipment of the courtroom was a challenge in itself. But she knew this moment was coming, so she'd made sure she knew how everything worked. It took her a bit longer than she'd wanted, but eventually the projector was on, lights were dimmed, the image of the first cell phone video was frozen on the screen facing the jurors.

"Is this the protest we were just talking about?" Talon had to ask for the record.

"Yes," Karim confirmed. "That's it."

Talon pressed play.

Everyone watched in silence as the two videos played back to back. She could have had Karim narrate along, but she felt like that would take away from it. The videos had sound, albeit mostly just a constant background of people yelling, although Karim's profane chant was also audible. This was the instant replay. Karim had told them what happened. Now the jurors could see it for themselves, to confirm the Hero had told the truth. They wouldn't be able to see everything of course, but having already heard from Karim, they could fill in with their memory of what Karim had described.

When the second video finished, Talon hurriedly turned off the projector and signaled to the bailiff to raise the lights. Then she stepped back in front of her client to finish her examination.

The problem with self-defense was that it was, literally a justification for something that was otherwise unjustifiable. It sounded like an excuse, but it was really an assertion that there was absolutely nothing wrong with what you did, and you'd do it again if you had to. That could sound cold, but it still needed to be said. Because if you could have done something differently, then you used more force than necessary, and that meant it wasn't self-defense.

"Did you want to kill Mr. Dank?" Talon asked solemnly.

"No." Karim shook his head. His face held an expression of true remorse. Talon knew it was genuine, but there was a definite possibility some or all of the jurors would think it was a practiced façade.

"Did you want to hurt him?"

"No."

"Do you wish he were still alive?"

"Of course."

"But now that you've told the jury what happened, and watched the videos," Talon posed her last question, "is there anything you would have done differently?"

Karim hesitated. He lowered his eyes in thought and his mouth screwed into a pensive knot.

Just say no, Talon thought. *The answer is no. He left you no choice.*

Karim finally lifted his head and nodded. "Yes."

"Yes?" Crap.

"Yes," Karim repeated. "I've thought about this every day since it happened. Every single day. I don't want to be where I am right now, and I really don't want him to be where he is. I wish it had gone down differently. I wish he had tried to talk to us. I wish he hadn't grabbed me. I wish he hadn't hit his head. I wish he hadn't died."

Another pause. Another nod. Then he turned to the jury. "So, I'm going to say yes. I should have turned the other cheek. That doesn't mean looking away and forgetting about it. It means offering up your body for more abuse, rather than react with physical force. In the moment, I was just trying to get him off of me, but if I'd known he was going to die, I never would have done it. I should have let him assault me. I should have let him hurt me. I should have let his guards beat me up even more than they did. I would have gladly suffered all that if it would have kept a person from dying."

Talon stared at her client for a moment, then nodded and smiled just a bit. *Okay then. That's what a Hero would say.* "No further questions."

She made her way back to her seat. Hoping the jury was as impressed by Karim's answer as she was. But then Cobb stood up and ruined the mood.

"You killed James Dank." Not really a question.

When Karim hesitated to answer the non-question, Cobb pushed forward. "He's dead because you pushed him."

Again, not technically a question, but Karim answered anyway. "I guess so."

"You pushed him intentionally."

Karim considered for a moment. "More reflexively, I would say."

"But not accidentally," Cobb pressed. "You weren't swinging at someone else and he walked into your hand, right?"

"Oh, right," Karim agreed.

"So, intentional." Cobb said. Definitely not a question because he didn't give Karim any chance to answer it. "So, did you realize he could die from you pushing him, or were you just extremely indifferent to that?"

"I didn't realize it, and I wasn't indifferent to it," Karim insisted. "In fact, the entire reason I was there that day was because I care about the life and dignity of every huma—"

"Thank you, Mr. Jackson," Cobb raised a hand and cut him off, "but you can let your lawyer give the speeches. I have no further questions."

Karim looked at Talon. Judge Harvey did too. Cobb was a jerk, but he hadn't done any damage. Not really. And it was never good to keep your client on the stand any more than was absolutely necessary.

"No redirect examination," Talon informed the judge.

Judge Harvey excused Karim from the witness stand back to his seat at the defense table. Then he looked to Talon. "Any further witnesses?"

Talon thought the answer was yes, but she wouldn't be sure until 9:00 a.m. the next morning.

"Not today, Your Honor," she answered.

Judge Harvey seemed to understand. He turned to the jury. "Ladies and gentlemen, we will now adjourn until tomorrow morning at nine o'clock. Please assemble in the jury room no later than eight-forty-five. Court is adjourned."

The judge banged his gavel, and the courtroom broke into the noise of people packing up their things and leaving. Talon scanned the scene as she gathered up her materials. When her eyes reached the front row of the gallery, they locked with those of Helen Hampton Montclair, who was staring daggers at her.

Talon smiled. Tomorrow was going to be fun.

CHAPTER 39

The next morning, Talon and Karim arrived at the courthouse fifteen minutes early. Any later, and they would have been cutting it a little too close for her own comfort. Any earlier, and it wouldn't have necessarily meant her witness wasn't coming just because the seats outside the courtroom were still empty. But 8:45 was the perfect time to turn the corner and see Donald Weathers waiting patiently for her arrival.

"You came," Talon called out as they approached.

"You served me with a subpoena," Weathers pointed out.

Talon shrugged. "Not everyone honors a subpoena. I'm glad you did, though. It speaks well of your character."

It was Weathers's turn to shrug. "I have the feeling I'm about to break a different legal obligation I entered into."

God, I hope so, Talon thought. "Yes," she took the offer and accepted it, "but for the greater good."

"The greater good?' Weathers seemed dubious.

"Justice," Talon explained, "or something like that."

Weathers laughed lightly. "'Justice, or something like that'. I like that. Is that your firm motto?"

Talon considered for a moment. "It may be now. I'll look

into getting my business cards updated." But time was limited, so it was time to get serious. "Has anyone else talked to you this morning?"

"No, I just got here," Weathers answered. "I haven't talked to anyone except you."

"Good," Talon said. "You'll get your chance to talk to a whole bunch of people in just a few minutes. But I need to go inside now to make sure that actually happens."

"I can't wait," Weathers joked.

"Cool," Talon responded. "Me neither."

Talon pulled open the door to the courtroom, and she and her client went inside. Cobb was already at the prosecution table. Hampton Montclair was already at her regular spot in the first row of the gallery, directly behind Cobb. They were both standing. They both looked Talon's way when she and Karim entered.

Cobb spoke first. "Any more witnesses?" he asked Talon.

Hampton Montclair remained silent, but her eyes were locked intently on Talon.

"One more," Talon answered. She set her briefcase down on the defense table as Karim circled over to his own seat. "Donald Weathers."

Cobb didn't ask who that was. Instead he looked to Hampton Montclair, who confirmed with a nod.

"Did I hear correctly?" Hampton Montclair interjected. "Did you say Donald Weathers?"

"You heard fine," Talon said to her. "And you already knew, because you knew whose name was in those records I tried to subpoena."

"Of course I did," Hampton Montclair admitted breezily. "What I don't know is how you found out."

Talon bared her teeth in a cold smile. "Trade secret."

"Well, then, Ms. Winter," Hampton Montclair huffed, "you must also know there's a non-disclosure agreement preventing Mr. Weathers from discussing the very matter I imagine you want him to discuss."

"And you must know, Ms. Hampton Montclair," Talon mimicked her haughty tone, "that I don't give a flying fuck about your N.D.A."

Hampton Montclair flinched at the profanity. That only confirmed for Talon to continue using it. "Well, I think you should, Ms. Winter, if you know what's best for you personally."

Talon's brows knitted together. "What's that supposed—?"

But her question was interrupted by the arrival of the judge. "All rise! The Pierce County Superior Court is now in session, the Honorable Robert Harvey presiding."

"Please be seated," Harvey instructed as he reached the bench. "Are we ready to proceed? Ms. Winter, is your witness here? I presume you have a witness. That's why we adjourned early yesterday."

"Yes, Your Honor," Talon confirmed. "The defense will be calling Donald Weathers to the stand."

"Well, the defense may be ready," Cobb interjected, "but the State will be objecting to this witness. This alleged witness did not observe the incident involved in this case. Rather, this witness, if allowed to testify, would testify to an unrelated incident involving Mr. Dank over seven years ago."

"Is that accurate, Ms. Winter?" Judge Harvey asked.

"Yes, Your Honor," Talon confirmed. "This witness used to work for American Correctional Enterprises and was assaulted by Mr. Dank under circumstances very similar to the facts of this case."

"So, yes, objection," Cobb repeated.

Harvey inclined his head at the prosecutor. "Objection

overruled. You agreed to this at the beginning of this trial, Mr. Cobb. Perhaps you shouldn't have, but you did. I'm not going to change the rules now."

"Well, then, I object, Your Honor," Hampton Montclair stepped forward.

Judge Harvey pushed himself back in his chair and laughed. "I knew it. I knew it was going to happen. I just knew it. But then we went the entire trial and now we're on the final witness, and I thought, 'Well, maybe it won't happen,' but I knew it would, and now it did. Ms. Hampton Montclair has finally inserted herself into the proceedings."

"I believe I have standing this time," Hampton Montclair replied stiffly, ignoring the judge's commentary.

"As the representative of James Dank's estate," Harvey asked, "or as the representative of American Correctional Enterprises?"

"A.C.E.," Hampton Montclair answered. "The witness Ms. Winter intends to call has signed a non-disclosure agreement with A.C.E. not to discuss the incident she wishes to question him about. Therefore, he cannot testify."

"The Sixth Amendment and the subpoena I handed him say otherwise, Your Honor," Talon put in. "He absolutely can testify. There may just be repercussions for him afterward. But Ms. Hampton Montclair's N.D.A. does not trump my client's right to a fair trial. My obligation is to my client."

"Well, then, you should enforce the non-disclosure agreement," Hampton Montclair practically squealed with glee. "It was drafted by our law firm while you were still employed there. That means you represented A.C.E. as well. I believe you have a conflict of interest, my dear."

Talon didn't know what to say. She didn't know her old firm

had negotiated the N.D.A.

"You can avoid the conflict, Talon," Hampton Montclair counseled. "Just don't call Mr. Weathers to the stand."

Talon's thoughts were flying too fast through her head. Thankfully Judge Harvey interrupted them and gave her something to focus on.

"Were you aware the N.D.A. was drafted by your old law firm?" he asked.

Talon shook her head. "No, Your Honor. The copy I saw was on letterhead from A.C.E., not Gardelli, High, and Steinmetz."

"It was signed by Roger Andrews," Hampton Montclair put in.

"I don't know who that is," Talon said.

Hampton Montclair gasped. "He was one of our most senior partners," she explained. "He died shortly after the N.D.A. was negotiated."

"Okay, so some ancient senior partner I never met drafted it," Talon threw her hands up. "I know I didn't work on it."

"But your firm did," Judge Harvey reminded her. "While you were employed there."

"I don't see the conflict of interest," Talon asserted.

"The Bar may disagree with you," Hampton Montclair warned. "Do you really want to take that chance?"

Talon just stood there for several seconds, trying to keep her breathing even and her fists unclenched.

"Ms. Winter?" Judge Harvey prompted. "What do you want to do?"

Talon took another moment, then looked up at the judge. "Can I have five minutes to consult with my client in private, Your Honor?"

"Of course," Harvey was quick to accommodate. "Take all

the time you need. We will be in recess for the next fifteen minutes."

He banged his gavel and Talon gestured at Karim to follow her into the hallway. Cobb was grinning, but it was nothing to the beaming expression Hampton Montclair wore. Talon ignored them both and stormed toward the door in the back of the courtroom.

"Stay right there," she instructed Weathers as she and Karim passed him on their way to an empty corner at the end of the hallway.

When they arrived, Talon laid it out for her client. "They want me to not call Weathers because they know it's going to hurt their case. They want me to believe there's a conflict of interest so I either don't call him or I withdraw to let another lawyer call him. But if I withdraw, this trial ends in a mistrial and the trial starts over again with a new jury and a new defense attorney, who, quite frankly, can't be as good as me. They want a mistrial because they think they might lose. And that's the absolute best reason to go forward. Understand?"

"Yes." Karim nodded. "But what about you? Could you really get in trouble with the bar association? Could you lose your license over this?"

Talon took a moment. "Could I? Maybe. Will I? Probably not. I hope."

Karim shook his head. "That's not worth it."

"It's totally worth it," Talon answered. "We are only going to get one chance for this. If you have to start over with another attorney, they will know Weathers is coming and they'll be ready for him. They'll be ready for everything we just threw at them. They might give it to a better prosecutor. They might get a different judge who makes better rulings for them. They're scared. That's why they're doing this."

"I'm scared too," Karim said. "I'm scared for you."

Talon looked at her client for a moment, then shook her head. "You really are a hero, aren't you? You're looking at thirty years in prison and you're worried about my bar card. I'll protect my bar card. But first, let me protect you."

"Why, though?" Karim asked. "Why risk it?"

Talon needed a moment. That was a very good question. She wasn't sure her answer was very good. But it was her answer. "Because it's the right thing to do."

Karim smiled. "Okay, then."

"Justice, and all that," she laughed, then she clapped him on the shoulder. "Now come on. Let's go win."

They returned to the courtroom and the bailiff fetched the judge. When he retook the bench, he looked down at Talon.

"How are we proceeding. Ms. Winter?"

"I already told you, Your Honor," Talon answered. "The defense will be calling Donald Weathers to the stand."

CHAPTER 40

Judge Harvey brought the jury in, then invited Talon to make it official.

"The defense calls Donald Weathers to the stand," she announced formally.

Talon had retrieved Weathers from the hallway prior to the jury entering the courtroom. He stood up from his seat in the back and came forward to be sworn in by the judge. Once he was sworn and seated, Talon began.

"Could you please state your name for the record, sir?"

"Donald Weathers," he answered.

"Are you ready to answer my questions, Mr. Weathers?"

There was still a chance he might change his mind again and invoke the N.D.A. after all. But he just smiled a little and nodded. "Yeah, I'm ready. Let's do this."

Talon returned the slight smile. "You used to work for American Correctional Enterprises, is that correct?"

"Yes, that's correct," he confirmed.

"What was your job there?"

"My title was Correctional Specialist," Weathers answered. "That means I was a guard. I worked at one of their small private detention facilities down near Olympia."

"What level were you?" Talon asked. "Correctional Specialist Four, or what?"

"I made it up to Correctional Specialist Five," Weathers answered.

"Nice," Talon acknowledged. "Is that the top level?"

Weathers shrugged. "Nah, it keeps going up, for whatever that was worth, which wasn't much."

Talon's brow lowered. "What do you mean?"

"I mean they gave us promotions in title, but not money," Weathers explained. "Higher level, more responsibility, but no more money."

"What about benefits?"

Weathers chuckled. "We barely got any benefits. Especially compared to real jail guards. Those guys get full medical and a pension."

"That doesn't seem fair," Talon offered.

"I didn't think so either," Weathers replied.

"So, what did you do about it?"

"I tried to organize," Weathers answered. "I tried to form a union."

"Oh," Talon said. "And how did that go over?"

Another dark laugh from Weathers. "Not great."

"Not great, like the other guards weren't interested?" Talon asked. "Or not great, like management was upset?"

"Not great, like I got my arm broken," Weathers said.

"Okay," Talon said. "Tell us about that."

Weathers nodded and sighed deeply at the memory. "Like I said, I wanted to organize. I was trying to get some of the guards on board. We had possible support from some of the larger national unions, SEIU, the Teamsters, you know, but first we had to show there were enough of us serious about it. But it was dangerous because all of us were at-will employees. That was as bad for us as it was for the inmates."

"Wait," Talon interrupted. "Explain that. Why was it bad for the inmates that the guards were at-will employees?"

"Well, if you can be fired at will for any reason," Weathers explained, "or for no reason at all, then you're not going to rock the boat. And you're definitely not going to go to bat for the inmates if the conditions are sub-par. If there's not quite enough food, if the linens aren't getting washed often enough, if the backed-up toilets don't get fixed for days. I mean, no one's going to listen to the inmates, but they'd listen to the guards—unless the guards are too scared to say anything."

"So, what happened with your organizing efforts?" Talon continued.

"Well, like I said, I was trying to get a few of the other guards on board," Weathers said. "We were having a meeting. It was over lunch, in the break room. On the downlow. A few of us adjusted our lunch a bit so we could stay behind after the others went back on shift. We needed to map out the strategy to hold a vote without management hearing about it until it was too late."

"Did that work out?"

Weathers shook his head. "No. Management found out about the meeting. Someone said something, either on purpose or we got overheard. But anyway, about a minute after everyone else left and we started talking, in walked the director himself."

"The director," Talon repeated. "And who was the director of that private detention center?"

Weathers took a beat. He knew it was an important answer. "James Dank."

A murmur rippled through the jury box.

"Objection!" Cobb stood up and slapped his table.

Hampton Montclair stood up as well and added her own, "Objection!"

Judge Harvey's eyes flashed. He pointed at Cobb, "Overruled," and Hampton Montclair, "Sit down."

Talon proceeded. "What happened when James Dank showed up?"

She was going to say the name James Dank as many times as she possibly could,

"He walked in with like five or six guards behind him," Weathers recounted. "Guys I knew. Guys I knew were more interested in getting promoted than getting a union."

"Did James Dank say anything?" Talon asked.

"No," Weather answered. "I mean he cussed, but he didn't try to have a discussion. He just marched right up to me and got right in my face. Because I looked like the leader, I guess. I was standing and everyone else was sitting. He grabbed for the little clipboard I was holding. I turned away, and he kind of tried to reach around me to get it, but it had people's names on it—people who would get fired if he got their names—so I held it away from him. His face turned bright red, he grabbed my other arm by the wrist, and…" He trailed off.

"And what?" Talon prompted. "What did James Dank do?"

"He grabbed my wrist," Weathers repeated, "and he twisted my arm as hard as he could. It broke my arm, in two places. Shattered my wrist and snapped one of the forearm bones in two. And it pulled my shoulder right out of the socket, tore all the ligaments. I had to have multiple surgeries, but it never healed right."

"Does it still hurt?" Talon asked.

"Yeah, when it's cold out," Weathers answered, "and more

now that I'm getting older."

"So, what happened to James Dank after he did that to you?"

"Nothing," Weathers grumbled. "I don't know, maybe he got promoted. But me? I got fired."

"You got fired?" Talon tried to sound as incredulous as she hoped most, or all, of the jurors were.

"Dank claimed I attacked him," Weathers explained. "They even got some witness statements from those guards who came in with him saying I started it."

"That's terrible," Talon sympathized, again hoping the jurors felt sympathy, too. And the opposite of that for James Dank.

"It was," Weathers agreed. "But I hired a lawyer, and we got a few statements from some of the other guards who were there. Not all of them, but some of them. Eventually, they backed down. I didn't get my job back or anything, and nothing happened to Dank as far as I know, but they agreed to pay my medical bills and give me a year's salary to drop the lawsuit and never talk about it again."

"Did you accept that offer?"

"Yep," Weathers answered. "They signed a check, and I signed the settlement agreement and a non-disclosure agreement."

"But you're talking about it here today," Talon pointed out. "Doesn't that violate the non-disclosure agreement?"

Weathers shrugged. "Well, you handed me a subpoena, so what choice did I have? Besides, what are they going to do? Have Dank break my arm again? He's dead."

Talon suppressed a wince. That was harsh.

It would have been an interesting place to end her examination, but she had one more question she was curious about.

"Looking back now, would you have done anything

differently?"

Weathers took a moment, then answered with an honesty no juror would have doubted. "Yeah, I should have punched that piece of crap in the face. I should never have let him lay a hand on me, let alone break my arm. I should have broken his goddamn nose." Weathers patted at his injured arm. "I didn't deserve what happened to me, but James Dank sure as hell would have deserved that happening to him."

And that was the perfect place to end.

"No further questions."

Cobb stood up on the invitation of Judge Harvey and took Talon's vacated space in front of the witness stand.

"That was a long time ago," Cobb said, "under very different circumstances, wouldn't you agree?"

"It was a long time ago," Weathers allowed. "I don't know about the circumstances."

"Right," Cobb said, "because you weren't there when the defendant in this case attacked Mr. Dank, were you?"

"I wasn't there," Weathers agreed, in part, "when whatever happened happened."

"Well, you have no information," Cobb challenged, "that the defendant didn't assault Mr. Dank, do you?"

Talon had to stop herself from jumping to her feet and calling out, 'Objection!' It was classic, and unethical, burden-shifting. The defendant didn't have to prove he didn't commit the crime. But she had a feeling Weathers would do better answering the question, than she would do blocking that answer.

"Actually," Weathers replied, "I do."

"You do?" Cobb was too surprised not to ask that question which he really shouldn't have asked.

"What happened to me, that's just who James Dank was."

Weathers grabbed onto his injured arm again. "I may have been the worst, but I wasn't the first. And I knew I wouldn't be the last."

Cobb just stood there for several long seconds. Talon wondered if he could possibly make it any worse for himself, better for her. He must have been wondering the same thing too. He finally turned around and muttered, "No further questions."

Judge Harvey looked down at Talon. "Any redirect examination?"

Talon knew the judge knew her answer, but she gave it anyway, because it was the first of two very important questions which were necessary to allow the trial to proceed to its final stage.

"No, Your Honor," she stood and answered the first of the final two questions.

"Does the defense have any further witnesses?" was the other question.

"No, Your Honor," Talon answered. "The defense rests."

And that ended the testimonial portion of the trial.

Talon sat down again as Judge Harvey explained as much to the jurors, then told them what was next.

"We will now be adjourned until tomorrow morning," he said, "at which time the lawyers will deliver their closing arguments, after which you will retire to the jury room to begin your deliberations."

Harvey was giving them the rest of the day to prepare their closings. That was kind of him. But it meant a long day and night ahead of Talon.

After the bailiff led the jurors out of the courtroom and Judge Harvey left the bench and the courtroom started to empty out, Karim stood up and grabbed Talon's arm, unable to suppress a wide grin. "That was awesome."

Talon allowed only the slightest nod. "Don't celebrate yet," she cautioned. "We're not done yet. Go home. Get some sleep tonight. Get here early tomorrow morning. Then we'll talk afterward."

Karim kept the smile. "Yes. Right. Perfect. Tomorrow." Then, he squeezed that arm. "Thank you."

Talon nodded again and Karim departed.

Donald Weathers was lingering. Talon walked up to him.

"Thank you, Mr. Weathers."

Weathers shrugged. "Honestly, Ms. Winter, I'm glad I did it." He nodded toward the gallery. "I saw that lady in the front row. She's gonna want her money back, huh?"

Talon laughed. "Yeah, probably."

"It was worth it." Weathers grinned. "You know. Justice, or something like that."

CHAPTER 41

The next morning couldn't come soon enough, but also came too quickly. Closing arguments presented their own unique challenges. On the one hand, they were probably the most important part of lawyering to the entire trial. The last time the lawyer got to speak with the jury and the grand summation of why they should win. On the other hand, their content was dependent on what evidence actually came out at trial, so while rough contours could be planned in advance, there were arguments that simply couldn't be formed until after the last witness was excused from the witness stand.

Unless you were a prosecutor, in which case you could always just give the same closing argument you'd been giving your entire career, just changing the elements of the offense.

"Ladies and gentlemen of the jury," Judge Harvey said after everyone was assembled in the courtroom and the proceedings were ready to commence, "please give your attention to Mr. Cobb, who will deliver the closing argument on behalf of the State of Washington.

Cobb stood up and walked over to the easel tucked behind the witness chair. It was for witnesses to draw diagrams during their testimony and held an oversized pad of paper on it. It was also fairly flimsy and unwieldy, so Cobb, having been given the attention of everyone in the courtroom, began by dragging the rickety apparatus in front of the jury and taking more than a moment to make sure it didn't fall over before finally flipping over the first blank page to reveal his own awkward penmanship in black marker. He held a red marker in his hand, cap off, at the low ready.

"Murder in the first degree," Cobb read the top line he had scrawled in advance of his presentation. He had copied the elements of the offense from the statute and, Talon knew, was planning on going through them one at a time, checking each off in turn. It was the classic prosecution closing argument. "One, under circumstances manifesting an extreme indifference to human life; two, he or she engaged in conduct which created a grave risk of death to any person; and three, thereby caused the death of a person. That is the definition of murder in the first degree, at least for this case."

That was part of his problem. The usual definition of murder in the first degree was the premeditated, intentional killing of another human being. But the other human being was part of their Team, so they overcharged it. Now Cobb was going to have to defend that decision.

"So, let's go through the evidence together," he continued, "and I will show you that each of these elements of the offense has been proven beyond a reasonable doubt."

A lot of lawyers seemed to forget that the jury had also been present during the presentation of all that evidence they were about to summarize. Imagine watching a movie, then having to sit through some lawyer recounting every detail of the movie you just watched. Oh, and you can't leave or speak. Terrible. And Cobb was going to do it three times, because he had also charged Karim with murder in the second degree and manslaughter in the first degree, as backup, in case the jury, as they should, acquitted him of the overreach of Murder One.

"Let's start with element three," Cobb said. He looked at his chicken scratch and read the element again. "Thereby caused the death of another person. Did the defendant cause the death of James Dank? Absolutely. That much is undisputed. James Dank would be alive today if not for the defendant's actions in violently pushing him to the ground. Dr. Smith came in here and told you, under oath, that Mr. Dank's death was a homicide and it was caused by the injury he suffered when he hit his head on the pavement after the defendant pushed him there. So," he leaned over and placed a check mark next to the number '3', "that element has been proven beyond a reasonable doubt."

He took a moment to glance at the jury, Talon did too. Normally she avoided staring at them too much. Nobody likes being stared at. But closing was a little different. The jury knew they were again the focus of the courtroom, despite the lawyers prattling on as if they were the center of attention. Talon looked for any clue as to whether the jurors were buying what Cobb was selling. Things like nodding or crossed arms. But it was early still, and they mostly just looked like they were paying attention. Which was good, she supposed.

"Element two," Cobb moved on and read again from his pad. "Engaged in conduct which created a grave risk of death to any person. Well, we have that here too. The defendant is a strong, strapping young man. He should have known that pushing a, well, let's be honest, not in great shape, middle aged man to the ground was the kind of thing that would create a grave risk of death. I mean, we know it created a risk of death because it did result in death. So, element two is also satisfied beyond a reasonable doubt."

Cobb leaned over again and put a check mark next to the number '2'.

"Now, the last element," he read, "under circumstances manifesting an extreme indifference to human life. Do we have that here? Well, yes, we do. As I just said, the defendant should have known he could hurt or even kill Mr. Dank if he pushed him onto the cold, hard pavement. In fact, he did know. He just didn't care. He was indifferent to Mr. Dank's well-being. He told you as much when he testified. He said he was only thinking about himself. He wanted Mr. Dank to get away from him, so he violently and viciously shoved him to the ground, not caring one bit whether Mr. Dank was hurt or killed. That is indifference to human life. Extreme indifference. And that means," he added a third check mark to his pad, "all three elements of murder in the first degree have been met."

He paused, and Talon took another moment to see if any of the jurors had crossed those arms or maybe raised a doubtful eyebrow. She thought she saw some dubious expressions in the jury box, but it was always hard to tell. Then Cobb started talking again.

"But, ladies and gentlemen," he said, "murder in the first degree is not the only crime you will be considering. Well, maybe not. I mean, if you convict the defendant of murder in the first degree, as you should, then you stop there. But if you decide he is not guilty of that crime, or you can't agree as to that crime, then you will consider the crime of murder in the second degree."

He flipped the page again and revealed his second set of handwritten elements.

"One, committed or attempted to commit any felony, including assault; and two, in the course of such crime, caused the death of another person. Pretty simple, right? So, again, let's look at the evidence. Did the defendant commit a felony assault? Yes, he pushed Mr. Dank to the ground where he cracked his head and lost consciousness. That's an assault, and the injuries are felony level. Did Mr. Dank die from that? Again, yes. So," two quick check marks on this second piece of paper, "guilty of murder in the second degree."

Cobb flipped the page again and read the next header: "Manslaughter in the first degree. Now, this one is a little different. The only element is, recklessly caused the death of another person, but then recklessness is defined as 'knowing of and disregarding a substantial risk that death may occur, and this disregard is a gross deviation from conduct that a reasonable person would exercise in the same situation.'"

Cobb must have spent a lot of time copying all those words over from the statute. It was a good thing he was reading them out loud, because his handwriting got worse and worse and the last part of that definition of recklessness was basically illegible.

"So," he tapped at that unreadable script, "did the defendant know there was a risk Mr. Dank would die if he smashed his head onto the ground? Yes. Of course. Did he disregard that risk? Obviously. And was that disregard," he looked at the pad to read the exact words, "a gross deviation from the conduct that a reasonable person would exercise in the same situation? Well, again, obviously. A reasonable person wouldn't push an old man to the ground. A reasonable person wouldn't kill someone. Killing people is a crime and reasonable people don't go around committing crimes."

Talon frowned a bit at Cobb's argument. She wasn't sure if it was circular, or bootstrapping, or both, but it seemed weak, at least to her. Another check of the jury box revealed at least a few expressions that suggested similar thoughts. Or so she hoped. She also hoped Cobb was almost done. He'd gone through the elements. That was the prosecution schtick. That meant he was probably done.

"So, in conclusion, ladies and gentlemen," he popped the cap back on his red marker, "the State of Washington is asking you to hold the defendant responsible for his reckless, intentional, and indifferent actions that fateful day. We are asking you to hold him responsible for the death of James Dank. We are asking you to find him guilty of murder in the first degree. Thank you."

He abandoned the easel standing in front of the jury and marched back to his seat. Talon really didn't want to have to fight with it in advance of her own remarks. Luckily, Judge Harvey wasn't going to make her. "Ahem," he cleared his throat. "Mr. Cobb. Could you return the easel to its proper place?"

Cobb, who had already sat down, popped back up. "Oh, yes. Of course. Sorry, Your Honor."

He walked back to it, but rather than simply drag it out of the way, he took a moment to look at the definition of Manslaughter One again, then nod at the jury. He flipped the definition of Murder Two over and did the same thing. Then again, with the definition of Murder One, taking a small step back, appraising the words, then giving the jury one more nod before finally dragging the apparatus out of Talon's way.

Talon waited patiently, fighting to keep her eyes from rolling back into her head. Once the space in front of the jury was clear and Cobb had vacated the floor again, Judge Harvey instructed the jurors, "Now please give your attention to Ms. Winter, who will deliver the closing argument on behalf of the defendant, Karim Jackson."

CHAPTER 42

Talon stood up. She buttoned her suit jacket. She stepped out from behind the defense table. She walked over to the jurors. And she stopped directly in front of the center of the jury box.

"Justice," she said.

Then she didn't say anything for several seconds. She wanted the jurors to sit with that word. That concept. That charge.

"Justice," she repeated. "That's why you're here. To seek justice. To speak justice. To make justice happen."

She looked over at the easel stashed inelegantly behind the witness stand. "That," she pointed at it, "is the law. But the law and justice are not the same thing."

She returned her gaze to the jurors. "At its best, the law is an approximation of justice. It aspires to be justice. But at its worst, the law subverts justice. It is a perversion of justice."

Bold words. True, but bold. She needed to back them up.

"The law used to be that women couldn't own property," she said. "The law used to be that Black people were property. The law used to be that Native Americans had no right to their own property."

Those were the big, societal examples. But there were more

specific examples. Criminal examples.

"The law used to be that you couldn't commit a rape against your wife because she had no right to say no to her husband."

That was true. And, Talon hoped, shocking.

"Laws aren't written in a vacuum," she continued. "They aren't unchangeable everlasting truths. For better, and often worse, they reflect the society around them. And as that society changes, the law changes too. Slowly. Eventually. Hopefully. When I started out as a lawyer, there was a mandatory day in jail for possessing even the smallest amount of marijuana. Now, we could all go out on our lunch break and buy as much of it as we want from the corner pot shop."

She nodded and admitted, "Of course, murder isn't the same as weed. And if there is an unchanging everlasting truth in criminal law it's probably 'thou shalt not commit murder'. But the point is, the law as it's written is a guide toward justice, but the guidebook isn't the same as the destination, and you should, you *must*, strive to arrive at a just result in this case. The words on Mr. Cobb's scratch pad aren't the end of the inquiry. They are the beginning.

"When the legislature put those words on the page, they were trying to prohibit a particular type of conduct. But once written, the words have their own lives. They can be pushed and pulled and stretched and warped to try to fit situations the legislature never intended. And no one can stretch and warp words quite like a lawyer. I should know. I'm a lawyer." A pause, and a glance over her shoulder. "And so is Mr. Cobb."

How to impugn a prosecutor in a thousand words or less.

She turned back to the jury. "That's why you have to start with justice. You start with justice, you end with justice, and you stay with justice all the way through. It's not about checking boxes. It's about striving to reach an honest, fair, and just result. And if that's what you strive for, you'll see that those boxes aren't checked after all, and the only honest, fair, and just verdict in this case is not guilty to all charges."

It was all well and good to give a speech about justice, but she needed to actually address the facts of the case too.

She went over and picked up Cobb's easel and a black marker. She lifted the easel and carried it confidently back in front of the jury box. No awkward, rickety dragging for her. She flipped the top page over and pulled the cap off the marker.

"Extreme indifference?" she recited from the top element. "Please." She crossed it out. "This phrase is designed for people who shoot a gun into a crowd, with no specific intent to kill any particular person. It is not designed for people who are attacked and choose to defend themselves, as is their right under the law." She crossed out the words. "Mr. Cobb tried to stretch and warp that phrase to cover Mr. Jackson's actions. Mr. Cobb is wrong. And Mr. Jackson is not guilty of murder in the first degree."

She flipped the page.

"Committed any crime including assault," she read aloud. "Well, ladies and gentlemen, it is not an assault to defend yourself. See, that's where justice creeps back into the law. The law says you can't use physical force against someone. Justice says you can if you're defending yourself. Justice says you have a right to stand your ground, you have no duty to retreat, and you can use force to stop an attack against you, so long as you use no more force than is reasonably necessary to stop the attack. And that's exactly what happened here. James Dank laid hands on Karim, and Karim broke free. He didn't punch him. He didn't even shove him. He broke Mr. Dank's grasp. But that grasp was so tight that when it was broken, Mr. Dank stumbled backward on his own, he lost his balance on his own, and he hit his head on his own. Mr. Cobb wants you to draw a line from that fall to Karim's actions, but the line goes farther than that. It goes all the way to Mr. Dank's own action of grabbing Karim in the first place." She scratched out the words 'committed an assault'. "And he is not guilty of murder in the second degree either."

Talon flipped to the last page.

"Manslaughter in the first degree," she said. "This is when you kill someone accidentally, but it's still a crime. This is where justice and the law really do come together to try to figure out how to deal with situations where someone does something terrible, but not on purpose. When does justice require the State—the government, cops and prosecutors, judges and jail cells—when does justice require a person to be thrown in a cage for actions we all agree were not intentional?" She tapped the nearly undecipherable definition of recklessness at the bottom of the page. "When a person knows there's a risk. That the risk is a risk of *death*. That it's not just any risk, but a *substantial* risk. That the person disregards that substantial risk of death. And when doing so is a *gross deviation* from the conduct of a reasonable person. Death. Substantial. Gross deviation. Individually, any lawyer, including Mr. Cobb, can check off those words and claim the crime has been proven. But together they show you the intent of the legislature. They show the desire to punish only when doing so would be just. They show a longing for justice."

She glanced over at Karim. "Karim Jackson sits here on trial for murder. The State knows he didn't mean it. They know it was an accident. But they've charged him with a crime anyway because the victim was part of their team, and you don't hurt someone on their team, even if it's an accident. If he is convicted of any of the charges the prosecutor has put before you, he will be punished, just the same as if he had committed the crimes intentionally. The prosecutor tells you, that's the law. I tell you, that's not justice."

She turned back to the jurors. "I want you to recall what Karim said when I asked him if he would do anything differently. He could have said no. He could have said, I'm sorry Mr. Dank is dead, but I was defending myself, and I had a right to defend myself, and I would defend myself again. But he didn't say that. He said he should have let himself be hurt rather than hurt another person."

The Hero.

"I want you to remember what Donald Weathers said when I asked him the same question. He said he wished he had defended himself. He shouldn't have just let himself get hurt. And he said that was just who James Dank was."

The Villain.

"So, ultimately, ladies and gentlemen, you are being asked to find justice in this tragedy. The tragedy of a man who died before his time. And the tragedy of a man on trial for a crime he didn't commit. The prosecutor claims he wants you to follow the law. I ask you to follow justice. And if you do, I have no doubt you will return verdicts of not guilty to all charges. Thank you."

Talon turned and walked back to her table. She sat down next to Karim, who leaned over and whispered, "Thank you."

Talon nodded. It was over. She'd done everything she could. Now they had to wait to see if it would be enough.

CHAPTER 43

The waiting, as they say, was the hardest part. Deliberations took as long as they took. An hour, a day, a week, maybe more, and anything in between. Karim's future was, as they also say, in the hands of twelve people too stupid to get out of jury duty. All he and Talon could do was wait. And make contingency plans.

After court, they went back to Talon's office. Shayla tagged along. Curt checked in excitedly to see how everything went. Paul checked in cautiously for the same reason. But Talon kicked them all out of her office. She needed to talk to Karim. Alone.

"Close the door," she instructed him as the rest of the team exited. "This needs to be attorney-client privileged."

Karim nodded and complied.

Once the door clicked shut, Talon got right to it. "I cannot advise you to go to Canada now, but I can explain what will happen if you decide a quick trip to Vancouver sounds like fun. When the verdict comes in, one of two things will happen. You will either be acquitted, or you will be convicted. If you're acquitted, it won't matter whether you're in the courtroom because the case automatically terminates upon the verdict and the judge would have no reason or legal authority to issue a warrant. If you are convicted, and you are in the courtroom, you will be arrested and will not get out of custody again until the end of whatever sentence the judge gives you, which, if all goes the worst it possibly could go, would be thirty years in prison. You will not be free again for thirty years. However, if you're in Canada, the judge would issue a warrant and international extradition proceedings would have to be initiated. And as we discussed before, they may not even be able to extradite you if the conviction is for, say, the felony murder two. After the conviction, it would be too late to amend the charges. You'd have to spend the rest of your life in Canada and never come here even for a visit, but you wouldn't be in prison."

Karim looked stunned. "Are you telling me to flee the country?"

"No," Talon was sure to say. "I'm telling you what would happen if you did choose to do that."

"But won't they notice if I'm not there when the verdict comes back?"

"They'll notice," Talon agreed, "but they'll still take the verdict. They have to know whether to issue the warrant."

CHAPTER 44

Two days, four hours, seventeen minutes. That's how long the jury was out before they notified the bailiff they had reached a verdict.

Eleven minutes. That's how long it took Talon to drop what she was doing and drive from her office to the courthouse.

Twenty-three excruciating minutes after that. That's how long it took before everyone was finally assembled in the courtroom so the judge could call in the jury and accept the verdict.

It was minute twenty-two when Karim walked in. He strode purposefully to the front of the courtroom and took his spot next to his lawyer.

"You showed up," Talon said.

"Run, beg, or fight," Karim reminded her. "Justice isn't given. It's fought for. You fought for me. I'm not going to run now."

Talon patted him on the back. "You're either brave or stupid."

Karim smiled. "I believe in you."

Talon smiled back. "So, both."

"All rise for the jury!" the bailiff called out.

The jurors walked in solemnly, heads down, and took their

spots at their individual chairs. One of them, a middle-aged woman in the front row, was holding the verdict forms, giving away her status as the foreperson.

"Has the jury reached a verdict?" Judge Harvey asked formally. He knew the answer, but he had to ask. A lot of trial work was like that.

"We have, Your Honor," the foreperson answered.

"Please hand the verdict forms to the bailiff," the judge instructed. "Everyone may be seated."

The bailiff accepted the verdict forms. Everyone sat down. The bailiff walked across the courtroom to the judge's bench. The bailiff handed the verdict forms to the judge. The judge read, to himself, each of the three forms in turn. Then he looked up.

"The defendant will rise for the reading of the verdict," Judge Harvey announced.

Karim stood. Talon did too.

"In the matter of the State of Washington versus Karim Jackson," Judge Harvey read from the first verdict form, "we, the jury, find the defendant..."

A pause. They always paused.

"Not guilty of the crime of murder in the first degree."

Karim exhaled audibly and smiled at Talon.

She didn't smile back. They weren't done yet.

Judge Harvey moved on to the second verdict form. "In the matter of the State of Washington versus Karim Jackson, we, the jury, find the defendant... not guilty of the crime of murder in the second degree."

Karim's smile had faded, but his eyes were still hopeful. Talon gave him a quick nod, but she wasn't going to say anything until the third verdict form was read. After all, she wasn't that lucky.

"In the matter of the State of Washington versus Karim Jackson, we, the jury, find the defendant... not guilty of the crime of manslaughter in the first degree."

Or maybe she was.

Now, she could say something. Or rather, she would have, except that Karim grabbed her in a bear hug. She almost made a joke about breaking free, but thought better of it.

"You did it," Karim choked back a sob. "You got justice for me."

Talon raised her arms as best she could and gave him an awkward hug back. "Or something like that."

EPILOGUE

Two Fridays later found Talon back at The Bar. A good Manhattan was a good Manhattan, and the bartender there had made one of the best she'd ever had. She felt at home in the aggressively neglected space. She could see it becoming her new place, even if it had actually been discovered by someone else.

"Paul." Talon shook her head at the sight of him walking through the door. Of course she would run into him there. But that was a good thing. He had turned out to be a Good Guy too. And he looked good with his tight shirt and fresh haircut. She waved him over to her spot at the bar. "Pull up a stool."

Paul grinned nervously and glanced quickly around the establishment. Then he shrugged and marched over to Talon. He didn't sit down though. "You're still talking to me?"

Talon frowned, but she supposed she deserved that. "Yes. In fact, I'm more than talking to you. I'm thanking you. And apologizing."

"For what?" Paul asked. "Start with the apology, then the thanks."

Talon smiled and took a sip from that Manhattan she'd come for. "I'm sorry I didn't appreciate your generosity and hospitality. I'm sorry I didn't acknowledge your talent and hard work. And I'm sorry I thought you were some sort of an enemy sleeper agent sent to murder me." Another sip. "Is there anything else?"

"You held me at gunpoint," Paul reminded her.

"Yes, that," Talon pointed at him. "Sorry I held you at gunpoint."

Paul smiled and tipped his head to her. "Apologies accepted."

Talon retuned the smile. "Good."

"Now what about those thanks?" Paul prompted.

"Ah, yes," Talon nodded. "Thank you for finding Donald Weathers. I wouldn't have won that case without his testimony. He won it for me. Which means you won it for me. So, thanks."

Another grin from Paul. "My pleasure."

Talon appraised the man standing before her. "I was wrong about you, Paul Delgado."

But Paul shrugged. "Maybe you were. Maybe you weren't."

Talon liked that response. "How do I find out?"

"Hire me for another case," Paul suggested.

"I could do that," Talon agreed. She knew she probably shouldn't do what she was going to do next, but those Manhattans were good for a reason. She pulled her phone out of her pocket. "Or maybe I could finally give you my number?"

Before Paul could respond, a young woman with black hair falling over her shoulders walked up and grabbed Paul by the arm. "There you are, Pauly. I got us a table in the corner."

The woman looked really familiar, even in the half light of The Bar. "Do I know you?" Talon asked.

"You do," the woman confirmed. She extended a formal hand. "I'm Erin. Erin Vandergraben."

A younger version of Talon.

Talon pointed at each of them in turn. "And you two are...?"

Paul put an arm around Erin's waist and pulled her closer. "We ran into each other at the coffee cart in the courthouse, and just, sparks."

Erin giggled and squeezed his bicep. "Yes, sparks."

Talon was speechless. She put her phone back in her pocket and watched as Erin and 'Pauly' made their way to a secluded table in the back.

Just as well, Talon thought. Paul was still a bit too much of a mystery, a fact her Manhattan didn't seem to appreciate. Talon may have pulled the gun on Paul, but somehow, she felt like she was the one who just dodged a bullet.

"Maybe I am that lucky after all."

END

THE TALON WINTER LEGAL THRILLERS
Winter's Law
Winter's Chance
Winter's Reason
Winter's Justice
Winter's Duty
Winter's Passion

THE DAVID BRUNELLE LEGAL THRILLERS
Presumption of Innocence
Tribal Court
By Reason of Insanity
A Prosecutor for the Defense
Substantial Risk
Corpus Delicti
Accomplice Liability
A Lack of Motive
Missing Witness
Diminished Capacity
Devil's Plea Bargain
Homicide in Berlin
Alibi Defense

ALSO BY STEPHEN PENNER
Scottish Rite
Blood Rite
Last Rite
The Godling Club
Mars Station Alpha

ABOUT THE AUTHOR

Stephen Penner is an attorney, author, and artist from Seattle.

In addition to writing the *Talon Winter Legal Thrillers*, he is also the author of the *David Brunelle Legal Thriller Series*, starring Seattle homicide prosecutor David Brunelle; the *Maggie Devereaux Paranormal Mysteries*, recounting the exploits of an American graduate student in the magical Highlands of Scotland; and several stand-alone works.

For more information, please visit *www.stephenpenner.com*.

Made in the USA
Middletown, DE
17 June 2023